HALF MOON BAY

*Betray humanity and risk insanity
to love a siren queen.*

RICHELLE MANTEUFEL

Praise for *Half Moon Bay*

"This story is so inventive that it seems like folklore uncovered, rather than told. Manteufel's writing is filled with rich imagery and detail, and her voice will remind readers of the best Gothic novels—lush and haunting, expressive and hypnotizing, but always clear about the most heightened moments... a dark fairytale. The combination of genres, influences, and the lovely melancholy creates its own spell. *Half Moon Bay* is a book about what happens when you chase monstrosity and you catch it."

—Ana Hansen, *Sparks Editorial*

"*Half Moon Bay* blends genres and offers readers intense romance that knows no bounds—a truly distinctive novel."

—*The BookLife Prize* (2025)

"As usual, Richelle Manteufel created a compelling Gothic love story that is as unique as it is intense."
—Elise Nelson, author of *The Light in Hades*

"Manteufel crafts a strong sense of place and mood, a brooding nautical vibe... the physical empowerment and freedom of the siren is a most delicious call, and I delight in this book's exploration of it."
—Arlo Z. Graves, author of *The Ice Moves for No One*

"I really enjoyed the dark, gothic approach to sirens... Laura is drawn to the feral, unrestrained, rule-defying way they live, and I can relate."
—Booksprout Reviewer (starred review)

"This book is gorgeous, it had me hooked from the beginning... the true definition of 'could not put this down.'"
—Goodreads Reviewer (starred review)

Half Moon Bay

Richelle Manteufel

MAN DEVIL PRESS

CONTENTS

"But a mermaid has no tears, and therefore she suffers so much more."

HANS CHRISTIAN ANDERSEN, *THE LITTLE MERMAID*

"Does evil come from within us, or from beyond?"

ROBERT EGGERS, *NOSFERATU*

*To my dear cousin Olivia.
And to the beautiful souls of my fellow womenkind gone before, who could neither publish nor even dare to write such a damnable novel as this one. Consider this book my rose placed upon thy grave.*

PART ONE

~Laura~

CHAPTER 1

M ist cloaked the ship as we prepared to sail past Half Moon Bay.

The pastor rambled on, unruffled, but I noticed him clench his holy book with increased fervor. His high-collared throat flexed with a gulp. Amused, I masked a smile.

"Almost there," Hyacinth whispered. Her arm was tucked in mine, yet she pulled me closer still. "Once we pass the bay, the weather should clear. So they say."

They being—as required in such cases—a secret count of unsound folk whose primary occupation is to gossip unchecked. I kissed my friend's pale cheek. "We have nothing to fear from sirens," I reassured her. "Their palette savors man-meat." Hyacinth made a pinched face.

I gazed across the converted mail ship. An altar to the High God Maltaros faced an army of deck chairs, all filled with devout women and their lady's maids. The elder of Maltaros was the only male passenger aboard. *"He'd* better not slip overboard, however," I murmured aside, "for I imagine seducing a holy man may taste better than sailors."

"Shh," Hyacinth cautioned, shaking her coiffed head. Darling brunette waves curled around her cheekbones. "I'm quite accustomed to your wicked sense of humor, darling, but what if the others think you in earnest?"

I bestowed a dry smile. Like my physical attributes, my grim attempts at warmth and humor were washed out. Even my strawberry-blond hair refused to be smooth and feminine and luxurious, preferring to humiliate me by forming halfhearted waves that would not be tamed. I tightened the bun, tucking my obstinate locks into the tight, gray collar of my traveling dress. I couldn't wait to change out of it. It caused my throat to itch, yet polite society must be placated.

"Why didn't you bring your new maid?" Hyacinth whispered. "I'd offer to dress your poor hair myself, but I have never touched anyone else's hair in my life."

Including your own. Another vapid smile creased my chapped lips. Hyacinth's high-born family name had blessed her since the day of her conception. I, however, with a humble painter for a father and a washwoman for a mother, had but recently acquired a modest inheritance from my aunt. She had lived and died stewing in the notion that our family did not prosper because we did not worship the correct god. But she loved me nonetheless and had high hopes for me. Perhaps because there is a part of me that's "impressionable."

As my immediate family preferred to ignore religion, we had precious little to comment upon the matter. But Auntie's dying wish was for me to sign my name as a passenger and board the *Saint Brigette* with Hyacinth so that I may, in the seas of mighty Maltaros, at last submit to conversion.

Firstly, I pitied her for wasting her last wish upon me. Secondly, I pitied the fact that religion must be tied to that wish. I am exceedingly unfit for religion. There is a shadow in my heart that I cannot rid myself of, nor do I wish to try.

What shadow? one might ask. 'Tis onerous to describe. To me, the beach at nighttime is far more beautiful than the beach in daylight. I'd rather stroll in a cemetery than preen in a ballroom; I'd far rather sing of freedom and frolic to invisible wood nymphs than warble undying obeisance in a church. I suppressed this shadow for most of my childhood, believing it to be the seed of sin. I strove to pray it away, but it would not go; although, I found I could lock it up.

Now, I shall not be parted from it.

My attention turned to the churning sea as the Maltaros elder called for new converts to come forward and receive his blessing. I sighed. Hyacinth darted a look of gentle chiding at me as she joined the others, bowing their elegant heads in prayer. I shunned the pretense (for in my case that's all it was and all it would ever be), leaving my seat to stand at the rails of the main deck.

As I watched the gray waters below, imagining all manner of sea creatures and predators teeming beneath the planks my feet so blithely trusted, the strange mist seemed to grow heavy upon my face. A sense of presence, of eerie suppression, caused the heat to rise and flush my cheeks.

I supposed it was my imagination, as one would. I was, by my loving parents' own accounts, wildly imaginative at times. I withdrew my handkerchief to blot at the salty beads gathering on my forehead, cheeks, and lips.

An unfortunate gust of wind ripped the lace-rimmed cloth from my hand. I swallowed back an exclamation and pawed for it in vain, predestined by the sea gods to watch my handkerchief fly away like a roguish gull.

I murmured some unladylike phrases. Of course, I'd left my new maid to do the packing, and she was young; she'd forgotten surplus handkerchiefs. I gathered my woolen skirts and turned, ready to stomp back to my seat in no amiable state of mind. Proper ladies *always* had a 'kerchief at the ready. Always. *I must ask Hyacinth for one. Ever a borrower and a beggar, even with my own inheritance.*

Peering over my shoulder for a final look, my lips softly parted. A long, scaled hand broke the glassy surface of the waves. Each finger was adorned with a red spike for a fingernail. It reached for my handkerchief and caught it. In the brief moment it took to blink, the monstrous hand drowned its prize. Claimed my handkerchief for Half Moon Bay.

The weather cleared. The sunset marbled over the ocean, rejoicing as if there was no such place as Half Moon Bay. The pastor forgot it, too, prattling away with his new converts in such a cheerful strain that I was tempted to join them. But nay: As it was his duty to convert and mine to oppose, we must only converse at cross purposes. And the older I became, the harder it was for me to hide my shadow. If I betrayed myself, I'd certainly stand alone upon this sanctified deck.

Instead, I approached the captain's mate and requested a spyglass. He raised his bristled brows at me (*"What does a young lady need a spyglass for, pray tell?"*), but he promised to seek one. He returned in short order and handed the instrument to me. I regained the rail and eagerly spied for the scaled hand. Night approached, and visibility was fading fast. *I must find that hand again,* I thought, *or perhaps, if luck permits it, the scaled body that is surely attached to it.*

"Looking at seabirds, Laura?"

I lowered the spyglass to confront Hyacinth. "And anything else I may find. How are you enjoying yourself?"

Dear Hyacinth's chestnut curls, as perfect as swirling, silk thread, blew across her peach-tinted forehead. Her charming eyes twinkled in the sunset rays. "It's wonderfully restful. I'm *so* glad your aunt persuaded you to come. Even if your mother was rather against it."

"She fears Half Moon Bay," I revealed without forethought. "So many ships have run aground and burst in its vicinity . . . Sometimes with every crewman lost." I paused, not overeager to contribute to Cape

Althea's superstition. "It's only the poor visibility due to the mist and high waves," I finished. Stepping back, I clapped the spyglass shut to emphasize my point.

"Surely," Hyacinth murmured. Her pretty head bobbed in agreement. "Although, I must admit to a *sliver* of disappointment. I hoped one of these handsome crewmen might become suddenly and irrevocably attached to me." She lifted one pearly hand to giggle behind it. "But when they so much as open their mouths, poor boys, Elder Yates stares them into silence. A crying shame!"

"Indeed."

To me, men were sometimes clever and, if adventurous and prone to frequent travel, quite interesting to talk to. Nothing more. I, myself, was determined to die a happy old maid surrounded by my books. "Pardon me, Hyacinth, but there's precious little daylight remaining. Be a dear and indulge my curiosity. I'll meet you for dinner." I held up the spyglass.

"Of course. Don't be late! Sea fare is particularly dreadful when it is cold."

She departed for the galley, leaving me to my madness. Wouldn't life be dreadfully dull without it?

The spyglass yielded nothing. At dinner, I was quiet and morose. After bedtime prayers led by the Elder, we were all dismissed below.

Wide awake on my straw cot, I listened to Hyacinth's even breaths echoed by her maid. The details of the hand prohibited any temptation to dismiss it as a mere vision. A dark ombre of iron melding into teal, shining with the greenish tints of the emerald sea on a clear summer day. And those *fingernails*! If they could be called that. Vicious red spikes, the claws of a hunter. I couldn't have imagined them, could I?

Maybe you are *mad, Laura Frances Rivell,* my shadow whispered. It rested its smoking arm over my shoulders like an old friend. *Fortunately, you're the sort of madwoman who can coexist happily with her madness. So be content.*

"I am content," I whispered.

Even so, I was restless. I rose from the cot and tiptoed to the door. I knew I would see little (if anything), but I longed for the nocturne waves sloshing against our peaceful vessel, rocking us to sleep as a mother rocks her infant. And perhaps . . . just *perhaps* . . .

Pattering up to the main deck, I floated to the railing in my cream nightgown and peered below. Those lovely, melancholy, silver waters were now black as ink, taunting me with a featureless void. I sighed again.

At least you're alone, my shadow comforted me. *You're content, but you must not let anyone know you are mad. You know where they will take you if you fail.*

I shuddered, refusing to let my mind so much as brush against that sort of place, even in theory.

They'll inject you with stupor. They'll tame your brain until it's soup, tame your spirit until it's chained, steal what little agency you have—

"Enough!" I whispered fiercely.

And then . . .

Bursting into my dark thoughts, a melody darker still.

A cascading, lyrical ripple, jumping from one octave to the next with neither strain nor pause. Then lowering, seething and decadent, terrifying and beguiling. A voice like a sunken harp playing a dirge for Maltaros himself.

I gaped like a fish out of water, my mind plagued with confused emotions. It couldn't decide if I was listening to a tune of Summerland or a dirge of Hellscape. It was neither. It was both.

Heretofore, my darkness was buried deep down, acknowledged but locked up. I didn't even have the key; I couldn't free it if I wanted to, and that was the crux of my peace. My salvation. My hope for a normal life.

This song . . .

This predatory aria was the key.

CHAPTER 2

When I came to my senses, I was lost at sea.

Somehow, in a state of complete disassociation, I'd wrenched one of the rowboats free, clambered in, and lowered it. How I'd accomplished it was beyond me. I was far from frail, having taken care of myself and walked instead of ridden in carriages most of my life, but I was no hardened crewman, either. My own strength surprised me.

Suppressing a surge of panic, I scanned the black horizon for the mountainous projection of the *Saint Brigette*. As I feared, there wasn't a speck to be seen. I cried shamelessly, for I could not read the stars, nor could I ascertain from the currents which direction

I ought to steer in. I would perish out here in this churning wilderness because of one ethereal song.

Though perhaps hearing it was worth dying for.

I pushed Shadow away with all the mental strength I could muster, which wasn't much. Shadow reveled in its first taste of freedom. And that melody yet echoed in my ears, buzzed in my veins, and teased Shadow into a gleeful dance. I wondered if that cursed tune meant to haunt me until I died.

Once I dried my tears on my sleeves, I stared at the dome of stars winking their brilliance overhead. There was nothing else for me to do. I could see nothing, do nothing, think of nothing but that song.

A scream wrenched my awareness back from the edge of oblivion. Peering into the dark, my eyes chased the sound of distant splashing. It was impossible to see. When another wail pierced the night, it beckoned me in its direction. The shattered cry prickled my skin.

A man was drowning. I gathered the courage to yell. "Where are you?" Raising my voice seemed a desecration to that sacred sea-night, though I struggled to ascertain why. I grabbed both oars and positioned them to row toward the victim, bracing my feet against the bow. "I'm coming. Call out again! Don't give up."

A lower, feeble murmur. I frowned and rowed faster, cursing my crazed state for grabbing neither my boots nor my coat. Enchanted humans are idiots, the lot of them. "I'm coming!" I cried out again. My voice sounded thirsty and lost.

My hands were already chafing against the oars. Ignoring the pain, I rowed faster. Suddenly the man's bleached, frightened face floated from the infinite void of ocean, framed by frantic hands and tossing arms. "Shark!" he gasped, eyes glazed with shock. "Hurry! For Maltaros' sake, hurry!"

Panic shot through me as I reached for him. His hands clutched my forearms. As I half-pulled, half-dragged him into the boat, a flash of chewed limbs and splattering blood echoed in my mind. Iron filled my nostrils. Coughing, I turned my head to gather my wits. *For the gods' sake, don't be sick.*

As the poor man trembled and raved from the stern, I first recognized his clothing. Then his face. He was one of the crewmen from my own cursed ship. I took him by the shoulders, pleading for him to calm himself and speak rationally, if he could. "What on earth happened? Did it sink? Did everyone . . . "

I couldn't bring myself to say it. *Drown.* My grip on his shoulders intensified.

Hyacinth.

"I must go!" he cried, sanity robbed from his person. "She has called for me, and I must go!"

Abandoning my questions, I tore my nightdress to wrap his most grievous wound; for the rest, his shirt must suffice. His left calf had gotten the worst of it. Steeling my nerves to examine it more closely, I was mystified by the round, dark pricks running the length of his leg. Whatever enormous needles had impaled him, they were as meticulously spaced and equal in breadth and depth as a weapon. From thence I analyzed the bite marks. They were small, though the tormented flesh and muscle was shredded . . . the telltale damage of a shark's serrated teeth. Yet the jawline was entirely the wrong size for a shark's wide mouth. *How odd.*

This was no shark, Shadow hissed. As cruel and careless as Shadow was, it was often right.

As I tended to the dying man (for from the relentless pooling of blood, I had no hope for him), his meaningless ravings quieted to a wheezing, warbling hum. I started, dropping the knotted end of his makeshift tourniquet to lean closer. Listening.

The melody that had driven me into the sea. It haunted *him*, too.

I was ashamed to admit that my first emotion was joy. *I am not mad!* I informed Shadow in a heave of great gladness. *He heard it, too. And it impacted him far worse than me from the look of it. It is a relief to know that I have a strong spirit.*

Or you're less affected by the psychic emanations of another being's madness, being so heartily accustomed to your own, Shadow responded with a caustic chuckle.

Can't let me have a single victory, can you? Well, I'll show you who leads who by the reins around here. I nestled close to the crewman and patted his hand, whispering encouraging words. Our only hope was that we hadn't strayed too far from the ship after all, or that a current might bring us back to it. And since I'd found this man, perhaps we weren't as far away as I'd feared.

Time passed. I knew not how long. Once the crewman fell silent and his head slumped against my shoulder, I knew he would not survive much longer. My desperate eyes awaited the gray sliver of sunrise touching the horizon. I hummed the haunted melody to keep myself awake.

At once, a knocking—*thump, thump, thump*—vibrated from the bottom of the hull.

I shrieked, bolting upright in my seat. The crewman slumped sideways and nearly capsized us. I hoisted him back into the boat, laying him down before looking over the edge and into the water, beyond terrified of what I might see.

Something like a cloud of dark gray seaweed floated near the surface. Puzzled, I hesitated before reaching out and seizing a handful of it. "So soft." The illustrious strands fluttered against my fingers. Before I could think better of it, I yanked it to the surface.

A head came up with it.

Then a long, slender, scale-speckled neck. Bony shoulders. Smooth, round, gray-green breasts with teal nipples, completely devoid of clothing. And flashing, indignant creature-eyes, wide with the brilliance of a nocturnal huntress. They were staring straight at me.

Luckily, I had the good sense not to shriek again. I released her at once and fell back into the boat, managing as much distance between us as possible. My hands brushed the unconscious crewman and came away bloody. "What are you?" I asked in a tremulous voice.

No answer. She lifted her right hand from the water—scaled, knobby, and tipped with red claws—to point to the crewman. The flash of her ruddy siren fins broke the surface before vanishing again.

"You want him?"

She jerked her iron-gray head in a short nod.

"You're going to eat him, aren't you?"

She tilted her head as if to say, "And?"

"I can't let you do that."

Her mouth curved into an amused smile. Her lips were dark, too, shaped with exotic curves and a delicious cupid's bow. I didn't know if she could speak at all, let alone in my language. But something about that flashing brilliance in her flexed pupils told me that she could if she wanted to. *Only* if she wanted to.

"Please, don't make him suffer anymore. Let him die in peace. Eat me instead."

Horror pooled in my stomach and blossomed outward, tensing every limb. *What did I just say?* Had I no control over my own tongue? What madness *was* this?

The creature laughed with a sweet, majestic gaiety that changed her from animal to angel in a matter of seconds. My body relaxed despite the warning screams of my conscience. *Row away, Laura! Row away if you value your life!*

But how could I hope to outpace her? Besides, a magnetic influence drew me to her; I could not resist staying. As I agonized over what to say next, the siren spoke. "What a charming human thou art. What dost thou call thyself, woman?"

Her voice was powerful. Oh, it caused me to tremble from the sheer magical power of it! She didn't speak loudly but with a lisping sort of purr. As she smiled at me, she exposed her small, serrated teeth, curved inward to prevent injury to her plump lips . . . streaked red with blood. Yes, she was the crewman's attacker.

And yet I was not afraid of her anymore. Not since she laughed. Despite the blood, I wet my own lips at the sight of hers, so full, so breathtakingly exquisite. "I am Laura Rivell."

She hummed as she seemed to consider how to respond. *She does not converse with humans often.* "I am pleased to make thine acquaintance, Laura Rivell."

I wondered if she talked in such an old-fashioned way because her schooling of English was outdated. "What is *your* name?" I all but pleaded.

In reply, she sang one long, low note rife with regal vibrato. I smiled and shook my head. "I can't say that. Or *sing* it, I suppose."

The siren shrugged—it was a rusty movement, yet surprisingly human. "Then call me what you like, Laura Rivell. I care not. But I am hungry." She gestured once more to my dying companion, "And thou hast interrupted my supper. Give him over, woman, or I shall prick thee with mine spurs, put thee to sleep, and take him anyway."

"Then you'll have to put me to sleep," I declared. "For I shan't give any man, woman, or child over to their death in my right mind."

"He is dying anyway. A long, slow death. You cannot save him." Her dark eyes glistened. Their color seemed to change with the churn of the water, shifting from dark silver, teal, green, blue, and navy with the utmost subtlety. I could watch them for a night and a day and not know their true tint.

I fumbled with my shorn nightdress. "Still, I cannot give him over."

"Very well." With one sweep of her tail, she lunged halfway over the boat and wrapped her wet fingers around my neck. I swallowed hard as she stared up and down my body, curiosity shining in her strange eyes. "Man after man I have beheld so closely, but never the body of woman," she murmured. She parted her lips and fastened her mouth softly on my throat.

The siren did not bite down as I expected and braced myself for. Instead, smooth pockets of flesh on either side of her mouth parted, disclosing minuscule fangs that pricked my skin. A gentle doze clouded my mind, muffling my memories.

Her hands trailed over my skin. Succumbing to an undeniable wave of pleasure, I shuddered, growing warmer at her exclamations of wonder over my shapely legs. She gently examined my stomach and breasts beneath the blood-splattered nightgown. "A woman is a beautiful creature, then." I thought I heard her say. "A pity . . ."

Afterward, the roil of sea water rocked me to sleep. I woke on the deck of the *SS Saint Brigette*, blanketed and baffled but safe. Unfortunately, the poor crewman who had been with me was never seen again. When the medical officer asked about the blood on my gown, I explained it was from a "shark attack," describing the man I had attempted to save.

I said nothing more about the incident.

CHAPTER 3

Cape Althea was best described as a stubborn old woman who refused to wear any colors except navy or gray. I thought its creaking buildings, staunch traditions, and persistent superstitions might strike some visitors as charming . . . if they did not mind catching the Melancholy that hung thick in the air no matter the season. It especially lingered o'er the dim sea cliffs, taunting you with its perilous overhangs and the echo of stones and chunks of earth breaking loose to tumble into the water below. It took effort to be happy here.

Once upon a time, my stern constitution was more than suitable for the task. But now with Shadow set free to assert its will . . .

I should not think of that.

For after returning from the revival cruise, I could not sleep. My pitiable mother tried everything to help me: potions, charms, even spells chanted over a holy candle blessed by a local Elder. But the haunted melody lurked in me, in Shadow, and we told no one about it. I snuggled it to my chest like a deadly treasure I refused to share.

While many of Cape Althea's residents might be delighted to accept my declaration—"I have seen a siren! Conversed with it! Been touched by it!"—I doubted my friends and family could conjure up sufficient belief to *not* toss me into a madhouse. And if I were locked up there—horror of horrors!—not only would the song plague me night and day, but Shadow would have its way with me as well. No. *I must mask more cautiously than ever*, I'd decided. *Must play pretend with every ounce of my being.*

So, I hummed through my chores, smiling. Donning my ridiculous paisley prints, I allowed my new maid to dress my hair and managed some cheerful conversation with her, still smiling. My cheeks began to hurt. I preferred to be serious or melancholy over perpetually smiling; I wondered how other ladies managed it.

One smile *did* ring true, and only one. The smile that crossed my lips whenever I thought of talking to the siren. True, she did not look quite as I believed mermaids ought to look. She was less human and more of a predatory fish than illustrations led me to expect. Yet her voice was pleasant, her hair thick and soft, and her touch gentle.

Her lips . . . I should not think of them.

The way her mobile pupils flexed and narrowed as they absorbed me. We fascinated each other with equal delight; her touch and exclamations betrayed her elation. She stroked me with the reverence of a countess admiring a bolt of priceless silk. I'd never been touched by anyone like that before. Despite the resulting blushes, my helpless mind played the sensation on repeat. I yearned to feel it again.

Eventually, I was able to persuade my mother to condone late-evening strolls in the hope of "tiring myself out" for bed. But, of course, they were my guise for snatching Father's spyglass, running to the cliffs, and keeping watch for my siren. For so I came to call her almost overnight—*my siren*—and it suited her so well that not even Shadow questioned it or teased me about it.

Beneath a broad wolf moon, I wandered by the seaside.

The sand gleamed silver, broken by black rocks among the silk. The waves greedily lapped the shore. I removed my shoes and stockings and waded barefoot. Lifting my skirts to keep them dry, I vocalized the haunted melody, loud and long, as I'd often done before.

Nothing ever came of it. Yet, I would not desist. *Could* not.

As the tune came to an end, my eyes swam with tears. My soul withered without my siren. I longed to speak with her again, to relish the otherworldly strength of her presence. What were friends and family compared to *her?* What was any human in comparison to such timeless magic? For it fairly radiated from her, though I hadn't understood it at the time. I'd never experienced magic before—only heard of it, wished for it. *Wanted* to believe in it. For surely the warm, undulating aura I felt in her vicinity had to be magic. Even if it consumed me, I would gladly die in its embrace.

"Please," I whispered, stretching my hands to the ocean. "Please, please. I'm waiting for you." I closed my eyes.

As I opened them, a striking woman broke the surface. The black, glassy waves parted to reveal moonlit ivory flesh, dark gray hair, and strange, shifting eyes. She shook her wild tresses out of her face and smiled at me. Her lush lips teased for my attention. I tightly pursed my own lips to keep them still, refusing to pant after her kisses. The temptation nearly strangled me. *Is this how it feels to be enchanted by a siren?* If so, it was the closest thing to heaven on earth I'd ever felt . . . despite also being the most vicious torment.

From her subtle expression—a certain regal quality of amusement—I knew instantly that it was her. This was *my siren*, though she did not appear to be anything more than a beautiful woman. Upon second glance, however, her uniqueness betrayed itself. Her eyes (albeit human) were abnormally large, dark, and glazed like sea glass. *Soulless* eyes, I supposed I might have described them, though that also seemed wrong.

Her hair remained the same, remarkably long and thick and of the deepest gray. Her skin was difficult to judge in the current nocturnal lighting, but with the aid of the moon I could determine its smooth, fresh human surface without a single glitter of her former armor-like scales. Throughout my assessment I blushed like a bashful child; she wore not a stitch of clothing.

She lifted her human hands to inspect them. "It has been many years since I assumed my land form. I had forgotten it. And so . . . " She astonished me by walking closer to take my hands into her own, as warm and smooth as the sunbaked sands. "Forgive me for delaying so long, Laura Rivell, but I have been seeking thine cure." She shook her head and smiled at me. "You are a strange woman, indeed, to be affected by the siren's call. For it to have taken root for so long is stranger still, but I've come to cure thee of it."

"I don't want to be cured of it!" I blurted out. My grip on her hands tightened.

She raised her fine, sharply-angled brows. "That song was not meant for you. It is a trap for human males. Human females are not affected by it—*should not be affected*," the siren amended.

"Then am I the only woman who has been affected?" I asked.

She glanced down at our linked hands and smiled again, tolerantly. "There have been other women in the past, but they are so few and far between. That is why it took me so long to rediscover the cure." Locking eyes with me once more, her tone changed from soothing to commanding. "Let me help you, Laura. You shall go mad for the remainder of your short life if you do not let me."

You want her, Shadow accused from the back of my brain. *You like wanting her. You like how wrong it feels, how deliciously against what is expected of you. You're just a rebellious child. How can you ever comprehend her, let alone truly love her?*

I trembled and released the siren's hands, watching them fall to her smooth, perfect sides. "Very well," I conceded, submitting to her will.

The siren's expression softened. "Thank you, Laura."

Kneeling, she waited until another wave pooled around her ankles and reached into it, withdrawing a length of twine with a single seashell hanging from its center. A necklace. "Wear this for three days and three nights. If you must remove it for any reason, you must continue again for three days and three nights. No more and no less."

"I understand."

She straightened and handed it to me. I tried not to look at her as I knotted it around my neck, uttering a soft gasp as I felt the seashell vibrating against my skin. Now that it was close, I heard a quiet continuous note ringing from inside. "Thank you, Lady Siren."

We both laughed at the phrase. "That sounded positively strange," I giggled. "Might I give you a human name?"

"If you wish. As I told you when we met, I care not."

I stepped close once more to evaluate her face. "So otherworldly . . . I couldn't possibly call you something ordinary. Let me see. How do you like Eramyne?"

"Air-ah-mine?" she sounded out, puzzled. "What does it mean? I have not heard this name before."

"Oh, it's just a character from human myths." I did not tell her it was after the goddess Eramyne, mistress of love, light, and lyrics. Nor did I confess that I'd already chosen this name for her the night before.

She nodded. "I suppose it shall do, but my real name carries well underwater. This one is as useless as exhaling tiny bubbles."

"Then it's meant for your human form only."

"Yes. We call such names our land-nomen." Eramyne frowned, kneeling again and scooping seawater to pool over her arms and legs. "My discomfort grows in this frail body. How are you not freezing to your demise?"

I laughed. "Your language is a bit less old-fashioned now. Were you studying?"

"A little. You humans have such rudimentary languages." The siren slipped back into the water, changing almost instantly. Silver, teal, and flashes of bright red shone dully in the moonlight. "I must return, for I have much to do." Her sidelong gaze trifled with mine, then drifted aside. "I cannot linger," she said in a low voice, almost a whisper. Dared I imagine it? Was that quenched gleam in her eyes . . . reluctance?

"Wait!" I pleaded as her tail propelled her away at lightning speed.

Her head surfaced with a sigh. "What is it, lovely one? I have work to do."

I flushed. *I do hope she calls me that again.* "Will I see you again? Please say yes."

She stared at me for a long moment. Her pupils flexed, then narrowed, just as they did when we first met. "Yes." Her smile was brief yet divine, ripe with the ruddy bloom of certain *meaning*.

My heart fluttered, an eager little bird in its ribcage. I waved to her as she dived back down. Her red tail resurfaced as she navigated the sandbar. Then, she was gone.

As I wandered back home, my steps were slow and hesitant. My fingers fumbled with the creamy seashell nestled in the crook of my throat. Its vibration was soothing, but I couldn't stop thinking about what would happen to me once I was *cured*. Would I yet long for her presence? Would I still feel so incandescently happy merely to see her, to talk to her? Or would the bedazzled glimmer that hung over her presence like a cape be torn from her, never to be donned again? Ah, the beauty of the sea goddess! Words truly could not do Eramyne proper justice.

CHAPTER 4

Over the prescribed three days and nights, I thought of her incessantly—of the underwater world she lived in and ruled over, if I was any judge of character and poise. Regal power flowed from her movements. Queenly training lined her alluring posture at all times. I mourned that I would never be half as captivating as her, not even if someone handed me a genie in a bottle with three wishes.

Despite this logical conclusion resolved during daylight hours—namely, the realization that even if I *could* spend every waking hour with her, I would neither be her equal nor a useful companion—I yet dreamed. On the third and final night, I dreamed I truly was her "lovely one."

Somehow, I'd been changed into a siren, too. Eramyne took me by the hand and led me down, down, down deep into the fathoms she reigned over. The waters shifted from royal blue to dark purple, the bubbles twinkling around us like crystals. Submerged cliffs loomed like mountains, and hammerhead sharks paced above us but didn't dare to venture close. *We* were the monsters of the deep, not they.

The sirens dwelt not in shining underwater castles or coral coves but in sprawling, echoing caverns, sharing them with their fellow sea creatures in good will. Eerie music rang everywhere, with strange voices to accompany it. There were no demonstrations of rash opulence or royal feasts. They thrived in their power simply, humbly. Their locks flowed freely, and they did not cover their breasts with shame. In a word, Eramyne's kingdom was *freedom*.

In my dream, she led me to observe a complicated dance performed by members of her court. Their fins were cutting yet graceful, their spines and tales lined with bright spikes like Eramyne's, but of varying colors: orange and purple and verdant green. One siren, the loveliest of all, had a glittering tale of deep rose pink with rose-gold hair. But even her heavenly beauty amidst the deep did not awe me as Eramyne did.

'Twas in the midst of this court dance that I woke and cried for my unromantic fate: to live, suffer, and die upon the coarse, dry land. To never know anything as eerie or as enchanting as life alongside my siren.

By the time sunlight arose to dry my tears, I scolded myself, washed my face, and donned my prettiest dress. *Do not be a child,* I rebuked my reflection. *If you want to be admired, then be admirable.*

The seashell had ceased thrumming, so I discarded it as Eramyne instructed. I toyed with the urge to hide it under my pillow. However, this might have undone whatever disenchanting work the shell had wrought, and it was better to be wise than romantic. The fact that I *could* be wise convinced me that I was indeed healed, at least for the most part.

I still wanted her.

Fully dressed and hair arranged, I stopped dead at the threshold and considered my emotional state. *Calm.* I still thought of my siren, still longed for her fascinating company and powerful voice, but I no longer felt as if I'd perish without hearing it. I'd merely love her from afar and never love anybody else. Since I didn't *want* to love anyone before, this did not change my noble future plans to remain a spinster. It would hurt more, yet I would survive the pain.

"You look happy this morning." My mother smiled as I helped her prepare breakfast.

In answer, I hummed a few bars of a cherished tune. "I am." For I *knew* Eramyne's word was as trustworthy as the tides coming in and going out. I would see her again. After all, though I acknowledged this thought as rather audacious, it seemed to me that I had fascinated her just as much as she had intrigued me. I believed our curiosity was quite mutual. What did a siren queen think about human women when she thought of them at all? Did we appear silly, weak, and hysterical to her? Did she frown at our complete dependence upon men, the very creatures most likely to prey upon us?

I'd suffered an encounter from such a creature before. I kept that sordid memory tucked as far away from my conscious as possible. *Eramyne would have simply grinned and eaten him,* I could not resist thinking. That mental picture made me giggle.

Immediate shame followed as the ghost of the wounded crewman raised an invisible hand to grasp my skirts, pleading for the help that never came. Why did I not do more for him? Did I execute the bare minimum and not an inch more? Shadow laughed, gleefully demonstrating its consuming darkness. *You liked the drama of it, didn't you?* It sneered. *You liked seeing all that blood, fancying yourself a heroine. You only ever think about yourself.*

"Quiet, you!" I muttered as I kneaded the dough.

"What's that, dear?" Mother called over her shoulder.

"Nothing. Just thinking out loud."

The threat of navy gloom shaded the parlor. A rising wind rattled the trees, casting blue streaks over the yellow crockery and the scalloped china. Despite the sullen weather, our breakfast was a merry one, for I minded tempests not a whit. I liked them. They stirred up the sea to demonstrate her wild glory and reminded all the world that she was *not* tame and never would be.

I excused myself to change again, guiltily peeling off my best dress to replace it with a far more sensible alternative. Snatching my cloak, I pelted out of doors before I could be stopped and questioned.

Once I gained the outskirts of town, I pulled off my boots and stockings to run through the sand barefoot. My father would be scandalized, I knew, but I could not bring myself to care. I laughed as I lifted my skirts to splash through the shallows.

A fever of stingrays coasted to my right. I marveled at their grace as I waded beside them, careful to shuffle my feet to warn any lingering creatures of my intrusion.

"I'll only be a few minutes," I whispered in apology. "I'm waiting for my siren."

It was more than a few minutes, closer to sixty, but I was stubborn. Once Eramyne's iron locks broke the surface, I was soaked through, teeth a'chatter. My lips broke into a beaming smile at the sight of her, a pillar of regal beauty framed by graceful waves. *What a glorious subject for a painting!*

"What a silly creature you are," my siren's rebuke commenced. "I save you from the siren's poison so you may freeze to death on the shore, awaiting your poisoner."

In one mighty sweep, she propelled herself out of the water and somehow grew legs at once, catching me up in her strong arms and carrying me up the ridge. "W-wait! Stop!" I managed between chattering. "You c-c-can't. Someone will see you!"

She raised her glistening brows. "Why should that cause you alarm? I look like a woman, do I not? I even walk quite well," she added with pride.

Giggling, I kicked my legs, enjoying the sensation of being carried. "You're n-n-naked."

"Oh. So I am. A Tritoness in human form should be clothed, yes?"

"Quite so!"

"But you must be removed from this rain. Where shall I deposit thee?"

I smiled, finding myself increasingly fond of her relapses into quaint olde English. "I know of an old s-s-seaside church not far from here, half-collapsed and . . . abandoned. It's not m-much, but some of the roof is still intact. No one will see us."

"Very well."

I insisted upon walking, but Eramyne would not allow it. Her grip on my legs and shoulder increased. "I am aware that human women can be quite frail."

"I am *not* frail," I protested, kicking my feet again to prove it. She smiled, baring her tiny, serrated teeth. "Then think of this act as mine penance, lovely one. Be still!" I quieted—for after all, I liked being carried by her—and pointed in the direction of the abandoned church.

As she carried me there, the rain ceased. I immersed her in a flood of questions. "You called yourself a Tritoness. Are you related to King Triton?"

She smiled and shook her head, a bit clumsily, as if yet unaccustomed to the nonverbal communication of humans. "Sirens were born of the goddess Sofia. We are the physical manifestations of the dark divine feminine inherent to her nature, for which she was shamed and cast out. There are no men among sirens."

"No men?" I hugged her neck upon the pretense of slipping, moving closer to observe the faint, spider-web shimmer across her tender skin. It was more beautiful than a bolt of pure silk shining in the sun. "Then how are sirens conceived?"

Her slanted eyes fired an amused look. "Hardly a suitable subject for a young, unmarried lady." Soaked hair whipped about her face, drying quickly in the fervent wind.

I rolled my eyes, drawing another heavenly laugh from her. Eramyne complied, "Once we come of age, we either lure men from their ships or we come to land and lure men with the forms of human women." Eramyne spoke in a dreadfully matter-of-fact way that Shadow loved. "Depending on the location of the act itself, we may or may not consume them afterward. This has been our way since the male sirens became so rare. They are all but extinct."

We may or may not consume them. Disgust churned my stomach. Shadow was delighted. I kept it down with a firm mental *Hush!* An image of my father being ripped apart by creatures like Eramyne forced its way into my mind—their teeth ripping his flesh from his bones, their eyes matching their nature as they tore him apart: fierce, cold, and unsympathetic. I shuddered. "Can't you eat fish instead?" My voice was hesitant and gentle so as not to offend her. "Why the men? Your own mates?"

She shot me another sidelong look. One I could not read. "Only the men we have mated with, so they cannot band together to hunt us down. The siren's song suppresses their memories. However, every mind is different. The permanence of the suppression cannot be guaranteed."

"So, you're protecting yourselves and your future young," I supplied.

"Yes."

"But you *do* eat fish as a matter of course?"

"Yes. They are not so satisfying, however."

I exhaled in relief. Shadow shrank within my chest, disappointed. "Have you ever eaten a woman?"

She laughed again. The enchanting sound filled my heart with quick, eager pulses. "Sirens have nothing to do with women, and they have nothing to do with us. What can either species offer the other?"

The crumbling walls of the church peeked above a sandy cliff. *Almost there.* "Perhaps we can learn from each other," I proposed. "An information exchange. I can teach you about my world, and you can teach me about yours."

Eramyne said nothing until we reached the church. Ducking beneath a collapsed beam, she tucked me into a dry corner, wringing out my skirts for me. Her fingers brushed my bare legs. I bit my lip, concentrating on the cracks in the sand-blasted floor. "There is more risk than reward in trading such information," she finally said, her tone mild. "Many sirens dislike humans, and were you to tell anyone about me . . . about *us* . . ."

"Never!" I gasped before she could finish. A blush seared my face. *Tell anyone about us.* "I swear upon your goddess, Sofia, I will never tell anyone about you. Not unless you say it's all right."

Her cold, sweet smile both terrified and excited me. Such beautiful ferocity could not be described, but it was burned into my retinas for all time. "Not even to save yourself?" she asked with a low, seductive purr.

She'd locked our gazes together. My hands curled into fists. Shadow jumped up and answered for me. "Not even to save myself."

"Hmm." Releasing me from her predatory stare, Eramyne hummed a lilting tune as she used her own hair to dry my feet. Her delicious mouth teased me with its slow, deliberate smiles, our proximity breaking her queenly restraint. *She doesn't believe you,* Shadow crooned at my ear. *But she will.*

CHAPTER 5

I baited my siren with more questions. Once or twice, she bestowed an anxious glance toward the fading sunlight. Her face softened once I coaxed her gaze back to mine. For a fleeting moment, I thought of tempting her back to me with scraps of fish like a stray cat, which made me choke down a laugh.

"What amuses you, lovely one?"

I vexed myself by blushing again. "A passing thought, nothing more. Why do you keep looking at the horizon?"

"I must go. I only meant to speak with you for a few minutes to confirm that the cure worked as intended."

She'd been kneeling next to me, hunched over and clasping her knees. It could not have been a comfortable position, yet there she stayed for many minutes. *She doesn't know how to sit like a human,* I realized. She rose, her glinting eyes taking on a sudden seriousness. I knew what it meant. "Oh, don't say it!" I begged.

"Say what?"

"That we will not see each other again."

Her expression took on an additional gravity. "We cannot be friends, sweet Laura. Tales are already spreading of the wraith guarding Half Moon Bay. The people of your village might look for me." A minuscule smile touched the corners of her mouth. "Although being hunted down can make for excellent sport. The birthing season draws near; I cannot risk it."

And there you have it, Miss Rivell, Shadow sneered. *Do not fool yourself. You're not pretty, you're not amusing, and you're of no more than average intelligence. Why would a splendid creature like Eramyne want anything more to do with you?*

My siren knelt beside me once more, blinking with surprise. "Do not cry. For the goddess' sake, we have not known one another very long."

"I'm *not* crying."

"You are." She extended one long, shimmering finger and swept a tear from my cheek. I sniffled and turned my head away. "I have a headache."

"And this causes a human to cry?"

I laughed at her honest concern. "No, you are right. I am a silly goose crying over a siren I've just met. Satisfied?"

Eramyne gave me a long, solemn look. Her pupils dilated. "Then I promise I will come to see you. Look for me in the bay on the night of the full moon." Curious, she sniffed the tiny splash of a tear still on her fingertip, then licked it. Her long tongue was as dark as her lips. The animalistic impulse sent a shudder of pleasure through me. There was no hesitation in her urges, no habitual shame. She was such a beautiful contrast to the stiff, polite society I knew so well.

I burned to be with her more than ever. I might have informed her with no uncertain words that one night a month was *not* sufficient, but I could only nod. It was a grave risk to trust me—to trust *any* human—and she was taking that risk to please me. She couldn't stand to see me cry.

"I am grateful," I whispered. Our fingertips met in a ghost of a touch. "Truly."

Distraction rained down like a tempest. I weathered the storm as well as I could, yet my parents commented on the growing paleness of my cheeks, the nervous wringing of my hands. Thank the gods, I had but a few weeks to wait. Did she miss me as I missed her? Did she yearn for me? The constant resurrection of that question was torture—a ravenous thing that I kept killing, but it would not *stay dead.*

On the named night with the moon shining in all her splendor, I pushed my bedroom window ajar and clambered out, shoes in hand. I pulled them on once I'd gained a safe distance from the house and quickly slipped past the outskirts of town. The ocean breeze sang in my ears, and my heart danced light as a feather in my panting chest as I ran.

I gained the moonlit-crested waters of Half Moon Bay. Laughter broke from my lips as my head fell back. It was a brilliant night. The sand glinted blue-white, soft and silken against iron crags. The ocean seethed black and mysterious, crowned with diamond froth. And unless my ears beguiled me, I heard the strains of my siren's cryptic tune creeping ever closer.

Eramyne rose halfway from the sea. She remained in siren form, her thick hair glinting wet and tousled. Her little fangs bared in a monstrous smile. "Lovely one. You have been waiting for me."

"Not for long." I kicked off my shoes and waded into the water. "No need to transform again; I will come to you."

The Tritoness looked amused but said nothing about my imperiled skirt as I held it gingerly above the waves. "How have you fared?" she asked, tilting her head. "No more troubled sleep, I trust?"

"No. I have only been excited to see you again. So, you are tasked with guarding this bay?"

She nodded. "More accurately, the outer perimeter. We do not come too close to shore."

"Of course."

I struggled with what to say next—how to draw Eramyne into deeper conversation. I longed to ask her all about her world, *her* ocean. But would that be too personal? Too much, too soon? I hadn't the faintest idea what a siren's social protocol was.

"You are quiet tonight," Eramyne observed. She sank down into the water to cover her bare chest, staring up at me with her wide eyes. Smiling with her exotic lips. The dark water clung to her skin and polished her scales, reveling in her presence. I smiled back. "Has anyone told you that you're breathtaking?"

"No human has lived long enough to do so."

I tried to laugh despite the dread tingling down my spine. There was no jest in her tone. "Well, you are, and it is high time someone said it. You are beautiful."

"Thank you." Those diabolical pupils flexed and shrank, latched to me as if burrowing into my soul. It was a *swallowing* look. I loved it with a demented adoration that only Shadow understood. Eramyne drifted closer, touching my ankle with the barest trace of her tail fin. It tickled. Smiling, I dug my wriggling toes deep into the sand.

A pesky wave, larger than the ones preceding it, lurched up and smacked me in the stomach. Sighing, I relinquished my skirts to the sea. "No use trying to keep dry now."

"You may remove your clothing if you are uncomfortable."

Her cool words startled me. I shook my head, wide-eyed. The melody of her low laughter shrank my confidence further. "No need to gape like a frightened fish, lovely one. We never wear clothing; it would only get in the way of hunting and breeding. I have seen hundreds of bare bosoms. You are safer with me than with the most modest priest above the sea."

Her face was so very serene. She might have been a carven image there, half-drowned in the waves, motionless as marble. Despite my shaking fingers, I lifted my hands to start loosing the buttons. My face blazed; I suddenly wished the water was colder.

Eramyne fixed her pupils on the shoreline as I worked. Soon, I'd slipped from the sodden garment, bunched it up with my wet underthings, and tossed the whole of the pile to the sands. Still blushing, I sank into the ocean to the neck. It was certainly better than remaining at the mercy of the breeze. "Thank you," I murmured, flushing warmer still.

"It is no trouble." She returned her gaze to mine. The same intensity in her stare rattled me, making my toes curl. "Tell me, why did you want to see me again? Was there something you wished to ask me?"

"Not in particular. I enjoy talking to you."

"I see." She hummed a few gentle bars, side-eyeing me. "I am not convinced that the cure has worked to completion." She announced it with a sudden sternness that made me jump. "Why do you regard me so?"

"Who else is around for me to look at?" I fired back, stung by her perception.

She chuckled at my pique. Her tail brushed against my leg that time . . . a little higher, a little more lingering of a touch. I caught my breath. "Ah, thou art amusing, lovely one. However—and trust me when I say I do not mean you any offense— I am Tritoness. I am the primary guardian of the Nereid, Empress of Echo Trench. In human terms, you might call me a queen. I have many duties to attend to." She paused, regarding my facial expression with care. "To be frank, Laura, I do not have the time to spare for visits of pleasure. If you must summon me, I would prefer you to have a reason for doing so." Her solemnity clarified that she took no joy in telling me this, that she did not wish to hurt me.

Yet I felt hurt nevertheless. Anger and embarrassment fought for predominance. I crossed my arms over my chest, turning aside. "I understand. I'm sorry for bothering you."

Eramyne sighed. She drifted closer to me to stroke one hand down my arm. "It is not that I dislike your company," she murmured at my ear. "It is only that I have a great deal to do. I cannot neglect my tribe's needs for the amusement of one woman."

Both hands brushed against my shoulders, then gently clasped them. I shivered as her venom-red nails touched my bare skin. "Then tell me how I can make myself useful," I demanded, both to her surprise and my own.

She withdrew, tilting her head, bemused. "I suppose given enough time, when trust has been earned, it would be valuable to have a human informant. If you are interested in pearls, I would exchange them for the information I seek. Would this arrangement satisfy you, my strange, sweet little Laura?"

The barest trace of affection lingered in her address. Even when speaking playfully, a type of regal coolness was interwoven with her tone, holding her aloft from me. I found myself disliking it. *She's insisting upon this barrier between us. I will not have it! I will tear it down no matter how long it takes. I will earn her trust.*

"Yes," I agreed. "This arrangement would make me very happy." Though the promise of pearls shone but dimly in my mind compared to conversing with my siren.

Eramyne drew back with a coy smile. "Then you shall be tested." She writhed in the shallows with serpentine ease, her long tail generating clouds of sand. I wondered how much of her powerful tail was formed of muscle versus cartilage. *Can she navigate on land as easily as she swims in the sea?*

Freezing, I eagerly awaited the details, but the pull of water and a soft splash informed me of her departure. I groaned. She was such an elusive creature, but I already adored her as if I'd known her from my childhood. My heart fluttered at the prospect of helping her, serving her hidden kingdom. And while it would be lovely to adorn myself with pearls (or discreetly sell the main of them), it was the official alliance with my monstrous siren that thrilled me most.

For so long, I assumed my life would come and go with plainness—such heartbreaking normalcy that it might well make me cry some nights. Some half-feral desire in me keened after but a sixpence of greatness to clasp to my chest and call my own. I longed for adventure. Peril, even.

At long last, here it was.

CHAPTER 6

Eramyne did not make me wait long. Midway through an evening walk, the shriek of a wounded siren lured me to the sandbar. Although I had never heard such a sound in all my born days, it couldn't have been anything else. So plaintive and wild it sliced the heart. I dove into the breakers without hesitation, terror bounding in my veins. What if it was Eramyne?

It was not. A blonde siren with bright purple prongs and wide eyes flailed in the grip of a fisherman's net. She snarled at my approach, showing her fangs. I treaded water, well aware that I was risking bodily injury at best and a gory demise at worst, but confidence rose within me when I assumed this must be my test. Would I drag the imprisoned siren to shore, earning fame and fortune for decades to come, or would I release the wild thing at my own peril?

Speaking calmly to the siren, I swam close. To my shock, she quieted and stared at me with a fascinated gleam in her glassy eyes. "You are the queen's informant?" she asked as I struggled with the ropes.

I started back; I was not prepared for conversation. Somehow, it was easy to forget that these hissing, keening creatures could speak. "Yes. Am I correct in assuming you are part of Her Majesty's test? Have I passed?"

The siren smirked. She extended her claws and sliced through the netting. It dropped from her body. I stared at her, mouth agape. "Perhaps this was not your test," she crooned, reaching out to stroke her forefinger down my cheek. "Perhaps I was curious about you."

I withdrew, respectfully but at once. "What is your name, and what is your place in Eramyne's kingdom?"

The monstrous mermaid tilted her head. "Who?"

I sighed, trying and failing to recall the vocal arrangement meant to carry Eramyne's true name through the fathoms. "Do you serve the Tritoness?"

Her tone shifted. "You do not need to know who I am or what I do."

My eyes narrowed. "Then why are you here?"

"I told you," she said, a touch miffed. "I was curious."

"If you presume I'm the sort of human that believes what she's told at face value, you are mistaken."

The smallest of smiles betrayed the siren's amusement. Her fangs flashed between her lips, mirroring moonlight. "How fortunate for the Tritoness to have cornered just the right sort of human. What a happy accident for Half Moon Bay."

"I don't suppose you'd be so kind as to elaborate?"

"You suppose correctly." She vanished in an elegant backward arch.

The corner of the sinking net brushed my feet as I tread in place, thinking. With a sigh, I paddled slowly back to shore, pondering what the siren had said. As I wrung out my drenched skirts, the steady thrum of masculine baritone halted my task. "Might I be of assistance, my lady?"

I recoiled. A stranger lingered in the sodden dark, his own cloak proffered, concern in his stern face. My attention was immediately drawn to his thick, slanted brows, shaped and sized in a manner that one could only describe as *villainous*, yet the eyes reposing beneath them looked gentle enough, albeit guarded. "Thank you," I managed, "I shall go home at once and change, Mister . . . ?"

"Burke."

I dipped my head in a cool nod and would have passed him without another word, but his following query stopped my progression dead. "I heard her, too. Was she wounded?"

His directness, chilly as the water dripping down the nape of my neck, drew a gasp from my lips. "I don't know what you mean," I persisted, clinging to denial.

"Yes, you do." Burke's stern demeanor doubled. I felt his scrutiny breaking into my soul, seeping in through its cracks. It brushed against Shadow and withdrew, curious yet taut with a lifetime of vigilance. "You neglected to mention *your* name," he dryly intoned. In one sweep, he secured the navy cloak upon his shoulders, crossing his arms afterward. Glints of budding silver reveled in his short, dark beard.

I lifted my chin. I would not back down. "We both heard the shriek of a coming storm and nothing more," I proclaimed, "and this is neither the time nor the place for proper introductions, sir. We are alone."

"Yes," Burke replied, the touch of a smile softening his grim face. "Quite alone."

I steeled myself for the anticipated scolding. Ladies ought not to be unattended—why was I out so late, was I not aware of the dangers of cold night swims, had I never heard of sharks, etc. My shoulders stiffened, but he said nothing more. I swore that an answering flicker of fellow mischief shone in his pupils. Surprise muddled my response. Such a collision of austerity and subtle friendliness I had never before, nor ever since, beheld in one person. "I am Laura Rivell," I murmured, like a sinner at the confessional.

"Happy to meet you, Laura Rivell." He offered his hand. I stared at it blankly before submitting my palm to his. He shook as cordially as a boon companion might. That brief suggestion of a smile flashed from his lips again as he acknowledged our mutual ice-cold fingers. "Lead the way to your abode, Miss Rivell, and I'll escort you."

"That's kind of you, sir, but there is no need. I grew up here; I come here often on my own—"

"I do not doubt it. Nor shall I scold you as you've preserved yourself admirably thus far." Motioning for me to follow with the tilt of his head, Burke drew me into step with him as we ascended the path through the cliffs. He impressed me with his cool-headed nonchalance, his easy emulation of masculine honor that so many *gentlemen* failed to attain. "Nonetheless, no man worth his salt would stumble upon a lone lady in the dead of night and allow her to walk home alone."

I liked his voice, too, so effortlessly smooth and self-assured. *If I were born a man, I'd want to be just like him.* "You're right. Thank you, sir."

"You may abandon that 'sir' nonsense. Burke will do."

"Very well."

Silence descended, thick upon the sea-night air, yet strangely pleasant. *Familiar,* I might have said. With one chance gaze, one knowing soul hailed another in respectful salute. I pondered it as I peeled my wet skirts from my soaked skin and tried in vain to hold them apart, wrinkling my nose.

Burke's quick intuition pierced the dark. "Have we far to go?"

"About a ten minutes' walk."

"Then we must distract ourselves from the chill via conversation. You grew up here, you said?"

"I did." Sporadic lamplight bloomed from the cobbled streets ahead, lighting our way. Buckets of sea oats and beach plums lined the path. My eyes returned to Burke as they resumed their study. Close-cut hair meticulously trimmed, dark but fading into ombre lightness as they hinted their peppered flecks of gray. Fair skin intermittently marked with smooth, brown nevi. One crowned his left earlobe in the shape of a heart. *Gods, that is charming!* I nearly choked on the contrast against his villainous brows, turning aside to indulge a polite little cough instead. "Do you live here in Cape Althea?"

"Yes, but just recently. I was born in Summerside."

Ah, Summerside. A flourishing white-stone town of spotless fencing and azalea clouds. One cannot picture Summerside without the proverbial painted teacups, seaside banquets, and ice-jelly jamborees. A playground for the wealthy and politically privileged. The only locale that could match Summerside was Rosa Rugosa in its zenith, but it crumbled into ancient bloodline obscurity years ago.

Burke sensed my reaction, raising a stoic smirk in response. "That is not who I am, Miss Rivell."

"I believe you."

Comfortable silence resumed. Our synchronized steps traded the *shush* of sand for the *clop* of cobblestone. Once the lamplight shone full in his face, I rapidly concluded that he was indeed an honorable man despite his guarded sternness. I was glad he'd found me. "And why did you trade the opulence of Summerside for the gloom of Cape Althea?" I asked, linking my hands behind my back. Seawater continued to drip from my coiled tendrils of hair.

Burke shook his head, lifting a corner of his cloak to offer it again. I shook my head back at him. "Stubborn," he said with a smile. His first full, genuine smile. I liked it and hoped very much to see it again. "Cape Althea suits me," he professed, lowering his hand. "Summerside did not. Besides, I am not on positive terms with some of my relatives. Respectful distance helped everyone concerned."

"Certainly something I can understand."

"I had a feeling you might." He studied my face in the lamplight as I had studied his. I returned his scrutiny calmly. "There's a touch of cynicism in your eyes. We *live,* you and I, while many others simply exist, barging head-on from day to day without a single significant thought. Is that not so, Miss Rivell?"

I smiled. I knew what he was trying to do—what conversation he was hoping to reintroduce. *We both heard that siren, and we both know it.* I shrugged and reached up to uncoil my hopeless hair, allowing it to drape down my back in tangled ropes. "Perhaps. Or perhaps you are projecting what you *wish* to see, nothing more, nothing less."

"Implying that what I wish to see has a certain merit of its own."

"I cannot deny that. What little we've seen so far . . . "

"I agree wholeheartedly."

Kindred spirits. Were there really such things? Did such bonds truly exist outside of fairytale friendships? I'd never bothered believing in them before, much less hoped to meet one. Yet here we were. Only time would tell if my strong first impression was true or false.

"We're close enough," I said, stopping and extending my hand to bid him farewell. "I like you, Burke, but not enough to disclose my address just yet."

He took no offense, only chuckled. His laughter was brief, like his smiles, but as low and smooth as his speaking voice. It relaxed me with unconscious ease. He released my hand. "I hope we meet again, Miss Rivell. Forward as the confession must seem to you."

"Not at all. I hope so, too."

"Goodnight, then."

He bowed briefly—in alignment with his smiles and mirth—and left at once, politely refraining from waiting to see which house I entered. I liked him all the more for it. "If there were more men like *that* in this world, I might entertain the idea of marrying one of them," I muttered and slipped quietly through my bedroom window.

Chapter 7

It was a sunny day in Cape Althea when I encountered the mysterious Burke once more. I'd dashed to the general store by Mother's request, basket in hand, list in the other. I had the crinkled paper clenched between my teeth as I yanked the door ajar; 'twas in this ladylike state that Mr. Burke greeted me. A man's hand, gloved in sober brown, propped the door ajar on my behalf. "Afternoon, Miss Rivell."

I recognized his voice at once and flushed as I extracted the list. "Afternoon, Mr. Burke."

"Just Burke," he reminded me, entering the store behind me to the jingle of the visitor's bell. "Been on any more interesting solitary walks, my lady?"

I flushed all the more, pointedly darting a glance at the shopkeeper. She was wrapping an order and hadn't heard. "Not in public, if you please. Wait until we're outside, and if I must call you Burke then you must call me Laura."

"If you insist."

"I insist."

"Then I'll let you shop in peace, Laura, and we'll meet by the sea oats outside."

"All right."

As I leisurely strolled and selected items, my mind buzzed with concern. He wouldn't let me dance around the subject this time. That much I knew. We'd discuss the blonde siren, come what may. I could outrun him, perhaps, but the stately Miss Rivell lifting up her skirts to run from a gentleman might result in inquiries. That would not do. As far as anyone else was concerned, we'd never been introduced. Best for everyone to assume that this meeting was our first chance encounter until I knew what he wanted from me. What his intentions were.

What did Burke know of the sirens? Had he ever seen one up close and personal, as I had? I doubted it very much. Both the blonde siren and Eramyne had given me the impression that no man looked upon their faces and lived to describe them. They were man-eaters to the core of their coldblooded, beautiful beings. I had no reason to assume the rest of their kind were any different.

I cringed inwardly at my poor choice of words. *Their kind.* Even as a willing informant-in-training and hopeful friend to Queen Eramyne, I subconsciously separated *us* and *them.* We weren't so different at the end of the day. We protected our own. We guarded our lands as they guarded their sea. I rebuked myself as I approached the register and smiled at the clerk, arranging my purchases on the counter. *I will be better than this.*

I expected Shadow to mutter an abusive reply, but for once it was quiet. I wondered why, silently hoping it would last.

As I left with my loaded basket, I saw Burke waiting by a silver tub of sea oats. They drooped over the basin in feathery, golden wisps, nodding in the wind. Burke also nodded to me in lieu of formal bowing. "I won't waste your time with superfluous chitchat. I know what I heard. *You* know what I heard." He lowered his voice, ensuring his words reached my ears alone. "I want to know what you saw."

His gloved hands grasped a simple cane. He planted it directly front and center, leaning his weight slightly into it and staring me straight in the eyes. I found I could not look away, as much as I wished I could. His honesty compelled my own.

"Before I answer," I began, placing the heavy basket to one side, "I must ask what you are doing here in Cape Althea. And you must answer me true, by any and all gods that you hold dear."

"I hold to none," the infidel replied, serenity unshaken (and, I began to suspect, unshakable), "but I shall answer you true because I know we can trust one another. I knew it from the moment we first locked eyes."

"Rather audacious of you to assume it," I airily responded. His short chuckle stirred a smile from me; something in its duration and softness told me this was not a man who laughed often.

"I've resided upon this earth for long enough that I can read one's countenance in an instant," Burke said. He traced an absentminded picture into the dirt with the foot of his cane.

"And yet you are not elderly," I stated, immediately regretting doing so.

Burke was not offended, only amused. He brushed his lightly graying chin. "Time comes for us all, though she's good enough to grant the silvering in her wake. Wisdom's mark."

What an odd way to phrase it. He was certainly not boring—the worst of human crimes. I smiled and tapped the heel of my boot against the street. "And here you promised me you wouldn't chitchat."

"So I did. Forgive me." He straightened his shoulders, switching his cane behind his back and staring at the sky. "I came to Cape Althea to privately study one location: Half Moon Bay."

I nodded. "For the sirens."

"For the sirens."

The sea breeze stirred our hair as it whistled between us. He ceased his perusal of the clouds, if such was his aim, and looked back at me. "Time and time again, I have heard them. Their cold, clear voices are unmistakable to me; I distinguish them from the roar of the sea or the crash of thunder with an aptitude that would surprise you, Miss Rivell, and yet I have not laid eyes upon one. I suspect that *you* have."

I smiled wistfully. Burke's chestnut eyes glittered in the afternoon sun. His multi-shaded hair and pale, clear skin were so at odds, aging and eternal youth proclaimed in the same body, warring for dominance. "How do you know you are not mad, hearing voices that do not exist?" I asked.

Shadow started to laugh at me. *Keep quiet!* I internally hissed.

"Very well. I shall rise to your challenge," Burke answered. His expression remained sternly neutral, though his eyes gleamed. "Tell me I imagined this tune, my lady."

He hummed the hypnotic death chant that had driven me from the SS Saint Brigette that fateful night. Although his voice did not carry the same mesmeric quality of Eramyne's, I shuddered from the memory. I reached down and clutched the basket handle tightly, needing something to grasp.

"There is no mistaking your response." Burke moved to sit on the empty bench near the basin, indicating for me to join him. I did so, balancing the basket on my lap with shaking hands. "But how were you affected by it? Men are a siren's prey, not women. They do not respond to the siren call."

"I do not know," I snapped, quite unwilling to explain certain personal orientations. Even to potential kindred spirits. After all, most religions deemed such preferences as corruption, little devils to be cast out. I supposed Shadow was to blame, but I'd never really know. "And if we're going to ask questions, how were *you* able to hear it and withstand it? Are you a ghost?"

Unruffled by my acidity, he pulled off one glove and extended his hand toward me. "Touch my hand and see. I am no spook."

"Never mind," I flushed, petulance already waning. Never before had I met any man so complacent in the face of my moods. He treated me as if I were truly *equal* to himself. That I could snap if I liked, sulk when I wanted to, and dance barefoot in the waves when I took the notion. "I'm sure you do not know how you escaped it, either. How *could* we know?"

Burke worked his hand back into his glove. "I have my suspicions, but alas, my research has a long way to go." He paused, eyeing me with a delicate glance. "That is where I think we can help one another, Laura. If you would be so kind. In exchange, I'll be happy to share what knowledge I've gleaned to date."

"I won't take you to her," I warned him. "Best we have that expressly understood here and now, Burke . . . What is your last name?"

That brief, flickering smile. "Burke *is* my last name."

"Then kindly furnish me with your given name."

"I answer to Burke sufficiently well."

"Stubborn." We exchanged short grins. "Not fond of it, I gather?"

"Nary a bit. Laura, however, is a perfectly fitting name and exempt from the possibility of costing its owner impudent remarks. I congratulate your parents' sound sense."

"I taste a pint or so of bitterness," I gravely teased. "Pray lend me a sweeter draft to wash it down. It would be a shame to part with a bad flavor in our mouths."

"In *your* mouth, you mean." He fished about in his jacket pocket and fetched a business card, pressing it into the palm of my hand. "My lady." He stood, bowed, and departed, his face instantly resuming the perpetual rigidity that seemed to be his default expression. It delighted me, like finding and befriending an especially cantankerous cat who hated every other human alive but myself.

I read the card aloud. "Bartholomew Burke of Burke and Sampson, 110 Foxglove Lane, Cape Althea. Well! I always thought Bartholomew was a handsome name, but I can understand his evident distaste for it. It's one of those names that seems to go on forever, particularly when one is writing it down. Unpleasant for business."

Hyacinth and I strolled seaside, admiring the dull glass-green glimmer of the waves beneath pooling clouds. The scent of fresh and salt waters colliding restored a flush to our cheeks and a spring to our barefoot steps.

"What if someone should see us, ankles full out?" Hyacinth whispered. I indulged in a giddy laugh or two. "Then you'd best pray to Maltaros they're so taken with your pretty white ankles they won't mind at all."

She extended her fan to swat me, but I purloined it from her grasp and ran ahead, forcing her to chase me for it. We laughed as the strong breeze mussed our skirts and faces. "You seem so happy lately," Hyacinth called after me, panting as she gathered her lacy peach skirts.

"I am." For I lived in a secret world, a wider world, fraught with possibility in every breath of wild sea air I breathed. Even Shadow could not deny it. It remained serene with wonder. Sirens were real. And I had befriended one.

And you're in love with one, Shadow reminded me.

I smiled, remembering our magnetic gazes, the way her pupils wanted to swallow me up. The way Eramyne coyly drifted closer to stroke my arm or tap her tail against my bare legs. She longed to touch me just as I longed to be touched. *Perhaps she's in love with me, too.*

CHAPTER 8

Half Moon Bay donned her best at twilight.

A radiance of purple clouded the waters' edge, churning and frothing among the black rock with silver bubbles. Clear, stone-blue fanned outward into somber navy, still as glass, and I stared at the motionless water waxing tumultuous as it closed upon the rocky shore. *So like the sirens themselves,* I whispered to my sleeping Shadow. *Stark, menacing, and regal, but with scales flashing colors mankind has yet to name.*

Shadow did not answer. My lips curved in a satisfied smile.

It was said by nonbelievers that a colossal shark roamed the bay. Since a few unfortunate swimmers had indeed been attacked, tasted by something with very sharp teeth, the danger was the same, be it sea beast or siren. Either way, the residents of Cape Althea never dared to swim in it. As I dipped my fingertips into the plum-tinged waves, I wondered why the sirens had claimed this bay for themselves—what purpose this location served.

Did the warm, shallow waters here (untouched by human frolics) taste better to them, as fresh mountain air tasted to us? Were the hunting grounds good here? Or perhaps the nearby fishing docks, though quite desolate and in need of repairs, offered better access to—

A soft ripple and splash drew my focus outward. Iron-gray locks rose from the sea, shimmering red from the light of the setting sun. I spoke her name affectionately and extended my hand to her. "Eramyne."

She hesitated a moment before floating forward and touching her forehead to the palm of my hand. I flushed, pleased with her answering affection, wordless as it was. She withdrew. "What brings you here tonight?" I asked, lowering my hand. "Did I pass the test to satisfaction?"

My siren's wide, monstrous eyes blinked twice. "I have yet to determine what manner of test would best suit thee, strange woman. What event do you speak of?"

My lips parted in surprise. A stinging spray wet them as a rogue wave smacked the rock I sat upon. "The blonde siren. With purple spikes. She called me to her—"

"Melusine."

"What?"

"Her name," Eramyne sighed, sinking back into the water until only her head appeared above it, the waving coils of her hair swirling around her long neck. "Melusine is the land-nomen she goes by when she is among your kind."

Your kind. Their kind. I tempered a cringe, reminding myself that I'd just voiced that unconscious divide not long hence. I would not throw it in her face. "From the way you speak of her, you don't sound surprised. What did she want from me?"

"From you, Laura? Nothing. She is merely poking her pretty little nose where it does not belong. As she always does." For the first time since meeting her, Eramyne's imposing voice took on the brittle lilt of annoyance. "She is what you humans call . . . exasperating."

She swept her tail and lifted higher from the sea. Water trailed down her scale-plated shoulders, an ombre of silver and teal and turquoise. It struck me at once that Melusine had not looked the same; she had no protective scales across her shoulders and chest. Her own chest had been bare. "Why do some sirens have protective scales, and others do not?" I ventured to ask.

"It depends on their position. What they are bred for."

"What they are . . . *bred* for?" My incredulity lifted my voice an octave. "You mean to say sirens are bred according to design?"

"Yes." A pause fell as Eramyne's vigilant eyes swept the coastline, ever on lookout for intruders. "Depending upon the phase of the moon and the sire chosen, and some other rituals attended to before mating begins. You need not hear all the specifics. We do not take breeding lightly, as you humans do. As the apex predators of the sea, we ensure that every siren purse we create has a safe incubation, and every siren a place in our world upon the night of rupturing."

I could practically feel my eyes shining with fascination. I drank in each and every word. "I *need not* hear them, as you say. But I wish to."

"Curiosity is a healthy trait we admire from the humans, despite all other . . . differences," Eramyne warily submitted, "but in this case, it would not do to unveil too much, too soon. Our mating ritual would seem cold and savage to you. It is sacred to us."

I nodded, indicating my solemnity in my gaze. "Thank you for sharing so much. Baby sirens are born from *mermaid purses,* then?" A short giggle escaped my throat before I stopped it.

Eramyne attempted to raise one brow as I had done, but could not manage it; it happened unconsciously or not at all. We both laughed. "Mermaids do not exist, Laura. Only monstrous sirens."

I noticed she stated that caustic word, *monstrous,* with all the calm of mentioning the evening's fair weather. "It does not bother you that we humans call you monsters?"

"I will not shy away from a term we merit. We are man-eaters; that makes us monsters by honest definition. Some of us prefer the taste of fish, oyster, or shark, but many of us thrive upon the flesh of men . . . particularly the sun-bronzed flesh of our lovers divinely consumed to bring life to the next generation." Her voice dropped to a dreamy, humming cadence. "There is no satisfaction like it in the sea nor beyond it."

A shudder I couldn't hold back stirred Shadow. I clenched my teeth together as my hands grasped my shoulders tight. *No! Back to sleep. Back to sleep. Back to sleep.* It fought me, eager to hear more terrifying tales from Eramyne's carnivorous mouth. I rocked back and forth, hushing it back to insensibility with every ounce of inner strength I possessed. *I did not call you. I do not want you. Go to sleep.*

"Laura?"

My eyes snapped open and stared into Eramyne's. Worry reflected from their inky depths. I tried to smile, but I feared the attempt resulted in nothing more than a ghastly grimace. "I'm sorry."

"I said too much." Eramyne drifted close to unclasp my grip and hold my hand in hers. Her palm was rough, and the smallest slip might result in a scratch from those wicked nails, but the pressure of her fingers was gentle. "I ask for your forgiveness."

"There is nothing to forgive."

We traded smiles before I remembered my mysterious new acquaintance. "Eramyne? Does the name of the human 'Bartholomew Burke' mean anything to you?"

She retained my hand as she tilted her head, contemplating. Both her thumbs smoothed back and forth over my skin as if relishing its softness. "I do not believe I have heard this name."

I shrugged, doing my best to ignore the repetitive trace of her touch and how it made me giddy inside. "He's just a man I happened to meet one night when I'd come here to think of you . . . To see you. Hopefully," I amended. I prayed for Maltaros to kindly send a breeze to cool my face. As usual, there was no answer to my prayer. One learns to live with it. "He seems to know that sirens exist, and somehow he knew that *I* knew it, too. He asked me what I have seen. And," I admitted,

"I'm very curious to know what he has seen in return. Is it all right if I visit him?"

Eramyne pondered for a minute. She shook my hand as if sealing a promise, rather preemptively, making me smile. "In answer, let me clarify your position as my informant, sweet Laura. I both command and trust you to inform me of any person, project, or development that may bring harm to the Nereid or to Half Moon Bay. Otherwise, I leave you to exercise your own judgment. As long as you understand that the fewer people who know of our existence, the better off we *all* are. You must convey this to him as well."

"Of course. Yes. I understand." A beaming smile overtook my demeanor. "You mean to say you won't be testing me after all?"

She pursed her dark lips before saying, "I think there is no need. Melusine provided the test herself, though she did not know it. But pardon me, Laura; I must take my leave."

She departed like a flash of silver lightning through a cloud, hardly making a splash or a sound, barely stirring the water. I shot upright, eager to visit Burke's address at once. I remembered just in time that it was far too late in the day for an unaccompanied lady to visit a single gentleman. I groaned and stalked back to the house, boots clattering impatiently against the cobblestone walk. There were times when being a woman was tiresome indeed.

"Laura! Where on earth are you going *now?*" My mother turned halfway, teapot in one hand and steaming dishrag in the other. She frowned.

"Just for a walk through town, Mother."

"Again? Seems to me that's all you do nowadays, go for walks . . . *alone.* Well, take your cloak at least, please. It may rain."

"You're right. Thank you." Subdued, I turned halfway to snatch my beige cloak from the rack and secure it around my tight throat. Burke had emitted nothing less than an aura of extraordinary, *otherworldly* calm, and yet I was nervous.

Thunder grumbled in the distance as I hurried down the street to Foxglove Lane. A series of business duplexes lay in wait, crammed and crumbling. *Burke must be just starting out,* I reasoned as I lowered my hood. My gloved hand clenched his business card. I scoured the slightly decaying signs swinging in the forthcoming wind. "There it is. Burke and Sampson."

I expected a bell to clink as I swung the door ajar. My brain stuttered at the silence. Glancing about, I observed a worn desk leaning against a wall, halfhearted seaside décor, and cluttered bookshelves absolutely stuffed with tomes of every shape, color, and size. There appeared to be neither rhyme nor reason to their arrangement. I sat in a dreary brown chair opposite the desk and waited. *The door was not locked. He must be here . . .*

A muttered curse confirmed his presence. Burke strode from a small back room—a washroom, presumably—with a razor in one hand. The other hand pressed a rag to his chin. I stood to drop a quick curtsy. "Are you hurt, sir?"

"No," Burke grumbled, apparently displeased by my intrusion. What *did* the man expect, waiting in his public office during daylight hours? Stainless solitude? "I did not expect to see you today. How might I be of service to you, Miss Rivell?" He pushed back his chair and sat down, blatantly ignoring my curtsy to forgo the expected bow.

I hid a smile. My cantankerous cat was feeling . . . cantankerous. "Laura," I reminded him, recalling that I'd forgotten my own part of our bargain. I'd called him "sir" again. Perhaps that had ruffled his feathers. I offered him my hand and a friendly grin. "You said we have much to learn from one another. I have thought it over, and I believe you are right. As long as we pledge complete confidence."

"Goes without saying," Burke sighed, but he shook hands with me, and the amiable gesture put him back at ease. His lips flashed their brief answering smile. He withdrew, continuing to press the rag close against his skin. "So, tell me, if you'd be so kind. What have you seen?"

CHAPTER 9

I rresolute, I stared mindlessly at the rag Burke pressed to his chin. He shifted his fingers to cover more of the fabric. *Afraid I'll faint at the sight of blood? Ha! I've been trapped in the company of a half-eaten man, dear Mr. Burke. I watched him die.* "We'd better agree not to write any of our conversations down," I proposed as my thoughts danced with morbidity. "At least not until we've secured a safe hiding place for them."

"Of course." He leaned forward, one elbow propped on the desk, but instantly leaned back again with a short frown. I found his unease perplexing. Little as I knew of him so far, it seemed alien to his tranquil nature. "Would you kindly lock the door before you begin?"

I did as he asked. Attempting to be as succinct as possible, I delivered my eerie tale free of fuss or effusive feathering. Burke absorbed it all without a single derisive squint. Any other man in town would have been obliged to tilt his chair back, kick his heels, and howl, but Burke listened to me with the gentlemanly gravity reserved for a respected coworker at equal level. It flattered me. "You named her well," were his first words post-narrative.

I blinked in surprise. "Thank you."

"Eramyne, goddess of love and lyrical muse. I am not a believer, but I can appreciate my classical education." I grinned at his deliberate refusal to deploy the word 'religious.' Man after my own black heart, Bartholomew Burke. "And yet from the physical description you gave me, she is . . ."

"A monster?"

"For lack of a better word, yes." Lost in contemplation, he started to lower the rag and immediately lifted it again. Before it was obscured, my eyes drifted to the splatter of blood upon it. Astonishment creased my forehead. I dropped my gaze to my hands clasped in my lap before my face betrayed me. "And yet such a name implies you find her attractive," Burke resumed. "Do monstrous traits appeal to you?"

"Strange question." I grinned, again raising my pupils to meet his. I expected a mischievous glimmer in his eyes, but they remained as sober as the Vimmian plague. "If I confessed that they do, what would you say in response? Would you run away from me shrieking *'witch, witch!'*?"

The corner of his mouth twitched. The lightest touch of amusement. "I do not scare easily, madam."

"I don't imagine you do."

"Humph." A minuscule diamond-twinkle shone in his dark irises. "Thank you for telling me what you have seen. I am honored by your vote of confidence, as it were. In return," he rose from his desk and lifted a locked briefcase from one of the overstuffed shelves, "I shall tell you what I know of the sirens."

His fingers flew over the lock with impressive dexterity. I observed with bated breath. He snapped the lid open and exposed a messy sheaf of papers. Mostly notes, but also a few sketches and diagrams that my excited brain failed to interpret. "Where did *you* see your first siren?" I asked, eagerly perusing his stockpile of knowledge. "And I believe we've got our safe hiding place. Why didn't you mention this right away?"

"I reveal what others need to know when they need to know it. Not before. Saves time."

I nodded.

He pointed out a rough sketch that was vaguely reminiscent of the siren Melusine. "Most sirens look like your blonde friend," Burke informed me. I snorted at the word *friend* but did not interrupt. "The Nereid protectors and sovereigns are bred with plated scaling like Eramyne. It's beautiful to behold, like wearable gemstones, but it will cut soft human skin like a thousand tiny knives. I hope you haven't learned that the hard way."

"No. Eramyne is careful about how and where she touches me in siren form."

"Good. They don't normally take such care with humans. That is worth noting."

I blushed in spite of my strenuous effort to prevent it. Burke was good enough to pretend ignorance. "Did you succumb to the siren call, then were cured of it, like me?" I questioned to cool my face. "Is that why you were not affected when you heard the siren's song, too?

He hesitated. Rather a rare thing for him, I believed. His response was steady yet slow: "Yes, I am cured of it. I am not affected, even if the queen herself sang for me. Beyond that, I can say no more."

Interesting.

"But what fascinates me most about them," Burke continued, mechanically shifting through his notes, "is that they have never *once* (to my knowledge or according to my abstract research) consumed the flesh of women or children. Only men."

"Why should they have reason to?" I pointed out, sitting back down. "They only assume human form to seduce a willing mate, and part of their ritual includes consuming their lover once the deed is done." Once again, Shadow stirred, excited by the prospect of dark themes. I frowned and folded my arms, ignoring it. "Most of them haven't been close enough to a woman before, let alone a child."

"That's logical." After shuffling through a few more papers, Burke sighed and clapped the briefcase shut. It locked automatically. "As you can see, most of my notes are sheer surmise. It helps me to write out my thoughts and organize them." His tone waxed a tad sarcastic. "But as their preferred selection on the menu, I cannot get anywhere close to them. I'd all but given up . . ." his tone softened again, "until you."

That strange flash of kinship electrified the air between us. We both smiled. "I do not believe in the new gods, nor in coincidence," Burke elaborated. "I believe in what we humans refer to as fate. Mark my words, Miss Rivell. We were meant to find each other that night."

I deployed a cheery salute. "Consider them marked."

As we exchanged pleasant goodbyes and I regained the cobblestone walk, one final question buzzed in my brain like an impertinent fly. Had Burke's blood looked *purple,* or was Shadow warping my imagination as its revenge for being ignored?

The following night, I wandered the bay on lookout for my siren. She did not appear, but I did stumble upon a lovely piece of black sea glass prominently displayed on the rock I'd made my seat.

"Said to cast a protective shield around the wearer," Burke commented the following Thursday when I came to visit him again, armed with my sea glass and some fresh blueberry scones. My baking was received with grave politeness and a half-smile. "Carrying it will also help you communicate with clarity and confidence, though I don't believe you lack either."

"Kind of you to say." I folded our soiled napkins and tucked them into my basket. "I think Eramyne left it for me. I understand it is a rare color in sea glass."

"Yes. It is." Burke's demeanor doubled in gravity. I darted him a questioning look, but he only shrugged. "Out of sorts today. My business is not going well."

"Perhaps you'd better keep this, then?" I jokingly offered him the sea glass. He chuckled and declined. "Her Majesty may hunt me down. Thus far, I've taken great pains to study the sirens from out of reach. I don't intend to invite trouble."

"I'm *so* glad I can talk to you about her," I admitted, sweeping away the last reprobate crumbs. "I'm feeling a touch melancholy myself."

His fingertips met, steepling, and his hefty brows furrowed. A roguish look sparkled in his deep amber eyes. "Why and wherefore? I am all ears, my lady."

I relaxed thanks to his soothing voice. That alone improved my mood. "Why does Eramyne wish for me to be her informant?" Tapping my finger against my chin, I sighed. "What use am I to any of the Nereid, let alone the queen herself? I am hardly in a position of power. I despise politics, and this is Cape Althea: humble, gloomy, run down. Wouldn't she benefit far more from an informant in, say, Summerside? Or closer to Rosa Rugosa, at the very least." The royal bloodline was diluted, the family scattered from a myriad of catastrophes throughout its hapless generations. Still, the ruinous Rosa Rugosa was far more prestigious than the lowly Cape.

Burke ran his lower lip beneath the graze of his white teeth. His little '*I'm thinking*' motions were so unique to himself, just like his voice. "I judge not. For whatever reason, Half Moon Bay is Nereid territory and Eramyne herself frequently supervises it. Hence Cape Althea's legend of the sea wraith guarding the cove." He formed his forefinger and thumb into a soft *L* shape, stroking it along the length of his bearded jaw. "To be frank with you—because why wouldn't I be at this point— that's the real reason I moved to Cape Althea. To study the siren in Half Moon Bay. To find out why this cove is important."

"It may be a key location for one of their rituals," I suggested, crossing my ankles beneath the desk. My mother would have been appalled. "For surely their mating ritual does not remain their *only* work with lunar magic."

"Do you believe in solar and lunar magic?" Burke asked. According to our history, some humans were blessed with the ability to work solar magic, while beings like sirens and river nymphs wielded lunar magic. But as humans turned to science and industry, and sirens and nymphs faded into legend, not one shred of magical proof remained. Only old religious texts even mentioned magic anymore.

I tapped my fingers against his desk before replying. "I did not believe in magic until I came face-to-face with a siren. If sirens exist, and they perform rituals, it is fairly safe to assume lunar magic is real and sirens can wield it. Now, as for humans and solar magic. I'm tempted to believe 'solar magic' is merely a reference to our industrial progress. Our counter offering, if you will, since magic is outside of human reach."

"A refreshing perspective. You're more open-minded than most men I meet," Burke praised.

Beaming, I planted my elbows on his desk to prop my chin in my hands—daughterly crime the second! "And you're the most respectful, fair-minded man *I've* ever had the pleasure to know. You *are* human, aren't you?"

A peculiar stiffness edged his tone. "What do you mean? Of course I am."

"I meant to imply that you're an angel," I confessed with a laugh. "Why you seem to not only tolerate but *enjoy* this lowly feminine company of yours baffles me in the best way."

His tensed shoulders relaxed. Friendly affection stole across his mien. "Forgive me if this assertion comes too soon, Laura Rivell, but I believe you and I . . ."

"Yes?"

"I believe we are kindred spirits."

"I agree." And nothing more needed to be said.

We spent the remainder of our visit attending to Burke's topsy-turvy collection of books, reveling in the most benevolent silence of my lifetime. Despite the clammy, cluttered atmosphere, the dusty shelves, the sandy floor, the single candle (in lieu of a fireplace), and the lack of comfortable furniture, there was nowhere else I'd rather be.

Except for Half Moon Bay when my siren lingered near.

CHAPTER 10

As the empty nights passed without Eramyne, my longing for her grew until it was just as reckless and insatiable as Shadow. Despite Burke's kind reassurance reminding me that Eramyne was Queen and therefore must have many duties to perform, my spirits sank until even my patient kindred spirit could not abide them.

"I'll come with you," he insisted as I concluded our visit, voicing my intention to wander the shoreline again. "I'll withdraw if she is there and come straight back to my office. I swear upon the gods, old and new."

"You don't believe in them; swear on something you believe in."

"Very well. I swear upon Eramyne herself, Tritoness Sovereign of Half Moon Bay."

"That's more like it."

He offered me his arm and escorted me there. We chatted (I don't remember what about) until we reached the cove. Releasing his arm, I darted ahead. "Eramyne?" I dared to shout, raising the call over the crashing waves. A blustering, menacing twilight it was. Swirling navy clouds crowned the whole. "Eramyne!"

An iron-gray swell that I'd nearly mistaken for another wave emerged from the sea. A delirious laugh burst from my lips. I kicked off my boots, peeled off my stockings, and lifted my skirts, wading into the morose waters that groaned and dragged at my legs, as if hoping to separate us. I was convinced that neither sea nor sky, heaven nor hell, ever could. "Your Majesty."

"You need not call me that, silly Laura."

Eramyne rose even taller. She'd changed into her human form and was holding out her hand for mine. I took it just in time, for a threatening billow almost overturned me. I spluttered seawater and continued to grin at her, like the idiot I was. "I've missed you so much."

She hesitated. "I . . . have missed you as well." The sentiment appeared to surprise her. Stepping forward, she swept me up and carried me to shore. "You ought to wait for me to come to you and not drench yourself every time, silly Laura." Eramyne berated me again.

I kicked my cold bare feet, vastly pleased with myself. Her star-spun hair gleamed but dully on an overcast night such as this, but it gleamed nevertheless. I dreamily wondered if it was lit by lunar magic. "We can talk at the old church ruins," I said. "I sneaked out one evening and prepared a fire pit."

"As you wish." Eramyne gently lowered me to the shore. I instinctively sought Burke, wanting to ask for his cloak so we might cover my siren with it, but he'd been true to his word. He had vanished. "What are you looking for?" Eramyne asked, vigilant as always.

"Just Burke. He was good enough to escort me here. I thought he might lend you his cloak."

"I have no need of it. Our bodies adjust to the surrounding temperatures very quickly."

"I only meant if anyone sees you . . ."

How prudish humans are, her regal expression said, though her shapely mouth dropped not a word of complaint. "Then let's find this Burke of yours. I'd like to meet him."

"Next time, perhaps. He promised me he'd go straight back to his office if you were here."

"Why is that?" A vaguely coy smile lifted her wonderful lips. "Is he afraid of me? How delightful."

"Maybe a bit," I giggled. I did get so dreadfully *giggly* around Eramyne, like a giddy schoolgirl. *Must rein that in.* "But more than that, he respects our relationship." I cringed at my preemptive use of the word. *Why didn't I say 'friendship'?*

Eramyne's fingers laced with mine, her knowing look inciting my blush. I lifted my face to the darkening sky, thankful for its shadows, thankful for the wild wind and noisy spray. She gently tugged on my hand. "Let's go."

"I am *not* discussing this with a human."

"Eramyne! Do you not recall the night we met? You know I can handle—"

"I said no."

She chuckled at the petulant pout forming on my face. "I do not doubt your courage, Laura, but *why* do you want me to tell you how I enjoy consuming the flesh of your own kind?"

"We eat fish," I countered. My eyes strayed to where her tail would be were she not crouching far from the fire in human form, arms wrapped around her knees, hair cascading down her front and brushing the sand below.

"How amusing," Eramyne laughed again, and the rippling sound thrilled me. I'd commit many an atrocity to trigger my siren's mirth. "I do not know what we taste like, but I imagine we are hardly pleasant for a human's tastes."

"Now I'm curious." I flashed an impish grin across the golden flames. The siren shook her head, iron hair reflecting fire. "If you wish to shock me into lowering my guard, Laura Rivell, you'll be disappointed. Very little surprises me. Moonrise after moonrise has come and gone with every sunfall affixed, and there is nothing new in the world of men."

Her unique phraseology—*moonrise* and *sunfall*—begged my attention. "Sirens are nocturnal?" I guessed, turning to dry my clothing on the opposite side.

"Of course." She pointed one foreclaw at her wide pupil, her slender curving iris of deep-sea gray tinged with teal. "Eyes like these are meant for the night."

"Do sirens ever sleep?"

"No. We relax as needed, much like our pups do, in an anchored doze."

I tilted my head, tucking my hair behind my ear. "Your pups? Is that what you call your offspring?"

"'Pups' are our sharks. Many sirens tame sharks as their pets. They're rather like dogs are for you humans, I suppose, though sharks are far fonder of their independence. They can, however, be trained to come when called."

Fascination drew me closer. I unconsciously mirrored her pose, pulling my knees up to my chin. My crumpled skirts were hopelessly creased, but I didn't care. "Then you mean to say they're more like *cats*." As a verified cat lover, the comparison pleased me. "Limitless clear seas. Midnight frolics with my siren sisters. Evil men to devour. Sharks to tame. Oh, why wasn't *I* born a siren?" I lamented.

Eramyne's lips parted, then clamped shut tighter than a clam bearing a precious pearl. I encouraged her to say anything and everything that was on her splendid mind; she would not budge. "Perhaps another time," she kept saying until I finally submitted.

"Then I'll ask another question. What is your kingdom like?" Ere she replied, visions of coral castles, coves lined with sea glass and ruby-red flora, and rainbow cascades of seashells flooded my imagination. My cheeks flushed and my eyes glittered as they would were I presented with a chest of gold. I believed I would gladly drown to see such a world.

Eramyne interpreted my silent assumptions with a smile. "Banish your little mermaid fancies, sweet Laura.

We like the dark, gloomy caves and the bone-littered shipwrecks of Echo Trench. We'd rather watch the graceful migration of the hammerhead sharks than sit on large rocks and brush our hair. And we certainly do not kiss sailors to save them from drowning, though if such a charming remedy were real, I'd save *you*." Sirens did not blush, but from the way her eyelids fluttered and her lips fell slightly apart, Eramyne was surprised at herself. She shook her head quickly, as if to clear it.

I swallowed hard, twirling my thumbs to give my hands something to do. Sparkling warmth gathered in my veins, pooling in my beating heart. I'd never known that mere words could weaken one's muscles and put them under a spell.

Eramyne locked me in place with her hypnotic gaze. "My kingdom is dark because we are dark creatures. I am sorry to disappoint you, but I will not lie to you, even if it pains me to see your flushed cheeks pale and the excitement quenched in your pretty eyes."

"My eyes are . . . pretty?" No one had ever told me so before. No one but my parents.

"Yes. Such a lovely, golden-flecked brown, like a spiral shell I discovered and kept in my cavern."

Unaccustomed to compliments from siren queens, words failed me.

"You would make a beautiful siren. But more importantly you would have what a great many of us lack, even myself. Compassion."

I scoffed at that, tossing my hair. "I don't believe that. You *are* compassionate."

"To you." Eramyne unraveled from her crouched position, shifting elegantly to her knees and clasping her hands in her lap. A silvery shimmer highlighted her matchless skin. "You are an anomaly in my long life as Tritoness. I've never cared about a human before, male or female, rich or poor, upon the land or sailing across the sea. Yet here you are. And here am I."

"Here we are," I echoed softly. I longed to touch her hand again but restrained myself for once. *Why* did I crave physical contact with her so endlessly? "But surely if you had met other women before me, you'd have made other friends."

"I would not be so certain," Eramyne answered with a grim smile. "Most would faint at the mere sight of me. Others would scream and recoil. To be honest, Laura, I'd be disappointed if they did not. *You* screamed to satisfaction the night we met, and thus our relationship began according to my liking."

There. Eramyne herself said it: *our relationship*. I laughed at her blunt honesty, joy leaping in my heart. "The jest is on you, wicked siren. I relish a good scare. Shakes me out of ennui."

"I noticed. I admire that about you."

"And I admire how regal you are. Poise, posture, eloquence. You were certainly born and raised to be a queen."

"Queen and more besides," my siren clarified. "A Tritoness is blessed by the goddess Sofia to raise and lower storms, to calm or stir the ocean itself. I tame the sea for the benefit of my tribe. It is a humbling power to bear. That is why . . ."

My respect for her increased tenfold. I blushed with shame at the wanton dreams I'd entertained of her, forgetting that she was more than just an enchanting siren. So much more. Sovereign protector and daughter of a goddess. Lunar magic flowed through her veins. I shuffled back a few feet, biting my lip. "Forgive me," I whispered.

Eramyne's pupils narrowed as she focused on my expression. "For what, Laura?"

"I have not been as respectful toward you as your station demands. Shouldn't I be calling you 'Your Majesty,' at the very least? What does one call a Tritoness?"

One silent pause later, my siren laughed the most charming, unguarded laugh I'd yet heard her utter. I noticed then that she was so careful to be calm and regal, unruffled in any way, that her *true* laugh was almost never exposed. Delight cascaded through my body that I succeeded in unmasking it. "Officially, I am Tritoness Sovereign of the Agenne Sea, Firstborn of Goddess Sofia and Empress of Echo Trench, the Guardian of Half Moon Bay. My tribe calls me 'My Sovereign,' but you are not of my tribe, so you needn't call me that. I like the human name you've given me."

"I'm so glad."

She might have said more, but the rustle of footsteps and the murmur of men's voices made us both start and shrink into the shadows.

CHAPTER 11

E ramyne backed against the rubble of the church wall. She grabbed me by the elbow and tucked me close beside her, one arm around my shoulders. We waited in breathless silence for the intruders to pass.

Suddenly, a familiar voice said, "This way, gentlemen."

Burke?

I longed to peek over the ruins and confirm what my heart already knew. What was he doing here? And with whom? Was he leading them to . . .

No. Burke is not a traitor.

More brusque male voices shattered the silence. "Someone has a fire going."

My fault. Eramyne hated fire, but I was soaked, and she insisted upon having one for me. She caught my agonized glance and firmly shook her head. *No, Laura. Do not blame yourself. I will not have you catching pneumonia.*

I nodded in mute submission.

"Best see who it is," a second unknown voice chimed in.

"Waste of time." Burke's soothing baritone wrapped around my siren and I like a cloak of safety. Our tense shoulders relaxed. "Most likely just a bum. If you'll follow me to South Leed, sirs, you'll find the evidence I mentioned..."

Their footsteps and voices faded into the distance. When it was safe to do so, I rose to my feet with a relieved sigh, extending a hand to help Eramyne up. "He's leading them away. I owe him a fresh batch of scones next time I visit."

She clutched my hand and stood up. "Bartholomew Burke, I presume?"

"Yes. If there was any doubt remaining that he meant to expose us, this erases all suspicion."

Eramyne looked down at our hands, still clasped together, but made no movement to extract hers. "He might not have known it was us."

"True. But he has some manner of sixth sense when it comes to me."

"I see." She released my hand and proceeded to retrace our steps back to the bay. "This was a pleasant visit, but I must return."

Her tone was clipped. Abrupt. I stared after her in astonishment before willing my feet to move, slipping after her in silky sand. "Burke and I are only friends," I blurted out.

Eramyne turned halfway. Her thick iron hair twirled around her hips. I averted my eyes from the enticing twin dimples on her lower, bare backside. "I did not say anything."

"I'm not a half-wit, Eramyne. I know jealousy when I see it."

"Jealousy? Why would I be jealous of you *humans*?"

The sneer on her beautiful face froze my advance. Her barriers, which had just begun to crumble around me, slammed back up, forcing me out of her personal circle. I winced, having nothing clever to say in response. As she slipped back into the sea, her freshly-formed tail rebuking the waves with a sharp slap, I wondered how I could convince her.

Several days later, the same question continued to revolve in my mind. I accompanied Hyacinth to a seaside concert, guiltily drifting in and out of conversation while imagining Eramyne sitting at my left-hand side instead. Sweet Hyacinth, however, did not have the piercing perception of either Eramyne or Burke and quietly prattled away to no offense.

I missed my siren.

Upon reflection, I found it disturbing that no one else's company fulfilled me since meeting her. Burke came closer to it than anyone else, but I still wanted *her*. Whether this was a result of lingering obsession triggered by the siren's song, or whether I simply found the company of a siren queen fascinating, 'twas difficult to say. Since Shadow had ceased to bother me, I grudgingly admitted to myself that it must be sheer fascination.

"And what's wrong with that?" one might ask. I supposed there was nothing *wrong* with it. Eramyne had even admitted that sirens generally admired the curiosity of humans. Yet, our . . . friendship . . . was strictly anathema—a willing breach of the wall between heaven-bound humans and heathenish sirens. Legendary predators that most of Cape Althea denied the existence of, and the rest believed were *leviathans* or sea wraiths or some other equally "soulless" creature.

As the wind and string instruments flourished their notes on high, I stared out upon the sea and mentally constructed Eramyne's Echo Trench. The water there must have been stained with such a dark navy hue that one would sink into it like a velvet pillow. The prowling siren sisters could hardly be seen despite their scales of many colors. Next, I summoned the craggy walls of the trench itself, descending to the bone-strewn abyssal plain, down farther still to the oceanic trench level, scattered with scarce sea life.

Ascending once more, a shiver of 14-foot sharks weaved in menacing cobalt shadows, glassy eyes, jagged teeth. I imagined the sirens calling out for their pets, stroking along their rough backs and swimming directly above them, their dominant hand placed lovingly on their dorsal fins. The whole of the image was so eerie yet serene that I wished I could join them more than ever.

Luckily, there was a handsome young man of Hyacinth's acquaintance who kindly redirected her attention from me. After the concert, I wandered the shore, nursing a gloomy state of mind and wondering if my siren was still upset with me.

No. That didn't seem like her. She was a queen. She had a million matters to attend to that had nothing whatsoever to do with me or with our petty, trifling landlubber concerns. Even so, I kept searching for a break in the ocean surface—a scaled hand of red spikes, a spiked ruby tail, a sprout of gleaming iron-gray hair. Even when I told myself *not* to look, I looked.

Since my siren was out of reach, my thoughts wandered to the only friend I had with whom I might speak of her: Burke. But it was late in the evening. Would it be strange for me to seek him out? Wrong? "Perhaps not," I murmured to myself, twisting my aquamarine ring around my forefinger, a family heirloom and my latest birthday gift. "He might be at the bay, in which case we'd be meeting by accident." Religious propriety ruled over Cape Althea despite the fact that its sister region, Summerside, was comparatively liberal.

I slipped away, glad that Hyacinth was otherwise engaged. Her aunt played chaperone with no amiable expression, her bejeweled cane clenched tightly between her hands as if readied to strike. I did not envy my friend.

"So, you're in love with her."

In most contexts, Burke's particular bluntness served him well. There were no white lies, no guessing games. Yet something rippled across his expression as he said it, something that rendered me ill at ease. Something close to sharp curiosity, but darker. Deeper. It both wounded and frightened me; I'd never before seen such a look on his face, and I did not know how to interpret it. "It isn't love. It's the lasting effects of hearing her death song," I objected. "Eramyne is not even human. How can I be earnestly in love with a . . ."

"A monster?"

That indefinable look overshadowed Burke's face again. I turned my head to watch the misty bay, muttering a low curse—rare for me—then returned my pupils to his, unhappy with his expression but equally unhappy with my need to search for Eramyne. I was powerless to stop the driving instinct. It was as potent as a trained hound set upon the hunt. "She has admitted herself that sirens *are* monsters. Man-eaters."

Burke's expression reverted to calm inclemency. An oxymoron to wear on anyone else's face but perfectly sensible on his own. I breathed a sigh of relief. "'Do call things what they are, Laura dear.' Is this what she said to you?" He inquired.

I shrugged, tucking my arm into his. "More or less." We strolled just out of reach of the lapping black waves. A cream-colored crab scurried in front of us. I pulled us to a stop until it had passed, carefully considering what I should say next. More importantly, what I should *not* say.

Burke studied my downcast manner. He pressed his hand over mine. "Rest assured that I will never judge you for who you love. I know better than most that our natural cravings are often beyond our ability to control." He quickly removed his gloved hand, as if afraid he'd already touched me for too long. I smiled to reassure him. "Do you think," I whispered, clutching his arm and flushed from head to toe, "Do you think there's any hope for it? Or should I cast myself into the ocean right now and end it for both our sakes?"

He considered my question for a solid minute before replying. There was no attempt to deliver false consolation, and I cherished him for it. "If Eramyne were only a siren and not Tritoness, I'd say your love might work. Even then it's risky for multiple reasons. First and foremost, the Maltaros faith—prevalent in Cape Althea, as you know—preaches against same-sex coupling, which is obviously to benefit the religion's growth. Maltaros priests encourage their followers to produce children, resulting in the next generation of converts with no extra effort on their part. Built-in members equals built-in profit." He waved a hand dismissively. "But that may be my cynicism talking. I digress.

Secondly, even if your family accepted her as your lover, if anyone realized she was a siren, her life would be in danger. Your sanity would be publicly questioned. And thirdly, Eramyne is not only a siren. She is the siren *queen.* Eramyne told you that the sirens' mating rituals and breeding are zealously controlled, correct? Then is she not destined to pair with another?"

My flushed cheeks were drained of warmth. "I never asked. I assumed that sirens do not mate for life . . . including Eramyne . . . that all mating bonds must be temporary."

"Your assumption is correct. Only your knowledge is lacking, and I can remedy that." Burke fumbled with his beard before resuming. "When sirens take a male lover, it's strictly for breeding. Unlike humans, they can feel the instant the seed takes root. That's when they know to complete the ritual by consuming their lover. The 'mermaid purse,' which sustains the infant siren, requires the nutrients of the flesh, heart, and most importantly the liver. In a way, they cannot help themselves; it is a driving instinct far keener than a pregnant woman's cravings."

A driving instinct. Interesting how that exact phrase entered my mind this night. Unlike before, I did not shudder at the thought of a man being consumed. I was slowly adapting to the sirens' rationale, their need to provide sustenance for their little ones, the necessity of eliminating the immediate threat to their safety: their own clueless, lovestruck lover. "Then sirens never have lifelong partners," I stated, unable to mask my sadness.

Burke smiled his sympathy. "Some of them do. They either choose a fellow siren, or . . . Well, this is extremely rare, but a few sirens resisted the urge to consume their lover and revealed themselves for what they were. Incredibly brave of them, you must understand. In two cases out of three, the man is terrified and instantly kills her. But in that rare third case, the man accepts his siren, and once she lays her purse in guarded waters, they live happily ever after on land as a human couple."

A tiny chill slipped down my spine. "There are sirens living among us in plain sight? Fighting their urge to consume human flesh day after day?"

"Precious few," my friend comforted me. "It is hardly a pleasant life. Sirens stay in the ocean where they belong, unless loyalty to their human partner compels them to remain ashore. And as I said, that is very, very rare indeed." Now it was his turn to shrug. "There is no proof that sirens can fall in love as we do. If the Nereid are no more than highly intelligent predators without souls, as most humans think (the ones that believe in sirens at all), then I fear you must do everything in your power to abolish your love for Eramyne. It cannot be reciprocated."

This speculation was met with grim silence. I bit the end of my thumb to relieve the anxious pressure stewing in my body. "How do you know all of this?" I demanded.

"A great deal of clandestine reading, my lady."

I winced, withdrawing my thumb before blood flowed. "You must point me in the direction of those books sometime. It's incredibly lucky that you came across them."

Too lucky.

CHAPTER 12

Many lonely days and nights passed, rife with overthinking and fitful tossing and turning. Another humid summer in Cape Althea began. Mother expected me to aid her in preparing and dying fabric with dye made from royal purple urchins. She would sell this fabric in bulk, greatly bolstering our household income for the coming winter.

My good-natured parents blamed my flagging spirits on seasonal depression. Winters may be dim here, full of broken sunshine and blustering storms, but there was something hardy about Cape Althea's wintertime. A time of neighborly potlucks served in warm parlors. The crisp wind and accompanying sleet whipped life into you, heedless of whether you hated it. But in summertime the clouds took on a sluggish navy weight, the humidity clung to your skin, and the waves moaned and dragged themselves onto shore as if exhausted by the effort.

It seemed Eramyne disliked it, too. For a time, she visited me less often and her behavior turned brittle. Short. I thought about what Burke had said—that there was no proof sirens were anything more than soulless creatures without the ability to love anyone, but especially not a human. Their own young were left to hatch and navigate the treacherous seas alone, most likely never meeting either of their parents. Reminding myself of all this, I tried to match Eramyne's emotional distance, even outdo it. I failed miserably.

Her voice stirred something in me that no other voice could touch. Her simple, "Good evening, Laura," sparked joy down my ears and through my entire body, curling my toes. And when we were having a good visit like our first visits had been, the feeling of her fingers interlocking with mine caused my heart to dance with glee. It didn't just feel *good*. It felt *right*. I questioned whether she felt it, too. Thankfully, I soon had my answer.

One day while laughing at some odd joke (most likely at human expense), we plunged into the sea together. Eramyne laughed at my "feeble attempt at swimming," impressing me with her graceful leaps and turns. She culminated her display by curving her tail beneath me like a chair and propping me up, capturing me with her arms and enchanting mirth alike. "You are a dear, sweet woman, Laura," she exclaimed in an unusually affectionate burst. She kissed me on the cheek. "I believe this is what you humans call a *kiss*. Did I do it right?"

I gasped out some manner of positive confirmation. She was acting so differently than before, my poor heart fluttered madly. Eramyne noticed the confusion on my strained face. "Oh, forgive me. I believed good friends—*chums*, I recall the word—might kiss each other on the cheek with impunity. Am I wrong to think so?"

"No . . . no. I am surprised, that's all. You were different before. You've been so stiff with me lately." Resting my cheek against hers, I marveled at its softness. Her scaled body balanced my water-lightened weight, careful not to pierce my skin. "I thought you were angry with me," I murmured.

"With *you?* Darling . . ."

Darling.

The world stopped. The ocean could have turned to ash and blown away and I wouldn't have noticed. All I felt was her strong, feminine curves holding me so tenderly. All I heard was her soft, deep breathing, the wind instrument playing to the drumbeat of her pulse.

All I saw was her fierce, huntress eyes gazing into mine as if she would protect my life until the last drop of her siren blood was spilled. "I was never angry with you, Laura. Despite how utterly free a siren queen's life must seem to you, there are great burdens to bear. I feared Half Moon Bay would be taken from me, but another battle has been won. And now I can rest. Praise Mother Sofia!"

She kissed my cheek again, placing her beautiful lips so near mine that my mouth parted in another soft gasp. This time, a gasp of barely-repressed delight.

Kiss her lips, Laura. You know you can't resist much longer.

I shuddered, pushing myself out of Eramyne's arms in shocked silence. Shadow. Eramyne's kisses stirred it back to life, prodded it to the forefront of my consciousness. It was wild, ravenous, well rested. "What will you do?" I panted aloud, clasping my forearms as if that would trap the beast inside. "What will you make me do? Maltaros Almighty, help me!"

"Laura?" Eramyne drew me back into her arms, her white and silver forehead creased with deep concern. "What are you afraid of? I will never hurt you, sweet Laura."

"I know." I choked back a sob, refusing to indulge in tears. I believed Shadow was gone for good. I was an idiot. "But Shadow might hurt *you*."

"Shadow? Please explain what you mean. How can a shadow hurt anyone?"

Cradled in her arms, her hair drifting around me, surrounded by the sweet-and-salty scent that clung to her skin, I told her. I burst forth with the awful, damnable truth like I'd never done before. Not even my parents knew. Not really. And yet I longed for my siren—my *monster*—to know. I needed her to understand what I really was. "All my life, I've struggled with this darkness within my heart. No matter how wonderful my life was, filled with peace and family love, nothing was good enough for it. For *me*. Because of Shadow, I crave disturbance, violence, and *blood*. I despise it, yet I cannot part from it anymore than I could cut my true shadow free from my body. It is the sin I cannot purge; I know my soul is damned."

By the time I finished, the soft palm of her hand was gently rubbing up and down my back. She was careful to keep her spikes well away from my skin. Her loving caution broke the dam, and I cried in her arms with abandon.

"Tell me something," her melodic voice intervened. "Why do you think Shadow is bad?"

I sniffled, drying my tears before staring at her, wide-eyed. "What?"

"Did someone tell you that your own conscience—your Goddess-given nature, your instincts, desires, and sense of self-preservation—is *bad?*"

As I considered the implication of her words, Eramyne flinched. Her siren form melted to reveal her human form, a few remaining scales shimmering like abalone shells as they sank. Only a minor downturn of her brows betrayed the pain of transforming so quickly. She carried me to shore and lowered me onto a large black rock, still warm from its long hours in the sun. Fetching my clothes, my siren helped me to dress. Her fingertips brushed my skin, pinking my flesh with their lingering touch. "Shadow, as you call it, is part of you. It *is* you. It is your unadulterated self, untouched by societal expectations or religious restrictions. Do not be ashamed of it. And do not hide it from me." Once I finished dressing, she cupped my chin in her hand, fastening our gazes. "I want to see it. To see *you.*"

Goosebumps prickled my skin. I leaned in close. Her wide pupils took in my slender nose and my quivering lips. "What is Shadow telling you now?" she murmured. Her long fingers caressed my chin. "What does it want?"

But she already knew.

I broke our mutual stare, scrambling down from my perch. Eramyne observed my deep flush with fascination. "I must go home," I insisted, clutching my scarf. "I can't keep staying out this late. My parents will notice that I'm not in my room."

Eramyne hummed her assent. That contented purr of a sound weakened me, and I fled before Shadow seized control. My siren called out after me, "One of these nights we will not run away, darling." That haunted me just as much as her song did.

Southwest Cape Althea harbored the teal gem known as Nixbane Lagoon. Like the remainder of the Cape, it was overcast and plagued by constant drizzle, but every so often the sun would beat through the navy clouds and shine some gold and sky-blue into the lagoon's depths, polishing its natural brilliance. I liked to row in it on such days.

"This is where one would expect the sirens to lurk," I announced to no one, "especially in the surrounding caverns. Perhaps that is the problem; it is too obvious." Plunking myself petulantly into the bow seat, I unwound the mooring line, propped an oar against the post, and pushed my father's fishing boat away from the dock sprouting with salt grass, sea lavender, and pickleweed. "Thank goodness the storm finally broke. If Mother mentioned my capricious behavior one more time I'd have run out shrieking, rain or no rain."

Feathery festoons of lichenmoss, purple with crinkled black edges, dripped into the shallows. I grasped the oars to execute firm strokes. My bare hands complained at the rough old wood, but I ignored the chafing. *You deserve the pain,* Shadow was kind enough to remind me. *You're an evil woman, full of secret lust and wild temptations. You'll act on them one of these days. You'll give in to me.*

I grunted, neither ceasing nor slowing my pace. "I won't. I respect her. That's enough to keep *you* in your place, Shadow."

But she's a monster. Does she *respect* you? Shadow chuckled, floating upward from the depths of my consciousness. It leered into my face. I could almost smell it like smoke, feel it like ash on my skin. It took on a sudden new awareness of its own, rising like an undead entity. *Remember how she lifted your skirt while you were half-conscious. Remember how she touched your legs. Was that mere curiosity? Or was it something far worse? What can she do to you with her tail, do you think? Would you like it, Laura? Would you want her to—*

"Shut up!" I yelled, yanking the oars back and plunging them deep. The boat coasted to a stop. I bit my lip hard, focusing on the pain so I wouldn't give in to tears. "Just shut up. Leave me alone," I whispered. "Why don't you leave me alone?" Dropping the oars into the boat, I curled up and hid my face in my knees.

Because you're mad, Laura. Simply, beautifully, irrevocably mad. Mad, mad, mad . . . Shadow's taunting rippled and rose like a melody. It worked the word into a tune like the siren's song, causing me to tremble and tighten my grip around my folded legs.

Clunk. Something bumped into my boat. Something *big.* I sat up straight with a gasp, unwinding my arms to grip the sides of the boat. *Who goes there?* Shadow shrieked in my inner ear, cackling with mirth at my grim expression. "What on earth was that?" I murmured instead, casting Shadow back down with forced serenity. I stared into the water. "Eramyne?"

The sinuous movements of a shark mesmerized me. It was a good size, to be sure, approximately fourteen feet. It had a wide, gracefully shell-ridged head—a scalloped hammerhead. Its golden irises shone around murky pupils, and its gills flared from the warm, still water.

"Unique coloration," I mused, unable to look away. "Sandy brown deepening to bronze. A touch of gold along the dorsal fin, though that might be the effect of the afternoon sun."

I remembered what Eramyne had said about sharks—that sirens liked to befriend them and travel with them, calling them their pups. "Are you a siren's pup?" I asked, desperate to talk to anyone or anything besides Shadow. Even something that certainly wouldn't talk back. "What does she call you, I wonder? Do they give you names?"

The hammerhead circled my boat twice, eyeing me strangely. Bored, it soon swam away, leaving the melancholy merchant's daughter in her brooding state. "Nice to meet you, too," I sighed, preparing to mope in solitude again. Or partial solitude, I supposed.

Mad. Mad. Mad.

CHAPTER 13

Mother poked her head into my bedroom, her ruffled cap slightly askew. Something quite distracting must have happened. "Laura? Laura! A gentleman is here to see you."

I knew who it was without inquiring. "Thank you, Mother. I'll be there in a minute." On my way out, I paused at the vanity to smooth my braided collar into place and fluff my black skirt. *Presentable enough.* No need to fix my hair; Burke was not coming to court me. That was certain as death itself. He knew better than anyone else in Cape Althea what my preferences were.

The ruffled cap intruded once more. "Don't make him wait, dear!"

"Heaven forbid," I muttered as I stalked down the hallway to the mahogany parlor. *Clack, clack, clack.* My heels announced my arrival before my father could.

"I don't believe we've been introduced," Father was saying. His countenance tempted laughter—a comical contrast of doubt (at Burke's advanced age compared to mine, though I was no débutante) colliding with relief (at Burke's middle class attire). In short, my father concluded that poor Burke was an established businessman, safe for proposals of marriage to his spinster-daughter.

My curving lips betrayed me. I was obliged to lift my handkerchief to hide them. From the brief twitch in the corner of Burke's mouth, I knew he was also swallowing back mirth at the absurdity of my parents' assumptions. "Bartholomew Burke," my kindred spirit announced, deploying an appropriate bow. "Your daughter and I have met at various social engagements. We know one another tolerably well."

"So it seems," Mother noted. Her deft eyes flashed from one victim to the other, interpreting our true connection with disconcerting ease. Luckily, she did not *say* so. She was a good mother—nay, a *wonderful* mother, the type of mother that inherently knows when to speak and when to stay prudently silent. "Welcome to our humble home, Mr. Burke. Please be seated here in the parlor with Laura, and I will put the kettle on."

"No need," Burke persisted as he seated himself. "I am not fond of tea, madame, but I thank you for the offer."

"Something stronger then?" Father's relief heightened to delight as he prophesied a fellow Scotch enthusiast.

"Yes. Thank you, sir."

Mother withdrew as Father made a beeline for his personal stash. I chuckled at Burke's clever ruse. "Now that you've so nicely ejected the eavesdroppers, what have you to tell me? Be quick; Father will return shortly."

Burke gravely removed his gloves and leaned forward, tossing his top hat into the empty chair opposite his. "There will be another battle for the bay. Tonight."

I paused, waiting to confirm the clinking of glass and Father's muttering as he hunted down the perfect specimen. I kept my voice low. "Eramyne mentioned something about almost losing Half Moon Bay but that she'd won it back. What's going on?"

"Turf war. That's common among siren tribes. Especially rival families with generations' worth of quarrels in their wake." He tapped his fingers against his knee, then leaned back to remove his coat and push up his shirt sleeves. I noticed the faint beading of sweat gathering on his forehead. "I apologize for being the bearer of bad news, especially straight into your own home, but I was losing my mind pacing back and forth alone. I had to talk to someone. And you're . . . Well, you are all I have."

He slumped in his chair, dark circles beneath his eyes. I patted his shoulder. "You did the right thing, Burke. I'm here for you. Is there anything we could do to help?"

"I don't think so . . ." He trailed off as Father re-entered the parlor, bottle and twin glasses proudly in hand. "You'll appreciate this, Mr. Burke," Father crowed. "May I call you Bartholomew? Or do you go by Bart, perhaps?"

Burke waited patiently until his glass was poured and secured. "No, you may not. Thank you."

I nearly choked again at Father's baffled expression. The former doubt crept back into his face. Burke's stellar bluntness was fresh as ever, even if the man himself was exhausted. *Why is he letting this turf war upset him so much?* I wondered, gazing at him steadily. *And how does he know about it? Those men he was with near the church ruins, when they almost caught me with Eramyne. Are they his informants, too? But wouldn't Eramyne have told me that there were more humans working for her than just me?*

Burke glanced at me over his empty glass and barely shook his head. *Don't say anything more about it.* I blinked slowly in affirmation. *Aye, sir.*

I'd sneak out again tonight and see what there was to see.

"Hurry." Burke grasped my arm so I wouldn't slip on the crag. Once we approached the edge, he released his hold to leap over the short precipice, much to my alarm. "Careful!" I gasped over the wind, clutching my cloak. "You're going to break an ankle doing that, ridiculous man."

"Nonsense." Raising his severe brows, he turned and lifted his hands. "I'll catch you."

I glanced down the brush-rimmed pathway curving around the cliff to our destination. "Why don't we just take—"

"No time."

How do you know? Annoyed, I jumped without further resistance. He caught me by the arms, steadied my balance, and practically *flew* to the bay, his cape flapping behind him like the wings of a crazed bat. I'd never seen Bartholomew Burke so worked up about anything. I might have laughed if Eramyne wasn't possibly in danger.

Your siren is not in danger, Shadow reassured me. *Her enemies are, though.*

Was Shadow being *kind* to me? How very odd.

The wind rose higher as we closed in on the bay. The waters seethed and burbled strangely, tinged dark purple beneath the glow of a full moon. A familiar siren's shriek rebounded across the bay. "Melusine," I muttered. What was that troublemaker doing here? Helping her queen, I could only hope.

A slight shiver beneath my feet heightened into a quake. I fell back, open-mouthed, suddenly face-to-froth with a massive wave that only grew as it roared nearer. "Burke! Come back, you idiot!" I yelled, breaking into a sprint and cursing my wretched skirts the entire way. I caught Burke's cape and pulled him back with me. He was yelling something but kept turning his head to watch the wave crashing toward us, his voice swallowed by its roar.

I tripped, and Burke fell on the sand beside me, panting. He pointed at the monstrous wall of water prowling ever closer. "She's controlling it. It won't hurt us."

I spared a millisecond to glare at him. "For the third time, *how do you know?*"

He opened his mouth only to close it again. My focus returned to the wave. I instinctively scrambled back, clawing through the wet, packed sand. I considered a quick prayer or two to Mother Sofia, but I wasn't sure if the mother of sirens would care for humans much. I imagined not.

Just as my heart prepared to bound into my throat and choke me, a sleek siren head emerged from the top of the inky wave. She surveyed the approaching coastline with a short-fanged smile. *Eramyne.*

But not the Eramyne I knew. I knew Eramyne the monster, the man-eater. I knew Eramyne the enchanting woman with her graceful, sinuous manner of walking. But this was Eramyne the Tritoness.

Her wet, wild hair gleamed with moonlight, whipping around her neck and shoulders as if sentient. Her night-loving eyes flashed in her silvery face. She rode the wave as a pharaoh rode his bronzed chariot, her scales shining like the Usekh on a proud pharaoh's chest. I envisioned a twisted coral crown upon her brow and dreamily wondered why she was not wearing one. *Perhaps I shall make her one, someday.*

As the siren queen bore down upon us, I resolved it would be my honor to drown at her beautiful hands. I closed my eyes, a silly, dreamy smile yet playing across my lips.

"Laura." The queen's voice echoed over the mounting wave, though I didn't know how I could hear it. My eyes opened. Eramyne's fierce expression softened. She raised her hands, and the wave bubbled downward, dissolving into a swirling whirlpool that also dissipated.

As the wave fell, the queen assumed human form. She waded to me, and as she did, I noticed that dark purple tinge and froth was *blood*. Scratches, bites, and slashes adorned her body. I stumbled to her with an outraged cry, once again ignoring my drenched clothes. "Eramyne!"

Eramyne halted and seemed confused. "I am all right."

"No, my darling, you are *not*." I unfastened my cloak and bunched it up to dab her bleeding wounds. "You are the queen, Eramyne. Why did you come here to fight in a bloody turf war?"

The Tritoness simply laughed, musical and sweet. Shaking my head, I continued to staunch the bleeding. "If you were built like this, dear Laura," she raised her hands to indicate her predatory physique, "would you be able to resist the smell of skirmish? To hear the siren battle cry from miles away and not answer it? Bloodthirsty we may be, but let it never be said that we are cowards." She grinned her fierce grin, causing my skin to crawl despite my love for her. "Is this your friend Burke?" she added, staring behind me.

I turned with a smile, nodding as Burke trudged up to us. He kept his eyes politely fixed on Eramyne's face, well away from her bare form. "I'm honored to meet you, Your Majesty." He bowed.

Eramyne reacted strangely. She sniffed at him, deliberately absorbing and assessing his scent. The animalistic motion was mirrored by Burke, who did not act surprised or offended at all. I stared from one to the other, mystified. Was this some kind of siren greeting of which I was ignorant? *How does Burke know about this, too?*

"Well met, Bartholomew Burke," Eramyne said once their odd exchange concluded. For a fleeting second, I thought I saw a sparkle of wonder and excitement in Eramyne's blown pupils, but it vanished before I could be certain. "Laura has told me a little about you. You are a loyal friend to us."

"I am indeed, my Sovereign."

Whatever else he might have said was drowned by a final chorus of skirmishing sirens. Eramyne flicked her finger in their direction. A small whirlpool formed, prying the defaulters apart and driving them away from each other. "Pardon my frenzied sisters, my friends. They cannot always stop of their own volition."

"Why are they fighting over Half Moon Bay?" I asked.

A long pause intervened as Eramyne tucked my hair behind my ear. The tender motion contrasted strongly with her savage appearance. Goosebumps prickled my arms as the lightest scrape from her vermilion nails grazed me. *She's always so careful not to prick me with them.* "I shall tell you someday soon, but not now. Were you worried about me?" Her eyes shone like eager stars. *I knew you'd worry about me,* they said.

I chuckled, catching a lock of her hair and tugging it. "Of course." I tilted my head toward Burke. "I think he was even more concerned than I was." *Why, I cannot venture to guess, but . . .*

Burke spoke up. "Forgive me, my Sovereign, but Half Moon Bay cannot be exposed. By and large, the residents believe a sea wraith or shark guards these waters, and so they stay away. Let them continue to think that." He lightly shook his head at Eramyne. *Brave of him.* "We can't have shrieking siren hordes and tsunamis looming out of nowhere. You cannot be so reckless, Your Majesty."

The siren queen was not amused. She took me by the arm and turned her back to him. "Accompany me to the ruins, Laura. I want you."

I blinked at her candor. The drive of battle yet clung to her bearing and solemn voice, though her eyes and lips shimmered with delight. I smiled. *Changeling creature.* "Certainly, my queen."

"I am not *your* queen," the siren laughed. "To you, I'm Eramyne. Just Eramyne. Do you understand?" She held my hand, drawing it close to her soft hip. I caught my breath as I dared to brush the back of my hand against her curves. "Yes," I whispered.

Her hungry pupils absorbed my blush. "Good." She leaned to kiss my cheek. Both flustered and flattered, I inspected her claws as if they were suddenly the most fascinating things in existence. "Be careful of them," she advised. "Have thy fill of looking but do not touch them. They wield a potent venom, hence their color; it is a warning."

I lifted the palm of her hand to my lips and kissed it. "You are magnificent."

Eramyne hummed with contentment, eyes aglow.

CHAPTER 14

My dreams of Eramyne intensified.

In one, we explored the splintered bones of a sunken ship, happening upon pirate spoils and weaving around cracked cannons. In another, we wandered the shoreline hand in hand, laughing at everything and nothing. And in a third . . .

In the third dream, I spiraled into a dark whirlpool. Cold and naked. Eramyne's hand reached for me through the flurry of bubbles. She caught me and drew me from danger, but not without her venom claw slashing my skin. Bright red blood pooled through the current, carrying it straight to a familiar form steadily gaining on me. The scalloped hammerhead with the golden eyes.

"Do not be afraid, sweet Laura. He does not consume humans," Eramyne said with a fierce smile. Yet, the wisping coils of my blood through the water drew more sharks. And more. And more still.

The venom clouded my vision. I fought to swim upward, aiming for the dreary gleam of the moon on the surface. "Sleep, Laura dear," Eramyne murmured. "I will keep you safe. Sleep."

As the nearest bull shark gaped its jaws to receive me, I gasped and jolted awake.

No more rest for me that night. I gathered my cloak and pried open the bedroom window to slip out. Tears gathered as I stumbled to the bay upon sheer instinct. *Will she love me? Will she kill me? Will she love me? Will she kill me?*

Or will she love me and kill me anyway?

For a wonder, Shadow had nothing to add. I could sense it sneering but it did not utter a word. Perhaps it knew I was doing a magnificent job tormenting myself. No further contributions were necessary.

As I stood in my drab nightdress and cloak, gazing out to sea, utter despondency inundated my soul. *You're in love with her,* Burke had persisted. *You're in love with her,* Shadow echoed. *You're in love with her,* the waves whispered as they swelled around my bare feet and slowly dragged away. Up and down. Up and down. Up and down.

You love a monster.

I took one step.

Then another.

I sank in to my waist, my shoulders, my chin. I stepped again. The black water of the bay, streaked with silver moonlight, felt deliciously warm compared to the breeze. I kept moving forward, no longer bothering to shuffle my feet and warn any nearby rays of my intrusion. *This torment shall all be over soon, Laura.*

Shadow's caustic voice arose. *Don't be a coward, Laura! Is this how you want to die? Is this how you want your parents to find you? Is this how you want to leave Burke behind? Get out, Laura. Don't be a fool. Get out . . .*

Then Eramyne's firm, melodic voice: *Who told you that Shadow is bad, sweet Laura?*

Was it bad? Was *she* bad? Was she truly a monster any more than a shark was considered a monster, merely adhering to its nature? Are *any* of them monsters?

Or are we *all* monsters?

Thunder rumbled in the distance. Despite my frantic thoughts telling me to *get out,* my heart weighed as heavily as a stone in my chest. I sank down further still. The bay was beautiful . . . warm, calm, and quiet. It held me as gently as a baby in its mother's arms.

I only wished my final sleep would be induced by Eramyne's venom instead. I wanted to feel her lips on my neck one last time.

Something rough scraped against my throat. A crash resounded overhead, followed by calamitous thunder that shook me to my core. My heavy eyelids were forced open by fear. I gasped and choked. My pupils rolled madly about as I took in my immediate surroundings. *Where am I?*

Yet at sea. The storm that heralded its approach as I contemplated drowning raged overhead. My rescuer leaned close to my neck, one scale-backed hand gripping it as the other supported my lower back. *Eramyne?*

Eramyne, the monster. The monster I loved. Her claws lingered above my flesh. The feeblest resistance prevented them from puncturing the victim's skin. Her large huntress pupils were blown even wider as she took in my scent. Her low, deep breaths attested to her eagerness. I was utterly helpless. For the first time, my siren was forced to stare her nature straight in the face. To ask herself if she would yield or resist.

My gods. This is how I die. Eaten by the siren I befriended. But I liked it better than drowning. Shadow forced me to stare her down, refusing to permit me to close my eyes. I would drink in her beauty one final moment.

Eramyne studied my pale lips as I parted them. "Take me," I said.

Her wild demeanor tempered at the sound of my voice. Her pupils narrowed and drilled into my eyes. "No, Laura."

My siren's gaze trailed back down to my throat and to the predatory hand still gripping it. She withdrew it, and I trembled as her claws lightly traced my chest. "No," she whispered. "I want you, Laura. I want you *alive.*"

A drop of salt spray clung to her lower lip. I stared at its perfect, plump shape, my mind and body adrift. The gentle yet firm support of her hand on my back was the only thing between me and a slow drift into the ocean's turbulent, lightning-littered embrace. Yet I was not afraid. I felt more at peace than I ever had since hearing her hypnotic song.

Just then, a massive wave menaced our heads. I straightened and clung to my siren's shoulders, returning to harsh realities. She wrapped me in her muscular arms as if the motion was just as intuitive as my instinct to cling to her. With the powerful sweep of her tail, we whisked over the waves toward the shore.

"Wait," I called out, putting my mouth close to her ear to ensure she heard me. "Not yet."

"Do not be foolish," Eramyne replied. She navigated the churning water with supernatural grace and ease. "What in the nine seas were you thinking, Laura? What are you doing out here? Where is your boat?"

I never had one, I should have admitted; I knew that it was best to tell the truth and get it over with. After all, she knew about Shadow. But explaining would oblige me to confess *why* I'd felt driven to do what I'd done—that I was not just obsessed with her due to some lingering effect of her song. No, it was far worse than that.

"Capsized," I said, averting my gaze.

"You will catch your death in this storm."

"I'm sorry . . ." My breath shuddered, snagging on its way up my throat. My eyes returned to hers. "I wanted to see you."

"I thought as much." Eramyne sighed. "You've been a touch mad since we met, darling, but it seems to me you are getting worse instead of better. Perhaps I should make another healing necklace for you."

It won't work.

"I shall transform and carry you straight home."

"There is no need—"

"There *is* need."

Her insistent tone silenced me. I kept quiet as she flew over the sandbar and past the shallows. She winced as she transformed, emitting a short hiss of pain through her short-fanged teeth. Most of her scales vanished, but a handful of shining, abalone-bright laminae flashed in starlight as they melted into the waves.

I could tell by her stiffening shoulders and narrowed pupils that I was in for a lecture. Thankfully, she did not make me wait long. "Listen to me, Laura Frances Rivell. I will not have you continuing these mad midnight ventures, ruining all your clothes in the sea and romping around soaking wet. I ought to have put a stop to it at once, but I did not fully consider the delicacy of the human constitution." Her expression warmed. "You are so free in the night, sweet Laura. So beautiful." She shook her head, her locks clinging to her shimmering face. A face formed from the very definition of beauty. And yet, she had the audacity to call *me* beautiful! Eramyne was the mad one, not I. "From now on, *I* am coming ashore to visit *you*," she insisted. "I shall leave a sign on your window—something only you and I shall recognize. And I will meet you in the church ruins."

My brain emptied itself of all words. Something Burke had said rattled around in the sudden void of my subconscious. Something about sirens only risking coming ashore repeatedly for their beloved human partner. A scattered count of sirens so vague they were considered mere legends. "But if you're caught, Eramyne! If someone sees you—"

"If you would be so good, find a simple dress and cape for me and hide them near the bay. I shall don them every time I come ashore for you. No one will look at me twice."

I rather doubt that, my darling. Even cloaked in a simple gown and cape, Eramyne's stunning form would arrest any man's attention immediately, and some women's attention, too. *I ought to know.* "I'll find an ensemble for you," I promised, "and you're right. We should be more careful, for your sake as well as mine." I sighed as we passed the cliffs.

Soon, Eramyne was prowling through town. I started to direct her to my home, but she smiled. "I remember where it is."

She paused at my window, waiting for me to yank it open. She gently maneuvered me inside. "Take a hot bath," she commanded the instant my feet hit the floor.

"Yes, Your Majesty." I shot her a coy glance, which made her smile again.

Framed in my arched bedroom window, with that faint spiderweb shimmer over her skin, my alluring siren robbed me of breath. Neither of us moved. Her pupils blossomed wide like fresh, black pansies bright with dew, and I could see my own reflection in them.

Unthinking, I extended my hand for hers. She touched our palms together then raised them upright, interlocking our fingers. "Laura ..."

"Eramyne ..." The breathy, seductive quality of my voice made us both quiver.

She tugged me closer and guided me to perch on the windowsill, taking my other hand and leaning down to touch our foreheads together. "You smell so sweet," she murmured. The musical hum of her voice sent a tremor straight to my soul, like a harpist lovingly plucking the string of their beloved instrument. "Do you know, I do not want to eat you. I want to keep you in my home forever so I might permeate my cavern with your ethereal scent."

My lips trembled as I replied, "That would be unfortunate, as I cannot breathe underwater." My siren's lips had never been closer to mine. Their voluptuous, sweet-and-salty softness filled my head with damnable thoughts.

"Mmm. Yes, human corpses do not smell sweet."

I paled and drew back from her. *In love with a monster* echoed in my head. Shadow *tsked* and turned away, uninterested in my tiresome fragility. *Do something about it or forever hold your peace,* Shadow groaned.

A flicker of remorse narrowed my siren's pupils. She lowered her hands. "I am sorry. I offended you with my unfeeling comment. I do not—I *have not*—eaten women or children. And I never shall."

Small comfort for the consumed men, Shadow sneered. I sighed. "I suppose some restraint is better than none."

"Yes. I will leave now. Goodnight." Eramyne straightened and turned from the window, but I caught her slender wrist before she could flee. She tilted her head toward me, waiting.

"I don't think you're a monster," I blurted out. My grip on her wrist tightened; I feared she would slip away before I finished speaking. "If you are, then sharks are monsters, too. And tigers, and bears, and everything else carnivorous that we've normalized by giving specific names and categories for humankind's convenience. *Humans* are monsters."

Her fixed stare made me swallow hard. After a long silence, she leaned forward and pressed a tender kiss to my forehead. Anticipation shuddered through me at the brush of her angelic lips. "Thank you, darling. Do not forget that warm bath. I shall scold you thoroughly if I find you sick in bed."

Without another word, she slipped through the window, moving so gracefully and silently that I couldn't hear her bare feet moving over the soil. I gathered clean clothes and headed for the bathtub, feeling very much like crying.

Why didn't anyone warn me that love was pain?

CHAPTER 15

The next day, I relieved my perfect storm of feelings by painting.

I am not talented. I knew this painting was destined to go no further than my own bedroom wall, if it escaped the fireplace. It was certainly a step up from drowning, though, so I committed myself and gathered my stained implements.

Like most drawing rooms in the Cape, ours was simple. The walls were painted a grim stone-blue, contrasted by the warmth of cherry-stained oak—furniture that was more practical than pretty. The swirled, beige carpet mimicked the sand in the sea. It was a little ocean unto itself, and frequently just as roomy as it was seldom used, except when Burke called in the evening.

My father still held the conviction that Burke meant to court me. Burke and I thought it a charming jest, indeed, and indulged in a laugh or two at Father's deluded expense. I couldn't help feeling sorry for Father, though, even if he might well disown me if he found out whom I *did* love.

When I sat at the easel with a brush in one hand and a palette in the other, I had every intention of painting Eramyne as I perceived her atop that massive wave: dark hair ripe with moonlight, scales bright with starlight, and that wicked, delicious grin curving her wonderful lips. Alas, sheet after sheet burned merrily in the grate until I finally gave up and painted the scalloped hammerhead shark instead. That attempt was more at my level.

Satisfied, I leaned back and tapped the tail end of the brush against my chin, smiling. "You struck me a lazy beast the day we met," I informed him. "I shall call you Cimon."

I touched it up with gradual beige and bronze tints until I grew tired of it. I tried reading, but as had been the case of late, books held my attention for a meager five minutes. I was about to dash down to the bay again on an overwhelming impulse, but Burke's impromptu entry saved the day.

"And now I find you pacing and wringing your hands, just like the woebegone heroines of yore." My friend shook his head knowingly. He abandoned gloves, hat, and jacket, settling himself in the family's pet armchair—the one we all fought over. "May I ask (with all due respect, of course, twin spirit of mine), what you intend to do about this?"

"About what?" I creased my brows in defiance, but my tone was weak.

Burke paused as he chose his words with care. "It hurts me to see you suffer. Your pain grows by the day. If you don't take a decisive step soon, in one direction or the other, you may do far worse than pace and wring your hands, dear."

From any other man's lips but my father's, "*dear*" would have earned a frown and immediate dismissal. However, my friend spoke it with such gentle kindness, offense was the furthest thing from my mind. "She must know how I feel," I reasoned aloud, resuming my anxious pacing. "She's no idiot. I believe she's more intelligent than most humans. That's why I've been hoping *she* will introduce the wretched subject, not I. Depending on *how* she introduces it, I will know how to proceed. As it is . . ."

"As it is, you are uncertain. Floating in a dark sea without a compass."

I chuckled at his linguistic acumen. "If I *was* the type to court men, I'd be swooning in your arms about now."

Burke's rare laughter delighted me, as always. "We're not talking about me, sly little minx. We're talking about you and Her Majesty. If I were to run into her at the bay one night and drop a subtle hint—"

I flushed, then paled. "You would do that for me? No, no. I'm a grown woman, not a shy little girl with an inconsequential crush. I must talk to her myself. Please, say nothing."

"As you wish." Burke's subtle sparkle warned me of incoming banter. "But should you take the notion to write your lady siren a love letter, properly sealed and perfumed, it would be my honor to convey it forthwith."

"Don't you dare put such ideas into my head, thou menace."

"'Tis a kindly offer, nothing more."

"To be sure!" He made me laugh in spite of myself. "I wanted your company tonight. How did you know?" *As a matter of fact, how do you* always *know? It's uncanny.*

"We are kindred spirits, mon amie. There is no need for further explanation."

This did not satisfy me. However, I allowed the matter to lapse; the timing wasn't right. "Will you be attending the Summerside Jubilee next month?" I asked to change the subject.

He groaned and falsified collapsing in his chair, triggering my mirth again. "Oh, all my former colleagues will be inquiring about my *flourishing* career in the Cape. I'll be obliged to dispense a fib or two. Might I beg you to accompany me? I might tolerate it in that case."

I'd far rather linger in the bay than attend Summerside's annual gala, but Burke never asked for favors, great or small. Of course I would grant him this one boon. "Yes, but only if you promise to *smile* at least three times. You look positively Rhadamanthine in most circumstances. Even when *I* know you are happy. Why is that?"

"Once you've hit forty revolutions 'round the sun, my dear, you will not ask."

Pleasant chatter and the *clink* of delicate china pulled me in the direction of the jubilee. I batted my fan furiously in a vain attempt to stir up something like a breeze. "What will we say if people assume we're a couple?" I demanded of the grave-faced gentleman at my side.

He tugged his stiff, white collar, looking just as uncomfortable and apprehensive as I felt. *Maybe I should have come with Hyacinth.* Or maybe not. Mother had mentioned something about Hyacinth's new beau. Of course she'd be escorted, not in need of my companionship. For that matter, Hyacinth and I had ceased to write to each other, too. I flushed with guilt.

"Let them think whatever they want," Burke shrugged. "It is of no consequence one way or the other."

"You're right."

"I usually am."

I snorted in response. The corner of his mouth quirked in a half-grin as he sought an empty table. "I wonder what this year's entertainment is?" I asked. Centered at the head of the flowered tables, an embellished stage bore a large box, covered in white cloth.

Burke sighed. "Something expensive and useless, no doubt."

"My! How cynical we are today."

"Today and every day, if you please, Miss Rivell."

"Cynical *and* snarky. Watch your tone, Bartholomew Burke."

He openly cringed at my use of his given name. I laughed and patted him condescendingly upon the arm. "Fetch me a lemon ice, and I promise I will be good."

He grunted his grudging obedience and pulled out my chair for me. Left to ponder the mystery box in peace, I allowed my thoughts to wander all over creation until a sharp *bang* jolted me from my imaginings. I jumped, clutching the tablecloth and staring at the box. For there was no doubt about it; *something* or *someone* was inside that (apparently glass?) covered fixture.

I set to judging its size, weight, purpose, and probable contents. Some manner of sea creature, perhaps? A rare fish, an albino shark, a two-headed sea snake? As I deliberated, the distant grumble of a summer storm overshadowed pearly Summerside.

Bang! Smack. Bang! Whatever it was, it did not appreciate captivity. *It sounds strong and of a decent size. Wait . . . is it . . .*

Burke returned with a gilded cup of lemon ice. He offered it to me. "Laura? You look pale. Is something the matter?"

I stammered something unintelligible, pointing one shaking finger at the mystery box. "It couldn't . . . It couldn't be," I whispered.

"What couldn't be?" Following the direction of my finger, Burke's resolute gaze landed on the box in question. *Bang! Bang!*

His own start of surprise was all but imperceptible, but I was watching for it. "You don't think that's . . ." I tried again. No. I couldn't say it out loud. The consequences of such a possibility were *unthinkable*.

Burke adamantly shook his head. He lowered his voice, "It couldn't be. They'd rip apart any net, any human, any custom apparatus to shreds before they'd allow themselves to be captured alive. Even if they're cornered, all they must do is sing or utilize the venom in their spikes."

"Unless women captured them. Betrayed them," I whispered. *Normal* women. Women who didn't carry sentient shadows as I did. Women who didn't dream perverse dreams or crave forbidden futures. Poetic injustice, one might say, that they could simply steal someone I could barely get close to.

Who told you that Shadow is bad, Laura?

I sighed, wondering if Eramyne's innocent question would continue to haunt me until my final breath. In a way, I wanted it to. I wanted *someone* to believe that Shadow was not thoroughly evil.

"It can't be," Burke persisted. He pulled out the chair beside mine and sat down. His bulky arms crossed in a particularly stubborn pose. "The chance of it is so remote, it's not even in the single digits. It's hovering at the 0.05% range."

His confidence gave me hope, but every violent thrash of the creature against the glass shook my doubts loose again. "It seems to be the right amount of force and weight . . ."

"Then let us ease our minds about it." Burke stood and offered me his arm. "We'll take a casual turn about the perimeter, and once no one is looking, we'll get behind the stage and take a peek beneath the sheet."

"Thank you. That's brilliant."

His dark eye winked at the compliment. We faked idle chatter as we rounded the tea tables, waiting for our chance. When it came, Burke stood guard at the back of the stage as I knelt and worked my way up to the box, crouched over so the box itself was my cover. "Don't take too long," he whispered.

"I'll be quick."

Slap! Tap-tap. Bang!

I lifted the edge of the sheet with bated breath. A siren bared her serrated teeth at me, her luxurious hair swirling around her neck. I knew her face, her eyes, her coloring. Perspiration dotted my forehead as I inhaled sharply. My hands felt ice-cold.

CHAPTER 16

My worst fears confirmed, I stumbled back from the casket and scrambled to Burke on my hands and knees. Quite undignified, I was sure, but I didn't spare any thoughts on my precious public dignity. "Melusine," I exhaled in a fierce whisper.

My own rage echoed in Burke's flashing eyes. Relief flooded me as I reminded myself that I didn't have to deal with this alone. My kindred spirit was here. "We need a distraction," we both said.

"Let's start a fire," I proposed. Burke looked vaguely horrified. "No? All right then, maybe I can have hysterics and faint."

"That will gather a small crowd, but we need a bigger distraction than that."

"Starting a fire will do the trick. Did you bring your pipe?"

"You know I don't smoke; I have my grandfather's pipe, and it's a keepsake only."

"Fine, fine, but I don't have a book of matches on hand. How else can we get some smoke going and yell '*Fire*'?"

"Snatch a candle from one of the table displays."

I nodded. "And light the corner of the entryway banner to drive people out the exit."

"Right. Go."

I ran to put our distraction into motion. Burke stayed near the stage waiting for all eyes to be otherwise engaged. Once I cupped my hands and yelled, "Fire," Burke shifted the casket onto a makeshift cart secreted near the back of the stage, pushing it well out of sight. As I joined the alarmed crowd rushing for the exit, I prayed Goddess Sofia would keep Burke and the casket safe, allowing him to release the siren as close to the sea as he could manage. She would have to transform and run regardless, which would be extremely painful if she'd never assumed human form before, but it was better than a lifetime in a casket peddled at circuses and freak fairs.

Or worse: a rich man's personal *pet*.

Once the banner was extinguished and the jubilee was proclaimed safe to reenter, a general outcry arose as the fete attraction was declared missing. Absorbed in my own performance, I did my best to observe everyone else's reactions very carefully. The mayor of Summerside most of all, though he seemed just as astonished and unaware of the casket's contents as the general populace. Who, then, knew of the siren? Who had captured her?

And strangest of all, why wasn't anyone guarding her? It was almost as if they *wanted* her to be found and rescued . . .

As confusion descended, I slipped away and ran after Burke. I heard a scuffle and a shout before I rounded the bend, nearly smacking into Burke as he worked his rolled sleeves back down, panting. Two men sprawled across the sand, clearly unconscious, and clearly by my friend's own battered hands and bruising knuckles. "What?" he snapped as I stared at him.

"I'm impressed," I admitted with a smile.

"I do not condone violence."

"Right, but it was necessary. They came for Melusine, didn't they? Why did they leave her alone in the first place? Rotten bodyguards, these two. Maybe I'll spit on their faces into the bargain."

"Easy does it, tigress. I think they've had enough." Burke stepped around them and braced his hands against the casket. "Do you mind?"

"Of course." I pulled from the front while he pushed. Melusine watched us with a sort of grudging appreciation. It suddenly occurred to me that Burke might be in danger—perhaps he'd better cover his ears the second his hands were free—but the siren kept quiet. I doubted even a predator like her would attack her rescuers.

"This is far enough," Burke announced. "We can't risk pushing her all the way to the docks without being stopped. Melusine will have to transform here and run."

I didn't like it, but I knew he was right. We stopped the casket and lifted the lid locks together, swinging the lid back.

I covered my ears just in case, unsure if I was only susceptible to Eramyne's song or to all sirens' voices. I waited for Burke to mimic my precaution, but instead (true gentleman that he was), he extended a hand to help Melusine out.

I feared she'd bite him, but she merely sniffed at his hand, similar to how Eramyne had greeted him. Her eyes took on that same fascinated sparkle that Eramyne's eyes had. *There's something about Burke that sets him apart,* I reasoned, watching Burke's calm smile. *He stands out, but not for remarkable looks or outlandish clothes or an exotic lifestyle.* His presence was both intellectually captivating and emotionally comforting. I was eager to learn more about him as we continued this mysterious journey together. A trial not by fire, but by seawater.

As Burke lifted Melusine from the casket, we all turned to face the sound of a small group of runners quickly approaching. Eramyne (in human form) headed the gathering, fierce spear in hand, righteous anger simmering in her expression. Her gaze softened when it landed on me. "Laura. I knew you would come to help."

I ignored the thrill her unusually emotional voice gave me, pushing it aside for later daydreams. "How did it happen?"

"She swam too close to shore during daylight. As she *knows* she should never do." Eramyne fired a withering glare that even the bold Melusine shrank back from. "You know better than most not to risk human capture. Why did you do it? If you were caught from Half Moon Bay . . ." She resumed her rebuke as Burke and I looked anywhere else but at Melusine's resentful glower.

Burke was strong, but any man outside of extraordinary build would struggle managing the weight of a siren's muscular build and thick, spine-bearing tail. He grunted and lowered Melusine to the ground. Eramyne instructed her to transform so they might return to the ocean at once. Melusine glared back, her former audacity returning now that the Tritoness's guards gathered around us, ensuring safety.

"I've never changed before, my Sovereign, and I'm not about to do it here and now with all of you staring whilst I writhe and scream."

Eramyne huffed her exasperation and knelt to carry the wayward siren herself. I stepped forward to object. As one, Eramyne's guards lifted their venom-tipped hands to stop me. Burke took my hand and drew me back from them, wary of their beautifully savage appearances. "Stay close to me," he muttered.

"Don't be silly. Eramyne wouldn't let anything happen to me."

From the slight lift of his brows, I could tell he longed to debate that sentiment. Yet it was neither the time nor the place to try. "We'll come with you and make sure Melusine is safe," he told the siren queen.

"The fewer of us there are, the better we shall escape notice." Glancing around, Eramyne shifted Melusine in her shapely arms. An invisible green-tipped arrow pierced my heart. I stared at the ground, ashamed of my budding jealousy. "But I thank you, Burke," she continued. "I do ask that you kindly stay behind and misdirect any humans who come this way." She nodded toward a handful of curious men gathering at the cliffs, observing us from afar. *We're in big trouble if they come any closer,* I realized.

Burke's nimble bow acknowledged understanding and consent.

"This way." Tightening her grip on Melusine, Eramyne jogged back to the shoreline past the docks. Burke and I stared after the sirens, every one of them crafted of stunning beauty and strength. "God!" Burke exclaimed. "If only I were an artist, I'd paint a masterpiece unlike any other before it. Are you all right, Laura?"

"Of course."

"Not physically. You seem sad."

Sad wasn't quite right, but I nodded. "I wonder if this is how they went mad," I mused aloud for Burke's benefit.

"Who?"

"Everyone."

He didn't answer, only cocked his head. I wasn't precisely sure what I meant, either, although I knew the bite of the green serpent had something to do with it.

"Laura?"

Startled awake, I shot up in bed with a gasp. Eramyne's huntress pupils shone down at me, vaguely mischievous. I groaned, clutching the bedclothes around my chest. "This couldn't have waited? You could have signaled for me."

"I needed to thank you properly." Eramyne opened her hand, proudly displaying a silver coin with a gold-plated pattern braiding its border. The markings engraved into the coin were strange to me. "What's this?" I sat up. Eramyne caught her breath as my quilt dropped to the bed, exposing my décolletage. She stared a moment before dragging her gaze back to the coin shining in her hand. "This is from the *Agenne Reckoning.*"

I gaped at the mention of Echo Trench's most infamous wreck—a merchant ship carrying rare riches that sank from a storm, or so everyone had assumed. As I stared at the precious, yet somewhat rusted coin, understanding dawned. "Siren attack."

Eramyne was sitting quite close at the edge of the bed. She pursed her dark lips. "It was. I suppose," her tone was a touch sharp, "I suppose you shall lecture me now? We put the cargo to vastly better use than you humans intended for it, I can assure you. And my sisters were hungry. We feast every so often, in the proper seasons."

Feast. The Laura that Eramyne first met would have cringed. Berated. Scorned. Even in the throes of initial, immediate fascination. But Shadow was too well known to me now, too near the surface. I felt its hot hand upon my head, stroking my hair. Placating my irrational notions and commanding them to remain. "Don't you remember?" I soothed my siren, placing my hand over hers. "I told you that you weren't a monster. Because you aren't. You must eat, just as we do. You must hunt, just as we do. You protect your own, as we do. If you are a monster, then so am I. Our natures are one and the same."

Our stares locked. Her hesitancy melted away, summoning her brightest smile. "You really mean that, Laura. You are not merely saying it for the sake of our friendship." It was a statement of fact, not a question.

"I've always meant it. I always will." *And I'll always be here for you, Eramyne.*

I couldn't say the words, but my eyes said them for me. Eramyne leaned in close, inhaling the scent of my hair, breathing against the base of my neck. I shuddered, yet it was not the shudder of fear or apprehension. "You are the sweetest little thing," Eramyne murmured. "The sweetest woman I have ever met."

"The *only* woman you've ever met," I corrected her with a breathless laugh.

Her slight fangs bared in her answering smile. "And the only woman I'll ever care to know." Her long fingers slipped to the back of my neck. She pulled me in.

I can't . . . I can't breathe. Can't move. I couldn't do a single thing besides stare into her wonderful, terrible eyes. No one had ever looked at me like that before. With such a primal hunger and insatiable thirst trapped in one nocturnal flash, stabbing me through the heart. It hurt, tickled, accused, teased. Bled. Delighted. I could live by that look, die by that look. I'd never need anything else for the rest of my life.

But then she gave me even more. Sliding her elegant thumb below my jawline, she tilted my head slightly and pressed our lips together.

CHAPTER 17

The slow, sensuous kiss embraced not only my lips, not only my tongue, but everything about me. She tasted Shadow and relished its bitterness—tasted my cynicism and savored it; tasted my loneliness and kissed it away. A flurry of emotions caressed me just as her strange hands did. Tears formed in the corners of my closed eyes. My cheeks flushed as she broke the kiss to wipe my tears away. "Never fear, darling." She tucked her wet forefinger between her lips, tasting my bittersweet sorrow. *She loves even my tears.* "Every emotion is sweet to me. *You* are altogether sweet. I will taste nothing else tonight."

My muscles weakened from those heady words. "Please," I whispered, leaning in again, begging with my lips brushing hers. "I want you, too." I kissed her in return, loving the twisted combination of sweetness and salt. *We taste perfect together.* Felt perfect. *Were* perfect.

"Then lie down, my sweet girl."

Eramyne kissed me to sweet oblivion as a full moon shone over Half Moon Bay.

What have you done?

A mournful countenance greeted me in the morning glass. I washed my face and hands and returned to staring blankly at my reflection. I knew I had the touch of madness—Shadow dearly loved to remind me—but I didn't know I was *this* mad.

Mad enough to love a siren queen.

My siren stayed with me and rubbed my back until I fell asleep. She was gone when I awoke, but I expected that. She wouldn't risk staying late and being caught there by my parents. Eramyne is too cautious to give into the temptation.

Still, I already missed her, so I busied myself by tidying up my room. As I did so, I came across a purse of Hyacinth's that I had once borrowed, and dissolved into a burst of crazed laughter imagining the look of horror on her face if she ever found out what I'd been doing last night. *She'd never speak to me again.* Or would she secretly envy me? I often found that the root of female contention stemmed from jealousy. They *wanted to* but *couldn't,* so they gossiped. Not the rose but near the rose, if you will, though they would never put it in such a positive way. My cynical thoughts linked me to normalcy again; I felt better.

As the sun climbed higher in the fog-stained sky, my mood continued to improve. For my siren was no longer a cold, pristine gem in a locked case to be admired but never touched. Eramyne had given me the key. She bid me to extract the precious gem with my own hands and to wear it around my neck. It beat close against my heart. Alive. Growing.

I muddled through the day in a dazed cloud, spilling a bottle of my mother's special dye, tripping across the threshold, and adding extra salt to the bread dough instead of sugar, which formed a very interesting accompaniment to our evening stew. Father laughed and teased, but my insightful mother (bless her!) pierced me with quizzical brows and the like. I excused myself for my evening walk and rushed out the door with my cape slung over one arm, eager to call for Eramyne at the bay. Eager to confirm that last night wasn't some fevered vision that Shadow had created just to spite me. *It would, too!*

The soft ombre of sunset had already dimmed over the sea, but I could still make out Eramyne's silvery-white form and dark hair as she dragged something into the waves behind her. Something quite bulky and thick with soggy, stained fabric. Mildly surprised that she was in human form already, I parted my lips to call for her upon a breathy exhale, then stopped. Something sharp overpowered the briny air.

The iron scent of blood.

I squinted at the bulk she was pulling into the ocean. Head. Torso. Legs. All bloodstained and battered. Slashes over the skin. Teeth marks riddled across the pale neck.

"Eramyne?"

My monster dropped her victim and stepped over him, flying over the glinting sand to embrace me. "Darling! I did not mean for you to see this. Please, close your eyes until I tell you the task is done."

My hands trembled as they wound around her waist, steadying themselves. "No, I'm all right. I should . . . get used to such things."

Eramyne withdrew enough to kiss my forehead. Her sweetness edged with salt breathed over me; I relaxed against my own will. "This was the evil man who captured Melusine," the Tritoness explained. "Justice must be dealt, and who better to serve it than myself?"

"I understand."

She frowned at the emptiness in my voice, then kissed my forehead again, and then my cheek. "I swear to you that from now on, I shall temper my impatience and only fulfill such distasteful tasks while you sleep, darling. I shall never darken your beautiful eyes again with such a sight as this. Please," she traced my chin with such a velvet touch it almost tickled, "Please turn around until I come back. It will not be long."

"I will."

"Thank you." With a final hug, she leapt into the sea and transformed to drag the corpse down to . . . Best not to think of that. I shivered and secured my forgotten cape around my bare shoulders. It was ridiculous of me to choose *this* suggestive design of dress to walk along the windy bay, but trust me to be a fool in love.

While awaiting her return, I trotted down the shore to obtain the spare dress and cloak I had hidden for her. As she broke the surface, Eramyne swept her arm over the waves, silently commanding them to carry her straight to me while she transformed. I managed a trembling smile as I helped her dress. She laughed at the restrictions of female dress, but tolerated the clothing for my sake. "And now I am properly fitted for an evening stroll with my darling. Where shall we go?"

My darling. She stole the breath straight from my lungs. I no longer trembled. I slipped my arm around her waist; she mirrored my movements. We fell into step as if born to do it. "Have you seen Nixbane Lagoon? It must be stunning at night. Maybe we'll see my friend again, the sandy-colored shark with golden eyes," I enthused. "I named him Cimon."

Eramyne's monstrous eyes widened in the dark. Her melodious laughter sent sparks shooting through my veins, quickening my heartbeat. "Sandy-colored shark, you say? With golden eyes? You must mean my pup. He is a rare one, as befitting the Tritoness Sovereign. He's a lazy fellow and he likes circling the lagoon."

Somehow, I already knew. Hence his name, meaning "lazy." I smiled at the gleam of affection in her brilliant pupils. "He eyed me as if he knew me and didn't think much of me. What *have* you been telling him about me?" I demanded with playful spirit.

Her bright face sobered as she looked straight into my eyes. "That you are the dearest, kindest, most generous human I have ever met, and I would drive my war trident through the chest of any man who harmed a hair upon thy head."

My jaw dropped, but not a word spilled from it.

"Then feed him to Cimon," she smoothly recommenced, "for to be consumed by sirens would be far too great an honor for him."

I tried to laugh but failed at that, too. My adoration increased tenfold. Eramyne shook her stubborn head and tightened her grip on my waist. "I adore you, Laura Rivell. And I guard whom I adore without hesitation. You shall have my devotion until my final breath. Is this..." Suddenly, my steady Eramyne was shy. "Is this acceptable to you, lovely one?"

I uttered a short sob, "Oh, yes." We embraced and kissed as the waves tugged at our bare feet, slipping between our toes as they curled in the sand.

Were my siren anyone else, I might have continued testing the waters for months. I would have politely declined, recited the common rules of courtship, said it was too soon. But for once in my life, I threw caution to the salt-laden winds. My Eramyne was worth it.

My siren and I stole many precious moonlit moments. Strolling along the bay, hand in hand, remained our preference. We talked about anything and everything we liked. Yet there were times when Eramyne's strange eyes would take on a fiercer gleam than usual, and I knew she wanted more than mere *talk*. As did I.

Her powerful tail supported me as I writhed in the ocean, catching my breath as she kissed down my neck. The warm water embraced us, and the touch of her lips filled my mind with pink clouds of soft vertigo. Once the wave of dizziness passed, I stuttered "Y-you . . . You've done that before, haven't you?"

"Do not tell me thou art the jealous sort," my siren responded, merrily repeating her trail of kisses down my neck. I loved that during intimate moments she'd forget to speak more modern English, making me wonder how old she was. "I never would have supposed it of you, darling."

I flushed. "I didn't think I was, but how was I to know? You are my first—"

"Lover?"

The pink in my face deepened to crimson. "Lover."

"Then thou art a lucky woman."

Laughter bubbled from my throat. "Audacious siren *thou* art!" I sighed, and she wrapped me in her arms, holding me as we floated in the dark sea. Ethereal peace enrobed us. "If only I could become a siren, too, and stay with you forever."

Sensing the sadness in my wish, she tilted my chin up and kissed me again. "I love you just the way you are, Laura Rivell."

Despite my answering smile, I couldn't help the question that drifted into my mind: *But can sirens love?*

Lightning rippled along the horizon as Bartholomew Burke hurried through the empty streets. He repeatedly scratched the sides of his neck, his skin turning a dull red from the abuse it endured. Muttering to himself, he paid close attention to whether or not he remained unobserved.

The instant he found a tide pool, he knelt to soak his face and neck. Relief dispelled his anxious expression. Burke's dark eyes flashed wide and full as he fastened his lonely gaze on the stars.

A drop of deep purple blood seeped from his scratched neck.

CHAPTER 18

"Is it true?"

Eramyne smiled as I pestered her with more siren lore queries. I made her smile and laugh so often in those days, she claimed I made her face hurt. "That a kiss from a siren keeps a human from drowning? Truth be told, darling, I do not know. I have never tried it, and neither have any of my tribe. None that I am aware of."

"Never?" Confused, I tried (and failed) to banish all my presuppositions of sirens luring sailors with the promise of a kiss.

"What a silly waste of time for a single—" My siren stopped herself, shaking her head dismissively, far more smoothly than she used to. I adored her thoughtfulness, continuing to adopt both our verbal and nonverbal communications for my sake. "Let us just say we have never taken the time to confirm that belief."

Too busy eating, Shadow chuckled. I ignored it, dissociating from its wretched presence as I commonly did. I held my siren's hand a little more tightly. "There's a ball at the Whittaker's manor this weekend. The white marble balcony gleams like a star overlooking the sea. I don't suppose you could come?"

Eramyne sighed, then parted her jaws to remind me of her little, flashing, sharp teeth. Then she pointed to her abnormally wide pupils and strange, gray-green irises that no human on earth could genetically achieve. "That would be too risky, lovely one, even for you. Though I long to join you with all my heart. I have never *danced* before."

"You nearly have," I objected with a grin. "In the ocean with me, just drifting upon the waves in one another's arms. That was close to it, methinks."

"Must be close enough to suffice," Eramyne smiled. She spun me into a clumsy twirl, making me laugh.

"Let's try it right here," I insisted, imprisoning her free hand before she could protest.

She huffed a slip of iron-gray hair from her eyes. "I daresay I have no choice in the matter, stubborn woman."

"You haven't."

I taught her the basic waltz. It was rough going, dancing on the sand. We made do, giggling when we slipped or stepped on each other's skirts. Once we laughed too loudly and had to *shush!* each other, which only made us laugh more. "This dancing is pricking the bottom of my feet," Eramyne proclaimed. "Shall we finish for tonight?"

I did not get the chance to reply.

"Young lady!"

Eramyne and I slid to a stop. Her eyes flashed as she clasped me close, drawing me to her by the waist. Her teeth flashed as her beautiful lips rose in a predatory sneer. I quickly covered her mouth with my hand, pretending to flick away some windblown hair from her eyes. "Mother?" I stammered.

"I knew you were sneaking out," she began, holding up her skirts as she descended the dune. The lines around her eyes crinkled as her frown increased. "I assumed it was to meet some brazen young man for a clandestine romance. But who is this?"

I turned back to Eramyne and pleaded with my gaze: *Don't let her know. Whatever happens, don't let her find out.* She responded with a nearly imperceptible nod. Catching my breath, I took my siren by the hand—her long, bony, vaguely monstrous hand, which matched her uncommonly tall and bony build. I'd forgotten how *inhuman* she must look to others. "This is Eramyne," I cautiously supplied. I considered (too late) that I ought to have given her a simple name, like Helen or Sandra.

To no one's surprise, Mother gave my *friend* a cold, hard stare. Particularly in the moonlight, Eramyne's huntress glory shone all the brighter: pupils wide and dark as sin, lips of curved ebony, and untamable hair as free as the fae. Eramyne did her best to smile without parting her lips. "She doesn't speak English," I blurted out before the siren queen spoke. "Only ... Norwegian."

From the twitch of Eramyne's mouth, I guessed she did *not*, in fact, speak Norwegian. She was torn between laughing at me and scolding me. No matter; the damage was done. I hurried on, "She's new here and she's very shy, not only a foreigner but also quite tall and ... and rather masculine-looking compared to the other ladies. She wanted to be friends but wasn't ready to come out in public, and she wanted to attend the ball but didn't know how to waltz—"

Mother cut off my meandering splutters with a laugh. As I'd hoped, her generous spirit overcame her suspicions. "So, you sneak out in the dead of night multiple times a week instead of inviting your new friend to dinner? What strange fancies you take, Laura! Pleased to meet you, Eramyne." She extended her hand, at which Eramyne merely stared. "And do come to dinner at your earliest convenience. I'm sure Laura will be happy to escort you to our home." Mother withdrew her hand when she finally realized Eramyne wouldn't be shaking it. "Does she understand English?"

"Some," I gasped, unsure whether to laugh or cry at the absurd situation. My siren was not afraid in the slightest—only tense with pent-up diabolical mirth—but I was terrified lest her angelic siren laughter would charm my mother, as it had charmed me. *Come to dinner, indeed! How can she sit and smile and nothing else?* "It's getting late," I muttered, blindly dragging Eramyne toward the town. "I'd best see her home."

"I will come with you."

"No need, no need! I know the way, and it looks like rain again," I nearly shrieked, scrambling helter-skelter up the dunes faster than my mother could run. "I'll come home directly after! See you soon!"

Even sturdy Eramyne was winded by the time I slowed down. She caught my shoulders and commanded me to stop and catch my breath. "It is possible your mother is not far behind, following us. Where should we go? Perhaps you can pretend Burke's place is mine."

"No, it's clearly labeled for his consulting business," I panted. "Although, perhaps we could say you're renting a spare room from him. But that's not . . . That would be strange for a young lady to rent from a single man."

"Let them think I am strange, then—a foreigner who does not know Cape Althea's ways. Burke is our only trustworthy friend."

"True."

Once we arrived at Burke's door, I imagined a good deal of knocking would be required to wake him. He opened his door at once, dressed and wide awake. *An insomniac, perhaps*, I reasoned without further question. Eramyne explained our quandary in a few terse whispers. Burke nodded and waved us in without delay, bowing to Eramyne in a solemn way I thought comical, considering the situation. "My Sovereign," he intoned. Eramyne shot him an odd look. He straightened at once, clearing his throat and fixing his tie (which did not need fixing). "Please have a seat at my desk, you two. Want anything to drink?"

"No, thank you," Eramyne and I answered simultaneously. We traded tired grins.

"Then we'd better discuss what just happened and how we can best mitigate the consequences." Burke's brusque manner put me at my ease, his presence better than a warm embrace. Eramyne held hands with me again after we, unconsciously, pulled our chairs close together.

"My mother followed me to find out who I've been sneaking out to see," I confessed. Eramyne stroked the back of my hand in silent comfort. "Fortunately, I passed Eramyne off as a foreigner and a shy new friend, but now that Mother will be watching me . . ." My vision blurred as I imagined coexisting with my lovely Eramyne as a platonic friend with whom I could not even openly converse, let alone share a kiss. The tears flowed forth.

True to form, Burke didn't bother with false encouragement; he only reached inside his pocket for a handkerchief and offered it to me. Eramyne graciously absconded it and dabbed at my tears on my behalf, regarding each drop with reverence. "Do not be ashamed to cry, my dear Laura, for every drop manifests your sacred tie to Sofia's Kingdom." I supposed she meant the salt in my tears connecting me to the sea. "Take heart. We might whisper in secret all we like, and take walks together as we can manage. In fact, this means we can spend more time together than ever before. Out in the daylight and in the open. I can even come to your ball now." She gave me an encouraging smile.

"But not as lovers," I sobbed, drenching the handkerchief. "We would be outcasts. My parents could disown me. There are zealots in Cape Althea who think same-sex couples should be stoned in the street. By the laws of Maltaros—"

"A stingy, selfish, jealous god that doesn't exist," Eramyne insisted.

Burke shrugged in unspoken agreement. "Regardless of whether or not such a god exists, and whatever laws he may or may not have put forth—more than likely by men who did so in his name—what will you do about your love for each other? Deny it and never see each other again because of what *might* go wrong?"

I bit my lip as I contemplated such a future. "No," Eramyne and I both said.

"Good. For such a love as this does not happen twice." Burke's rare smile at our joined hands lifted my heart even more than his words. "And I pledge before you both that I will do everything in my power to help you." So saying, he bowed to Eramyne again. I made a mental note to ask her about his oddly subservient manners later.

"For now, I suggest taking advantage of your present cover story as new friends," he continued. "Why not take Eramyne out, show her around the town, take her to the ball? This is not only exciting and enjoyable for you both, but an excellent educational opportunity for our Sove—for the Tritoness." He drew in a sharp breath, seemingly irritated at himself. Eramyne offered the handkerchief back to him, which he declined. "Laura may keep it. You will need a proper dress for the ball, Eramyne, or they will not let you in. How much do you need?"

The ridiculous, well-meaning fellow actually dove for his wallet. I rose from my chair and caught his wrist. "You needn't fund our mad expeditions. I can take care of it myself."

"If you insist, my lady," Burke smiled, and I nodded. "Let me know if either of you need anything. *Anything.* Do you understand?"

"Yes, sir," Eramyne and I echoed, rolling our eyes. I laughed at my siren's exaggerated posing.

"Cheer up, darling. This is going to be fun!" Eramyne gushed. The predatory gleam in my siren's face excited Shadow. I gripped my arms and rocked back and forth until Shadow quieted down again, sulking at its continual suppression. *You won't keep me down forever, Laura Rivell.*

CHAPTER 19

A blur of beautiful first-times filled the week ahead of the Whittaker's ball. A look that lingered, a prolonged touch sneaking into our secretive chatter between bites of the local baker's baguettes. Bouquets of red dune flowers and bayside meanderings at sunset. Half Moon Bay relished twilight like no other bay on earth, and I loved watching the bubbling blackness ombre into amethyst and turquoise behind my siren's graceful form as she walked beside me.

As frequently happened in public, there were some whispers, a few side-eyed remarks, but no one loudly commented on Eramyne's appearance. Cape Althea saw so few foreigners that most people asked no more questions past that of her origin. And though

Eramyne still laughed at me for essentially dubbing her Norwegian, it proved quite helpful to pretend she spoke little to no English; she could not hide her teeth for long whilst she spoke, nor her dark tongue.

At first, my siren's nocturnal habits presented a difficulty. She lapsed into a restful lethargy in the middle of being measured for alterations. Eliciting a beaming smile, I explained to the seamstress that Eramyne was "quite the bookworm, prone to excessive reading late into the night." As we adjusted to the daylight stage in our relationship, I relaxed enough to make jokes to plague her as she was bound by silence. She menaced me for it later, but in ways that I rather enjoyed; I certainly didn't feel dissuaded.

Meanwhile, a silvery-white gown was lengthened to fit Eramyne. Truth be told, I could hardly contain my excitement. I'd never cared for ballrooms or parties before. In a way, it would be a first for both of us.

The night of the ball, we helped each other set our hair. Initially, I was disappointed that I was deprived of the joy of surprise. Eramyne explained (very sensibly) that we might give ourselves and our blooming love away in those circumstances. I grudgingly agreed.

My siren stunned my own parents into silence when she entered my dressing room a graceful, though somewhat out-of-place being, and reappeared regal and glittering with gems around her smooth neck, her eyes keen and brilliant, displayed to advantage by the light fabric. Her lethal siren charm shone in full force. She was helped into the carriage with looks of astonishment and awe from everyone around us, and I, myself, tripped on my turquoise ruffles staring after her bare back.

"How I shall pry myself away from you to dance with anyone else, I cannot say," Eramyne murmured as she kissed the back of my hand behind the carriage curtain. "You are breathtaking in that color, darling."

"No more than you in that gown," I sighed, incapable of looking elsewhere. Delicate silver veiling overlaid the white under-sheath, culminating in a mock mermaid tail sewn into the train. (That subtle addition *might* have been my idea.) "Tritoness indeed. I could never carry myself the way you do; it puts human royalty to shame."

"Nonsense." She silenced my impending rebuttal with a quick kiss, burning my cheeks. "There. And I promise another on the ride back home. Can you wait until then, pretty temptress?"

I huffed, folding my hands into my lap and sitting bolt upright. "Temptress? I don't know what you mean."

"Oh, yes you do, lovely one."

Ivory and silver dinnerware glimmered from the table as we were invited to feast. I defied convention by switching my neighbor's place with Eramyne's card, having her next to me, but I was beyond weary of the good girl I'd cultivated ruining the best moments in life. *I am in love with a monster,* I firmly admitted to myself. I was resolved to be bad and enjoy it.

Eramyne, of course, thought *my* version of "being bad" was nothing short of hysterical. She was good enough to smile and restrict the desire to comment.

A seven-course meal followed, every masterpiece of the palate crafted to echo beauties from the seashore. I loved the creamy bisque topped with a sweet-and-salty foam. Despite my singing taste buds, I could hardly tear my attention from the empress beside me. And I was not her sole admirer.

Her iron locks were braided and wound around her head. Two seashell combs held them in place. Glass contacts we'd secured at the last moment masked her oddly-colored irises, and poor Eramyne's frequent blinking attested to her discomfort. But they served their purpose well; her eyes were a cool, solemn green. Unusual, yet not plucked from the realm of the impossible.

Everything was splendid until the main course, upon which a mouthwatering square of fish tantalized the eager diners with its tender, flaky delicacy and spiced aroma. "I wonder what kind of fish this is?" I murmured in awe. I was not particularly fond of fish, but this specimen was exquisite. I had my fork posed to dive in when a jab from my siren's elbow sent the instrument flying. I shot her a low, alarmed look.

"*Do not eat it,*" she hissed, her hands clenched in her napkin-covered lap.

"What's wrong?" I whispered back. One of the diners across from me politely returned my fork. Eramyne didn't answer. Her culminating rage was palpable, tightening every limb, roiling within her like a brewing storm. I abandoned my plate at once, seizing her by the hand and rushing us both to the balcony. Once there, Eramyne clutched the railing as her human form threatened to grow scales. Her venomous claws burst through the tips of her elbow gloves. Fear constricted my throat as I cried out, "Eramyne! You can't; not here. What is it?"

"That was . . ."

"Was what, dear?"

She bit her own lip so hard she drew blood and moaned from the pain. Purple heat spilled down her chin. In reply, she simply lifted her hand and pointed at herself.

Horror chilled my veins. I grabbed the railing, too, gasping in gulps of air to keep myself from being sick. "Oh, Eramyne!"

"Hush, dear, and let me think."

Taken back by her tone, I stepped away. The enraged siren paced to and fro, her sparkling trail rippling in the rising wind. Below the balcony, the waves boiled, answering their mistress's beckoning.

"This is no coincidence," she muttered through gritted teeth. "Someone had captured Melusine. We freed her before she could be displayed. They answered our triumph by killing another and attempting to feed her *to me*." My siren hissed and snarled, causing me to cringe and recede further. More spikes protruded from the back of her dress, violently rending it. "Whoever did this has to be in the dining room right now. Waiting for me to expose myself. 'Ah, there she is, the queen!' they will say. 'We must kill *her* next.'"

I froze. *Or anger the siren queen enough that someone else will kill her for them.*

To my horror, Eramyne's flesh flashed with scales as she peeled the glass contacts from her eyes and burst free from her dress, her massive, powerful tail supporting her upright and propelling her across the marble like an undulating snake. I shrieked, forcing myself to run *toward* the monster rather than *away* from her. I clutched her forearm in both hands. "Don't!" I yelled, ensuring that everyone on the other side of that flapping double door heard me, but I didn't slow Eramyne down at all. She dragged me with her.

The Tritoness burst through the doors. One scream rang out. Then another. The room was in instant, blinding chaos, food flung aside as people ran to escape the siren's menacing path. Terrified, I turned my head aside just as a splash of warm blood baptized it. Eramyne had bitten someone. My monster was unleashed, and I could not stop her.

It couldn't be real. Couldn't be happening. *A nightmare? Surely, this is all a nightmare. I shall wake up any moment now. That's not blood, that's wine. Freshly spilled. Those are not screams. Just loud, loud laughter—*

I let go of Eramyne to hide my face in my hands. Someone wrapped their arms around me and pulled me to my feet, pulled me away. I couldn't process what he was saying, but I recognized his voice. *Burke.* Had I really enjoyed five courses without noticing his presence at the feast? Was I truly that far gone? *On a monster?*

Somehow, we were outside. Burke had me by the shoulders—he was saying something in an urgent tone. I nodded with no idea what I was agreeing to. He vanished into the fleeing crowd, in the opposite direction they were running.

He's going to try to stop her. Burke, it's so dangerous— She is so dangerous.

My poor, poor love. I couldn't begin to imagine the pain, the horror. I was not a siren and *I* was almost sick at the notion of eating—*Don't think about it anymore. You'll fall off the deep end. You'll raise Shadow from its slumber. You must remain calm. Sane.*

Helpful. Be a loyal, helpful partner. For once in your life do something worthwhile! Inhaling deeply, I pried my forehead from my hands and looked at the crowd. *Think. She said the villain must be in the dining room. Must be present to watch her. Who is calm right now? Is someone else not running away, other than Burke? Is anyone harboring a secret smile amid the chaos?*

Torn clothes. Bleeding gashes, crying, yelling. A ballroom slaughter. But was it a slaughter? To my relief, there were only wounded, not *dead*. Not *bodies*. At least not here. That didn't mean there weren't any in the ballroom, but there appeared to be many people outside. That gave me some hope. Perhaps she hadn't intended to kill everyone, as I feared. Perhaps she hadn't snapped *entirely*.

I rose to my feet and stumbled forward two steps. Three. I looked for someone, anyone, whose current behavior indicated anything other than stark horror and shock. One person did stand out to me: a pretty blonde in a strawberry-pink dress, surveying the chaos with the calm of a seasoned journalist, first to the scene of the crime.

Something about her struck me as familiar. She was beautiful. Very tall, thin, yet muscular and thick-boned, like my siren. *She's a siren in human form.*

And she didn't have glass contacts. Her own odd eyes were violet. She donned brown-lensed spectacles right before turning her back to me and raising her skirts to run.

Melusine.

Unfathomable. I mustn't be so daft as to suspect one of their own. Eramyne would think I was crazy for suggesting it, but it did seem out of sorts—how we'd found Melusine in that mobile coffin with no one guarding her, as if no one else knew she was there. That wasn't possible. How *jealous* she'd seemed the first night I saw her, as I freed her from the net.

Was she guiding Eramyne to target the humans . . .

Because of me?

CHAPTER 20

I t never happened like this in the stories.

Hidden mermaids stayed hidden. Sacred birthing coves never came to light. The pirates never located Mermaid Rock, no matter how diligently they searched. But Reality is ever a harsh mistress, and she struck hard.

All Cape Althea knew of the siren that infiltrated the Whittaker's mansion. She was a pretender, a foreigner. And worse yet, all Cape Althea knew I was the first human she'd duped. The naive little friend she'd made. And worst of all, there were locals aplenty who believed that I was on her side, helping her plan an attack. I was on the side of the bloodthirsty, soulless, man-eating monsters known as sirens.

And they were right. Partially, perhaps, but right enough.

I couldn't bear to go into town anymore, not even for basic necessities. Too many people sidled away from me, whispering. Too many religious devotees lifted their religious symbols and murmured prayers of protection. I hid in my room, entertaining no visitors, reflecting gloomily on how terribly my first outing with Eramyne had gone. Cursing myself for a fool. My own family tread carefully around me, treating me as if my sanity was a muddled yolk inside a fragile shell—a single misstep would crush it beyond repair.

There was one thing I could be grateful for. No one had been brave enough to attempt to detain "the mad siren," so she'd escaped. Burke was safe as well, but as for me . . . Laura Frances Rivell was not born indifferent. GUILTY might as well have been stamped across my forehead and branded on my chest. My terrified parents planned to send me away to some sanctuary for a while—in secret, or so they thought—but I overheard them and was so very tired, sad, and frightened by the whole affair, I did not think to make my presence known and object. *Yes, send me away,* I thought to myself, *Remove me as soon as you can. I can never look anyone in the face again.*

But leaving my poor, enraged, grief-stricken siren behind cut me to the soul. How could I resist the longing to hold her, to soothe her, which pulled me to her as the moon directed the tides? No. I wouldn't leave Eramyne.

So, in the dark of a June midnight, I wrote three notes, packed a bag, and fled.

I'd have to commandeer a boat to reach it, but I knew of a small island east of the Cape where I might live unbothered. No one would think to look for me there, and having been raised in the Cape all my life, I knew enough about fishing and scrounging for edible seaweed and "sea shrooms" that I'd survive. It might be very lonesome, but I daresay loneliness was more appealing than a lifetime of social scorn, which I was certain to receive. Abandoning Eramyne would gain me little to nothing; vanishing from society to join her might gain me some semblance of belonging, of protection, of love.

That is, if Eramyne could find it in her heart to love a coward like me.

After leaving one note for my parents, one for Hyacinth, and the last one for Burke, I struck out in some unlucky fisherman's boat. I'd miss them terribly, but I couldn't drag any of them into solitude with me simply because my misery would love the company. Burke especially had already risked too much for my sake. I could ask no more of him.

With every stroke of the oars, doubts struck my heart one by one. Did I really believe I could survive on so little? What if the modest stream of fresh water on that island had long since dried up? What if a hurricane rose and drowned the whole of the place, wrecking this boat as well? What if I called and called for Eramyne, but she never came? What if I starved? What if I became very ill? What if—

A long, black figure sliced through the water by the boat, and I uttered a shriek of surprise. One wouldn't think a lone shark could scare me—not after the horrors I'd recently witnessed—but I jumped anyway, only recovering once I recognized the gleam of golden eyes. "Cimon," I gasped, relaxing my death grip on the oars. "Don't frighten me half to death when I'm half there already. Have you come to take me to your Tritoness?" Upon my query, the scalloped hammerhead turned immediately; I didn't doubt that was his purpose. I turned the boat to follow him.

In time, I realized my worries had distracted me from the direction of the island, and sweet Cimon was directing me aright. "Yes, Eramyne would think of this island as well. She hasn't forgotten me," I sighed. It *did* worry me that she couldn't come herself, but the fact she'd sent her beloved "pup" meant she still cared. It was an undeniable comfort. I'd deserted her. When she needed me most, I wasted time by staring stupidly at the chaos of the crowd until she had fled. I wouldn't have blamed Eramyne if I never heard from her again.

The closer we came to the island (unnamed, for it was too small to be worth it), the closer I inspected a lithe, long-haired figure, naked and crouching near the shore as if in wait. My heart whispered to me that it was my siren, and my heart was right. Dragging the boat as far ashore as my strength allowed, I splashed my way into her arms, sobbing with unrestrained passion and relief. "I'm so sorry, Eramyne. I left you. I just left you there. I'm *so* sorry!"

"No, do not *dare* apologize to me, beloved Laura," Eramyne commanded, stroking my hair. "It was my outrageous behavior that ruined everything. *I* am sorry." She knelt to stare up into my face, her eyes taking on a precious, moonlit innocence. "I all but confessed love for you, unsought and self-serving. I seduced you that night when I visited your room. And now I, who claim to love you, have irrevocably ruined your life and forced you away from your loved ones, from your tribe. What have I done to you? Oh, my darling Laura, what have I done?"

She would have wept, had sirens the ability to weep. Instead, she wrapped her arms around my knees and kissed them, her beautiful wild hair brushing the tips of my toes. "I would tame every sea for you to cross unburdened, though it drained me of my last drop of magic. I would kill any human who so much as scratched you with a hatpin. And yet it is I who have ruined you."

"You have ruined nothing!" Gently detaching myself from her, I knelt down, taking her beloved, strange face into my hands. "I didn't get a chance to tell you, but it's long been my intention to live a solitary life. This has only escalated my plans. And it's not solitary after all, for I have *you.* I've met the love of my life long after I ceased believing in such a fairytale. And now you can have *all* of me, and I can have *all* of you. It's a blessing, darling, not a curse. Although . . ."

Something akin to hope stirred in her expression. "Yes?"

"You may have to bring me food," I unwillingly admitted. "I am not famous for my fishing skills."

Her smile beamed with pride. "That is precisely what I wish and intend to do, my lovely one. I will be your provider; you shall want for nothing. And when I am occupied in Echo Trench, Cimon can bring you fish and scallops and squid. However, I cannot promise he will not eat half of what I send."

The last sound I expected to hear that night was our laughter, yet we laughed. Joy refreshed my weary spirit. That first night of my island life was spent in the arms of my siren, and the ballroom bloodbath was well out of sight, out of mind. I feared no violence from those gentle hands, so cautiously keeping the venomous claws out of range.

My eyelids fluttered open with the sunrise. Pink, orange, and light blue marbling painted the sky, with gilt clouds scurrying across the canvas. Eramyne's arms were still wrapped around me, and I smiled as I felt her even breaths against my bare shoulder.

I sat up slowly. Sand rained down from every part of me. I chuckled, startling Eramyne from her lethargic state. "Good morning, darling," she murmured.

"Good morning, my love."

Eramyne rubbed my back as I yawned and stretched. "I need a bath before breakfast," I grinned. "All this sand is going to drive me insane. I must get used to it, I suppose."

She giggled softly, helping me comb the sand from my hair. "You can set up camp further inland."

"Yes; a thorough exploration is in order." I stood and dusted myself off. "Must locate that stream first, if it's still there."

"It is. I would not have directed Cimon to escort you here otherwise."

"Of course. Silly me." I smiled and extended a hand to help her up. We strolled to the stream arm-in-arm. "Pity there aren't more trees," I commented, pointing at the unenthusiastic clutch of palm trees basking in morning light.

"It does not matter, dear. I will get you anything you require. You shall have your own little house, all the food you can eat, and I shall order the court sirens to make you the most beautiful, comfortable gowns you have ever worn in your life. You will be the queen of this island. What will you call your kingdom, my lovely one?"

"Hmm. I'll decide once I've seen all of it."

That was a memorable morning. The sandy shores graduated to packed, sandy dirt with scrubby vegetation. Tiny crabs scuttled homeward, indignant at our invasion. The sand was silky and cool, the breeze salty-fresh. I sighed happily and nodded to the palm trees. "I should take advantage of that shade, meager though it is, and build the house there."

"Very good. I will instruct the court sirens to begin gathering resources immediately." So saying, she detached from my arm and waded into the waves, shifting to siren form just before plunging in. A minute later she resurfaced, flinging her hair back from her face with a contented expression. She curved her tail fins above her head to shade herself.

"You've already told them?" I marveled.

She wiggled her tail, cooling her face with droplets from her fins. "Yes. Sound travels far beneath the sea."

"So I've heard."

"Do you know what you'll call your kingdom, my island princess?"

I giggled. "Love Isle comes to mind."

As expected, her nose wrinkled with distaste. I laughed. "Isle Rivell will do, unless I think of something more creative later on. What's for breakfast?"

"You would like to know, would you not?" Eramyne smirked. Beckoning with her forefinger, a wave bristled onshore laden with fish. I squealed and rushed to catch them before they flopped back to safety. My siren's rare, precious mirth rang like wedding bells. "Do you think you can be happy here? At least until I can relocate you to a better island. I need time to determine which is best."

"I'll be happy anywhere with you, Eramyne."

She motioned for me to join her in the ocean for a kiss. I playfully complied.

CHAPTER 21

FOUR MONTHS LATER

I sipped palm wine from my hut. Rain pounded on the roof but not a drop slipped in, and a small, rosy stove kept the living room warm. I stared out the window with a smile. My secret island life wasn't glamorous—I was skinnier, often sunburned, and quite sick of fish—but Eramyne spent every spare moment improving my situation . . . which plagued me with persistent guilt.

How could I repay her? She was a queen. She not only had royalty but real *power,* an ocean at her command, the court sirens of Echo Trench beneath her rule. Eramyne insisted over and over again that my love was enough for her, but it wasn't enough for *me.*

"What would Burke do?" I murmured, tracing the rim of the hand-carved cup. I missed his steady counsel. The first couple of months, I watched for a boat approaching the island with Burke in it, cursing at his chafed hands yet determined to find me. But as the third month passed, and now nearly a fourth, I abandoned such daydreams and accepted that fleeing to a tiny island was so ludicrous a plan, even my kindred spirit wouldn't dream I'd done just that.

Or maybe he did dream I had and kept away to prevent anyone else from figuring it out, too. He *was* my kindred spirit.

"I think," I mused aloud, sitting on my oversized pillow in front of the stove, "I think Burke would tell me that the perfect way to thank Eramyne is to solve the mystery of the ballroom dinner. To give her the fiend who publicly antagonized her by serving her one of her own." I shuddered. "But I can't do that from here. I can't do *anything* useful from here. Yet if I told her I was leaving, and why . . ."

I groaned, burying my head in my hands. *I wish you were here, Burke.*

Would he tell me to stay here, safe and sound, protected by the Tritoness herself? Or would he tell me to be brave and return to Cape Althea for a little sleuthing adventure, which may or may not include murder when all was said and done?

I knew what I *wanted* to do. I loved my peaceful life, but it was getting too quiet. Even for me. Most lone islanders in my situation would be continually scrounging for food, fresh water, and supplies, but I had Eramyne to direct the court sirens to fetch me anything I needed. True, a handful of them scowled at me as they did so, but they dared not mutter antipathies in the Tritoness's hearing. Nonetheless, boredom was setting in. I missed my parents and Burke, and I longed to see them. I'd wear my new clothes and cover my hair and wear glasses; surely I would pass unnoticed. *You're in desperate need of some real fun,* Shadow persisted. *Just don't get caught.*

I marched down the streets with all the confidence I could muster. My siren-made wardrobe ensured that not a single person would know me by the way I was dressed. I was a complete stranger in the garb of unknown lands, veiled and all. *Not even Burke will recognize me,* I assumed with a broad smile. The large, tinted glasses I wore were cumbersome, yet necessary to further my deception. I pushed them up my nose and surveyed the manor of the ballroom catastrophe from afar.

Nausea arose at the memory. I forced it back, keeping my logic ahead of my emotions, keeping Shadow on a tight leash. I considered stealing a maid's uniform from an obliging wash line somewhere and sneaking into the manor, but I doubted I could get away with that. Best to start with household gossip. "The maids know everything," so they say; I'd strike up a friendly conversation with the manor's staff after inquiring at the door for directions. After all, the news had broken out all over town. It should be easy to reintroduce what was certainly the most exciting event Cape Althea boasted in its gloomy, secluded life. The Cape's whispered sirens were *real*. How could that ever be topped?

Luckily, my knock was answered by a trim young maid who was indeed terribly fond of gossip. The sole suspicious character noticed by anyone else (besides one Laura Rivell, of course, who'd actually *befriended* the murderous creature) was the same blonde, pink-gowned lady I knew to be Melusine. Other people took note of how calm she was. It surprised me that she'd been so careless, letting other humans notice her like that. She didn't strike me as simple or careless. Was it intentional?

But why?

I thanked the maid for her kindness and withdrew. I walked quickly down the mansion avenue, deep in thought. Finding Melusine and questioning her wasn't possible. *I must become a siren myself in order to track a siren,* I discerned.

No other leads. I fumed, kicking at pebbles, wishing again for Burke. He was an excellent sounding board for my troubles.

You could reveal yourself to him, Shadow suggested, bristling with anticipation. *You know he'll keep your identity a secret. He can help you.*

Every so often, Shadow sprouted forth a good idea. I shrugged and silently agreed. *He's the only person I trust enough. And I* do *need help. I haven't the slightest idea where to go from here. And I returned so sure of myself! I can be such a ninny sometimes.*

Yes, you can, Laura.

Keep quiet, Shadow.

Heading back to the heart of town, I pushed Burke's office door open. A client half-turned in his chair, apparently interrupted midway through his consultation. Burke looked mildly surprised as well. "Just a moment, miss. I'll be right with you."

Apologizing for the intrusion, I slunk back outside and leaned against the building. *Yes. I'm a ninny.*

Two minutes later, the door creaked open. ". . . Laura?"

I jumped. Burke closed the door behind him and stared again, harder this time. "It *is* you, isn't it?"

"How on earth did you know?" I exploded. My friend chuckled, shaking his dark head. "Because you're one of the precious few young ladies of my acquaintance who would burst into my office willy-nilly, walking in like she owns the world. So, how are you? How is Eramyne?"

Of course, he'd know I was with her. I flushed. "We're both very well. But that misfortune at the manor still bothers me. I thought I might be able to dig up a few leads. Silly of me; I let the trail get cold. I don't know why I got it into my head that I could do any good now." Actually, I did know why. By the power of sheer, unadulterated boredom.

Burke hummed and crossed his arms. "I did some digging myself after you left. Nothing but dead ends. Whoever covered their tracks did it well; I doubt it was someone working alone. It occurred to me that perhaps Melusine and other court sirens had staged the whole event, hoping to poison Eramyne's feelings toward you by proving to her what 'monsters' humans are. But I'd have to become a siren myself to follow *that* lead."

"I had the same thought." I leaned against him with a sigh. He patted my shoulder with brotherly sympathy. "If Eramyne is willing to come on land again for a while, that might draw the villains out of hiding," Burke suggested. "I think that's the only chance we've got, though. And I despise using anyone as bait in such a manner, especially our Sovereign."

"Why do you call her that?" I startled him by asking, standing up straight.

Burke frowned, leaning against his cane. "It's one of her titles. Is there something wrong with me using it?"

"It's what her tribe calls her. *My Sovereign*. You call her that, too."

A long pause supervened. I grew more surprised the longer it drew on; it wasn't like my friend at all. Finally, Burke sighed. "I'll tell you someday. I promise. But now is not the time. The siren killer is the priority, not me."

"Agreed."

The next line of inquiry was the local fishermen.

I had an easier time of it, as Burke's unfortunately severe demeanor put them off. He wasn't a lawyer, but he had the face and direct speaking style of one. I laughed in my sleeve at his attempts—all in good fun—then flirted with the fishermen, painful as it was; it put them at their ease and opened the floodgates.

Absolutely nothing worth learning surfaced. Burke and I met up after a long afternoon of fruitless conversation, swapping exasperating gossip and fanning ourselves from the seaside heat. "I still think Melusine knows something about it," I declared, panting and daring to unbutton my collar (oh the travesty). "She was far too calm about the entire thing, and why would she risk being there at all? We humans aren't *that* fascinating."

Burke removed his top hat, exposing a line of sweat where the rim perched 'round his head. He muttered something about the 'goddamn heat.' "Perhaps her goal was to corner a potential mate at the ball. It is difficult—I can almost say impossible—to resist the urge during the fertile phase."

"Oh. You've read about it somewhere?"

Burke colored, strange enough for him. "Yes. I did."

I gave him a long look before continuing. "Melusine might be protecting a friend of hers."

"That's likely."

An awkward blank followed. Burke coughed into his sleeve. I touched his elbow. "Burke? You can tell me anything. You know that."

He nodded, but his countenance fell. "I know. I . . . I'm not ready. I hope that doesn't offend you."

I inhaled deeply, staring at the boats as they drifted to and from the docks. *Unconventional hours. A consulting business that he doesn't take seriously at all, coming and going as he pleases. He calls Eramyne "my Sovereign." And he knows so much about the sirens.*

He might laugh at me. Insist it was impossible or absurd. But I had to ask. "Burke. Tell me honestly; I swear I won't tell a soul if it's true. Do male sirens still exist?"

It was my friend's turn to take a deep breath. He answered slowly, as if from the bowels of a dream. "Yes. They're rare. Several conditions must be met in order for a male siren to be conceived."

"Such as? If you don't mind telling me."

"No, I don't mind." Sighing, he brushed his fingertips against mine for momentary reassurance. A habit we'd forged without realizing it. "Among other requirements, the siren purse must be laid on the night of the second full moon in a month—a black moon."

"Seldom happens, I take it."

"Next to impossible. Multiple generations pass without one."

"Did you meet one? A male siren?"

"In a manner of speaking," he said rather dryly.

You are *one,* I inwardly declared. I did not say it out loud. Not yet. He'd told me he wasn't ready; I would not force his confidence. But elation pulsed through my blood and tightened my stance, driving Burke to raise one stern brow. "What is it?"

"It's just so exciting," I gushed. "Knowing you've met one of the rarest creatures on earth. Were you nervous?"

"Terrified."

The softness of that word struck me. I tried to imagine being terrified of my own reflection. Tears welled at the thought. I hurried to swipe them away before my friend perceived them. "What a lonely existence," I murmured.

"The loneliest of any creature in the sea."

I gripped his hand as we watched the boats. Incoming thunder grumbled in the distance, but we both smiled when we heard it. "I love a stormy sea. Don't you?" I grinned.

His hand returned my gentle squeeze. "At this point, I'd say you don't have to ask what I like."

CHAPTER 22

A flawless night to walk the bay alone, fraught with sweet memories. I missed Eramyne, but I knew she would find me soon. I was just thinking about her again when I sensed my love's presence. The deep turquoise froth of tumultuous sea carried her in its wicked embrace, and I opened my arms to it and to her, smiling madly.

Her siren form rose from a bubbling wave that loomed above me. "Laura. What are you doing here?" My siren's fierce rebuke was expected, but I did *not* expect the predatory flash in her eyes, initiating a primal fear within me. I shrank back with a whimper. "I wanted to help you."

She blinked, smoothing her expression. The wave lifting Eramyne sank closer to my height. "Help me? With what, my darling? I feared you would be discovered, perhaps imprisoned." She reached out to touch my cheek. "What could you do for me on shore, and back in Cape Althea of all places?"

I sighed, leaning my repentant head into the palm of her hand. "I hoped I'd find out who killed one of your sirens."

"My foolish, pretty darling." Still in siren form, Eramyne pulled me close to cradle my head against her scale-plated chest. Her claws combed my hair. "I have already dealt with the traitor, and his death sentence has been carried out. He was a pawn of Melusine, who hopes to reclaim me from your embrace by vilifying the humans. She has vanished but will be found very soon. She is my own cousin . . . she cannot hide from me for long."

Her dreadful eyes flashed again. I found myself in love with them, though they caused my heart to tremble. My siren was the enfleshment of the Agenne Sea itself: powerful, seething, beautiful, frightening. I liked her better as a monster than a woman, even while I quaked with primal fear. "At least Burke and I were right," I murmured, kissing her stern cheek. "It *was* Melusine. Her lack of tact is disappointing. I was hoping my first mystery would be more of a challenge."

"You would find it challenging to solve any mystery of the sirens before I do, dearest," Eramyne laughed, "but I am proud of you nonetheless. You are so soft in my arms, yet so strong in spirit and will, and intelligent besides. I am blessed to call you mine."

Picking me up, she cradled me in her arms, kissing me, and I melted into her strength as the ocean rippled around us. "I wonder what Burke is up to on a glorious night like this," I said once our lips parted. Just testing the waters, so to speak.

She tilted her head with a coy smile. "Fishing."

Yes, my siren *did* know. Of course she did. Was there anything she *didn't* know?

"Darling, there is something important I must tell you."

I shifted on the pinkish sands of our island. Eramyne lovingly caressed my cheek, but concern shone in her wide pupils. The Tritoness seldom showed such a fragile emotion. "Tell me," I commanded. Waiting for bad news made me nervous.

"Do not boss a siren queen," Eramyne chuckled. Her finger slipped down my cheek and neck to trace my collarbone. "Do you remember when I told you about sirens coming on land in the form of women to lie with a mate? That this is how our species propagates, ever since male sirens became so rare?"

"*Propagates.* What a cold way to put it!"

My siren smirked—something she seldom did. "Considering the fact that we often consume our mates afterward, dear, I think a cold description suits the practice."

"The *necessary* practice," I rapidly furnished.

Eramyne's smirk melted into a fond smile. "Kind of you to add, my sweet Laura, but what I mean to say . . . What I must tell you . . ."

My face paled at her hesitancy. Eramyne inclined her head, affirming my fears. "It will soon be my turn to fulfill this obligation."

I turned away from her, my stomach clenching. "No. You can't!"

Sighing, she gently tilted my face back to her, her gaze seeking mine. "You know I must."

"You can't. You're mine. And I'm yours."

Vexed by my own childish tears, I turned my back to her and curled up, arms wrapped around my knees. The image of my siren pleasing—or being pleased by—anyone else made my stomach wind itself in knots.

Shadow started from its hiding place as well, snarling, claws out, ready to shred any man who dared touch my siren. *I'll kill them. I'll kill them all.*

No. I desperately pushed Shadow's words aside, pretending I hadn't heard them ringing inside my head like a funeral dirge. *Be calm. Be rational. She wants to fulfill her duty, that's all. She would never betray me.*

"I would never betray you," Eramyne persisted, as if privy to my thoughts. She rubbed my back and arms. "You know I shall find no pleasure in it. Every moment I shall be aching to return to you. No one makes my heart sing like my sweet Laura."

"I know that," I choked. More tears dripped down my bare knees. "In my heart, I know. I just adore you, Eramyne. I *worship* you. You are *my* goddess, not anyone else's."

"And that will not change." My siren wound her arms around me, pulling me back against her chest and holding me tight. "It is for but an hour, if that, my beloved. It will be quick."

"Promise me you'll kill him," I demanded.

A brief pause—Eramyne's rare but profound shock. "I promise."

Thank Sofia.

She rocked me back and forth, mimicking the motion and hum of the sea. My grieving mind scrambled for something else to talk about. Anything at all. I had to distract Shadow from bursting out with other violent demands. "Is Burke part of your tribe?" I asked, uncurling my posture and leaning back against Eramyne.

She blinked down at me, adjusting to the sudden change in conversation. "So, he has told you his secret? Male sirens have no tribe. It is tradition."

"No, he didn't tell me. I guessed it." I frowned. "They're outcasts?"

"Yes."

"Why? That is so cruel!"

Eramyne merely smiled at the duality of my nature. Selfish one minute, sympathetic the next. "Because of the first male siren recorded in our history. His name was Zorstrom." She proceeded to comb and braid my hair as she told me the story. "He believed he was Triton, king of all sirens and answerable to no one, even the Tritoness. He usurped the head of his tribe and drove the nine seas into a bloody war. Year after year, the season for mating would come and go without notice, for it was not safe to procreate while rival tribes destroyed the birthing places. Many sirens died and few remained to replace them.

"At last, the newly-crowned Tritoness destroyed him and suppressed the fighting, but not without great struggle. The effects of the War of the Nine Seas are present to this day, including the tradition that any male siren is neither born into a tribe nor permitted to be adopted into one. But do not feel so sad for them," Eramyne added, tying off my braid with twine and stroking my arms, "for they enjoy more freedom than any of the tribe-bound sirens. As long as Burke respects tradition and does not expose us or bring us harm, he may live in whatever way he prefers. Most males choose a life on land and take human wives. In this way, they are happy."

I sighed. *Burke doesn't seem so happy.* He smiled often with me, but that was only due to the fact that we were so alike in preferences and temperament. Most of the time he was stern and solemn, not cheerful. "I wish there was more I could do to make Burke happy."

Eramyne kissed the top of my head. "You do not need to risk yourself for me, running about catching killers. And you do not need to 'make Burke happy.' I am certain he would agree if he was here. You can be yourself and do as you please."

"That's easy for a siren to say," I smiled up at her, cupping her cheek in the palm of my hand. "Humans have far more expectations to live up to."

"Then I am glad I am not a human."

"I'm glad you aren't, too."

Eramyne and I sent an invitation to Burke to visit our island. Burke rowed out to Isle Rivell the next day, "consulting businesses be damned," or so he said, making me laugh. During his visits, I was careful to avoid the topic of male sirens or give away that I *knew*. It became increasingly difficult, as I longed to see his siren form; for I believed that of all people on the earth, I was the last human who would look upon him with hate or terror. I was sure he must be beautiful in that feral siren way, but since he lived as a human, no one had ever seen him and had the chance to tell him so. It made me happy to know I'd be the first.

Unfortunately, the splendid reveal did not come about as desired.

Eramyne woke me in the night, whispering my name with her gentle touch. My palm-filled mattress rustled beneath me as I sat up. "Is something wrong?" I whispered, instantly alarmed.

"Yes, but the danger has passed and now he needs your comfort."

"Burke?"

"Yes, my darling. Will you come? I will guide you to him."

"Of course."

I dressed in haste. We hurried to my rowboat and Eramyne helped me in. I rowed after her as she transformed and swam ahead of me, the swipes of her powerful tail slowing to match my pace with delightful patience.

A siren clung to a mass of rocks near the bay. His poor face was twisted with anguish and self-loathing, and his vicious, dark eyes mirrored Eramyne's hunting demeanor with lethal depth. He snarled as I approached, ducking behind the rocks. His dark purple tail crushed them in its grip like the coils of a colossal snake.

"Aden," Eramyne called. "Laura is here. Please come out; she will not be frightened. That much I can promise you."

"Aden?"

"His land-nomen before coming to Cape Althea."

"Burke, it's me," I pleaded, outstretching my hand. "What's wrong? Please come to me."

For a long while, it seemed he would not come. At last the enormous tail loosened its hold, slipping into the sea, and Aden resurfaced near my boat.

Grotesque features contrasted with sublime coloration: rich purple, silver, and dark blue scales that shone in moonlight. Blue spikes lined his spine and tail, his matching claws crowning his fingertips in lieu of nails. "You're stunning," I gasped, meaning it with all my heart.

He withdrew, disbelief heavy in his gaze.

"Don't you call me a liar, Bartholomew Burke." My playfulness surprised him. His tail curled around my boat and drew it (and me) closer, the ghost of a smile tugging at his dark lips. "Well, I'm here. Is anyone going to tell me what happened?" I asked, patting and stroking Aden's shorn hair, for only its coloring had changed with his transformation. He sighed, allowing me to draw his monstrous head near and kiss it with a motherly gesture.

"It was me," he began. His voice had changed somewhat. It carried further and deeper, chords of an ethereal cello caressed underwater. It caused both Eramyne and I to break into gentle smiles. "My hunger drove me to madness; I feasted in the mortuary with abandon. I meant to leave the Cape and never return, but Eramyne found me and convinced me to remain. Oh Laura, Laura, how can I live with myself?"

Then, Burke—my stern, determined, steadfast Burke—wept into my lap, though his siren eyes produced no tears. I cradled his head and ran my fingers through his short hair, darting Eramyne an alarmed glance. *I've never seen him like this before.*

Give him time, my siren's calm mien replied. *Being with you is enough.* With a silent splash, she darted underwater, leaving me alone with my friend.

I kissed his brow when his head lifted. "Has this happened before, my poor Aden?"

A short smile answered my immediate adoption of his former name. "I . . . I prefer robbing fresh graves when my appetite overwhelms me. A morgue presents too great a risk. What have I done?"

I kissed his brow again and felt his great surprise and wonder at my kindness. It killed me inside to know how starved for affection he must be. "Surely it shall be attributed to some wild animal. There are many farther inland, so perhaps one wandered closer to the bay. It's conceivable. Please don't leave me, Burke. What would I do without you?"

He grunted. "Find a better, happier friend sans human-eating tendencies?"

"How very dull."

It was short and brief, but he laughed. His siren mirth was just as velvet-smooth and innately charming as Eramyne's, though more masculine, and I laughed, too. "Nothing can dissuade me from being friends with you, whether Burke or Aden or your lovely siren name that I'm sure I can't pronounce," I persisted. "So don't try to push me off. I will be very angry, indeed."

For the first time, the warmth of affection shone unguarded in his face. "I can never express how happy I am to have met you, Laura Rivell."

CHAPTER 23

The morgue was peaceful. Order and silence reigned. Cold bodies were frozen beneath their sheets, tagged feet unmoving; silver tables gleamed, bright and clean, topped with glittering implements ready for their next unfeeling patient.

The door shuddered from a massive impact. Again. And again.

It burst open.

A grotesque beast of a siren coiled over the floor, dragging itself by its hands and tail. His mouth gaped and panted with hunger. He snatched the nearest calf of a deceased woman, tore it free, and gulped it down in great chunks, shredding it like a starved shark in a feeding frenzy. The other leg. Then an arm.

I hated to watch. I cried out, turning my head aside, but something had my neck in a vice-like grasp. I was forced to watch as the siren moved on to a fresher body. Blood sprayed the immaculate white-and-silver room, warming my feet as it pooled around them. I wanted to sob but couldn't. A menacing voice I knew all too well inundated the scene: *Come feast with us, Laura Rivell. Aren't you hungry? Aren't you hungry?*

Go away, Shadow. Get out of my dreams. Wake up. Wake up. WAKE UP.

I jolted awake. Tears streamed down my face, soaking the pillow. I reached out for Eramyne resting beside me, yet I pulled away before my hands touched her.

She's a monster, too.

"When?"

Eramyne ceased nibbling her redfish—in which she obviously had no interest—long enough to tilt her head at my question. "When what, dear?"

My fork clattered as I set it down a little too forcefully. "When will you go ashore to find a mate?"

That put an effective end to her charade of dining with me. She pushed her plate aside with a sigh. Normally I'd be begging for her untouched fire-roasted sea shrooms, but my appetite was failing me, too. "Three days from now. We usually go ashore in the evening, once the sailors are drunk or well on their way there."

"I want to come."

A flicker of irritable anger stewed in her pupils. "Absolutely not."

"I won't watch," I groaned, casting my eyes to the ceiling, "I want to be nearby in case anything goes wrong. What if he realizes you're a siren and tries to kill you?"

"That never happens. We always pick the drunk ones."

"It *does* happen; you told me so yourself."

"They seldom survive the attempt."

"Then you'll need me to help you subdue him."

She tossed her hair from her eyes. "How many times have I told thee, beloved? I appreciate your persistence to be of help, but I do not require it. I have navigated all of the Agenne Sea and half its infringing lands without any help—*human* help, at least."

"Oh?" I pushed my own plate away. "You don't want *my* help because I'm a *human.* I understand."

"Do not do this," Eramyne grunted. "Do not pick a fight to keep me with you. You are a grown woman."

"It's *because* I'm a grown woman that I have the right to ask you to stay with me. To *expect* you to be loyal to me. Why can't your court sirens breed on your behalf? You are not the only siren left."

Her eyes narrowed. Her lips pursed as she repressed a sneer. "I am Tritoness, not just the head of the Echo Trench tribe. My strength runs deep. My breeding is pure. It is my responsibility to produce strong offspring for the Nereid. If I succeed, my hatchling will be a princess, her place in the Agenne Sea fully secured. The court sirens do not carry Sovereign blood; they cannot breed a princess for me."

"That doesn't make sense. You're Tritoness, so you can do whatever you want." My eyes widened. "Wait. Doesn't Melusine carry Sovereign blood, as she is your cousin?"

Eramyne snorted, looking away. "I cannot simply live however I please because I hold a position of power. You mistake me for the selfish Zorstrom. And no, my *distant* cousin holds no serious claim to bearing royal blood."

I pushed away from the table and left the hut. As I glumly observed the sunset, Eramyne approached me from behind, touching my elbow. "It could be different for us," she said.

I held my posture stiffly as I turned, arms crossed. "Different?"

Eramyne sighed, hesitation delaying her response. "There is a siren witch in the caverns. Her land-nomen is currently unknown to me, so I suppose the Witch will suffice."

Hope fluttered my eyelids open wide. I uncrossed my arms. "What can she do?"

"Many things, including changing a human into a siren. She perfected this technique to rebuild the Nereid after the War of the Nine Seas."

"And the human would be changed forever?"

"Yes."

I trembled at the possibility. "Why didn't you tell me this earlier?"

Eramyne sighed and looked out to sea. "I had to be sure you would truly want it, Laura. Want *me*. I could not risk that you would make such a decision in the thick of limerence."

My face reddened. "That's not what this is."

She faced me again to touch my shoulder. "I am not disputing your love for me, darling, but I had to be certain. That is why I am telling you *now; I am* certain."

Despite my resolve, her touch alone weakened my stiffened muscles. My hands fell to my sides. "And you waited for me to learn about Burke," I guessed.

"Yes, although I was hoping he would tell you himself. I can understand why he did not. You will have another friend in the sea besides myself, which makes me very happy."

I crossed my arms again as I considered it. Besides my parents and Hyacinth, who had all benefited from my disappearance since the siren attack (even if they wouldn't agree), I had lived such a quiet, sheltered life that I had no other acquaintances besides Burke. And Burke, as it turned out, was a siren himself. I lost little and gained much by becoming one of them, so it seemed to me. "When can you take me to her?"

She laughed, tucking my hair behind my ear. "Slow down, beloved. Take more time to think about it. Once you are changed, you cannot be changed back."

"Fine. But you should know I've all but decided already. I want to be with you forever. I *will* be with you forever."

"You might change your mind the minute you see Echo Trench," Eramyne chuckled, kissing my neck, then lightly grazing it with the outer curve of her glinting teeth. I trembled with pleasure. "There are caves full of bones, not sparkling coral palaces. You can hardly imagine how different your life will be—how dark and full of strange sounds your surroundings will be—how limitless, yet rife with danger. I dearly hope you are not afraid of sharks in constant proximity; we love our pups."

I scoffed at that. "Banish the thought! And surely there are lovely, sunny places, too. It can't *all* be dark and gloomy. Besides, I like dark and gloomy."

"To visit, perhaps. But to abide in? Are you sure, my love?"

"Yes."

"Then once my unpleasant business on land is concluded, I will take you to the Witch."

No other sentence in my life thrilled me half as much. I pulled her into an enthusiastic kiss, relishing her low, muffled mirth before I tasted her tongue.

Tense with my joyous news, I relayed my plan to Burke, bright-faced and beaming. Rather to my surprise, he balked at it. "You can't be serious, Laura."

"Why not? What's wrong? I thought you would be happy for me."

Burke, as I thought of him while in human form, frowned and rubbed his beard. "You're telling me you're *choosing* to become a monster. There's no dancing around it; that's what we are. Nobody sane would *choose* to be like this."

Shadow snickered at the implication. "Maybe I'm not sane," I suggested, finally allowing Shadow's insights to break the surface. I felt Shadow inhale deeply and stretch its grimy limbs to the fresh air, vastly pleased. *I'll deal with you later,* I informed it.

Burke shook his head. "Don't be so frivolous. Besides, there's not a single witch alive—either on earth or in the sea—that won't expect you to pay a high price for such a spell. Did Eramyne say what she will ask for in exchange?"

"She didn't mention it." Unease stirred in my stomach as I wondered why. "Maybe she doesn't know?"

"Hard to imagine the Tritoness not knowing *that.* As our Sovereign, she must have overseen some of the human transformations herself. She *must* know."

"Then I'll ask her." *Right after I'm done keeping an eye on her through her mating ritual.* It would be gruesome, no doubt, but as her *real* lover I was determined to follow her and ensure her safety. So I told myself and Shadow, anyway.

"Tell me what she says," Burke requested. "I trust Eramyne, but I'm not altogether convinced you shouldn't remain as you are. You have a charmed life on that island. Eramyne loves taking care of you and sees you all the time. What's wrong with keeping things the way they are?" Burke fumbled with his cane, frowning at it instead of me.

Because it's boring, Shadow sneered. Who wanted to be trapped on an island for the rest of their life?

Sunset on the third day.

I rose and donned a cloak. Slipping quietly into my boat, I rowed to Half Moon Bay and moored it out of view. *She'll be haunting the inns along the shoreline.* I dodged from shadow to shadow, wary of the laughing, smoking men catching sight of a lone woman. The last thing I wanted was to cause Eramyne trouble by getting caught myself.

Unfortunately, I had no choice but to start peeking through inn windows. This offered up several sights I instantly desired to burn from my brain. Most of the windows were covered or just nonexistent, however, so this did not suffice. *I'll have to casually walk past the rooms and see if I recognize her voice.*

I searched two inns with this method. No luck. The third was also cleared without any sight or sound of my beloved siren. I was halfway through the fourth and considering giving up when I recognized her soft, enchanting moans. My hands trembled, then clenched into fists.

Acting on subconscious whim, I gripped something I'd snatched from the first inn. The door was locked. I tested the latch and slipped the blade in the crack, wedging it upward with ease. *Cheap inn latches. What a joke.*

His face was buried between her legs.

Mine. Mine. MINE.

She didn't scream. She just watched as I painted the room red, starting with the head nestled between her thighs.

CHAPTER 24

Once I'd finished my painting, chest heaving, red-faced, suddenly Eramyne's knee was digging into my gut. Her incredibly strong fingers pressed against my throat, pushing me against the shabby floor. She'd knocked me down with lightning speed—Shadow laughed. "Thou art impeding my sovereign charge," she said, her breath hot and dangerous against my ear. "I do not like it."

I like this, though. I savored the rage in her narrowed ebony eyes, her hand wrapped around my throat, even her knee menacing my stomach. I liked being pinned to the ground. *We should try this more often.* "You are so beautiful when you're angry," I said.

My siren hissed. "I told you not to follow me. I ordered you not to come."

"If you thought *I* might be in danger, and I told you not to come, would you listen?"

"... No."

"So there."

"You are a human. I am a siren. That is different."

I smiled. My bloodstained fingers grasped her wrist. I knew from the pulse rampaging through it that she was still primed for release. "There are a few very nice ways I can apologize, my love."

"Good luck getting up. You cannot overpower me, infuriating human."

I kissed her. She grunted against my lips, attempting to raise a resistance, but my tongue knew hers intimately well. Her hold on me weakened.

Infuriating human. I hoped to give her more reasons to call me that. Enough times that she'd be all too pleased to see me become a siren.

I closed the door of my island hut, humming with contentment. I washed, changed, and soaked my bloody dress in cold water, not that I had much hope in its salvation. It was likely stained beyond repair.

Still humming, I skipped into my bedroom. My tune fell silent at the sight of a blonde woman sitting on my bed, awaiting my return.

A blonde *siren*. I stepped back, but not in time. Melusine pressed a stony dagger to my throat, smiling sweetly. "And here I believed you'd done all the damage you could do. Now you will keep our Sovereign from breeding, as well? I've had enough of you, and so has half the court."

"I don't believe you," I gasped. The chilly blade pricked my skin.

"Not as if you would know either way," she coolly replied. She walked forward, forcing me to back out of the bedroom and exit the hut. The scrubby vegetation scratched my bare feet. "You have no choice but to believe what I tell you. Or not. Soon it won't matter at all."

My face reddened. "I want to help Eramyne and the sirens! You don't know what you're doing." Step by step, she prodded me at knifepoint closer to the lapping waves. I realized her intent with a shudder—the undertow was formidable.

"If your intention is to help us, then kindly go and drown without a fuss. You're an interfering, self-absorbed brat of a distraction. *Eramyne,*" she pronounced my cherished name for my siren with disdain, "will breed, lay her purse, and return to Echo Trench where she belongs."

As she spoke, Melusine waded into the sea, dragging me with her as she transformed. She bit back a cry as her legs thickened and molded into a writhing tail, her spikes burst free, and her pupils widened. All the while she managed to keep hold of me in her devilish grip. She pulled me in deep, far too quickly for me to resist. The waves reached my midsection . . . my collar . . . my ears. "Goodbye, Laura Rivell. I trust a burial at sea is romantic enough for you."

Water filled my ears, my nose, my mouth. The undertow seized my body in its wild clutches. For a moment, I fought to free myself from the current, but I remembered to preserve my energy and allow the currents to take me wherever they wished. *Not today. Not by her hand. I'm not going to die today. Eramyne, where are you?*

The hazardous minutes ticked by. No one came. I fought to keep my head above water, treading desperately. *Not today . . .*

My limbs grew heavy. My eyelids fluttered closed; the darkness fell.

I love you, Eramyne.

Warm lips were pressed to mine.

My weighted lungs suddenly felt lighter than air. I inhaled a shocked gasp. A pair of arms encircled me, muscular yet feminine. *Eramyne.*

I realized her hair was floating around her head, and I blinked in confusion. *We're still underwater? But how am I—*

A kiss from a siren saves you from drowning.

I laughed with pure delight. It cascaded from my mouth in golden bubbles shooting to the surface. Relieved, my siren embraced me and spiraled her tail around me until I felt smothered. I winced to convey it to her, and she guiltily released me. We nuzzled one another and held hands, happy to bask in Eramyne's world. At long last, I would see it as she did.

Every shade of blue, green, and gray shifted around us in veils of living color. Stingrays scoured the ocean floor while seagrass waved and clumps of dark orange seaweed ferried marine life. Even the jellyfish—of which I was deathly afraid—were beautiful, shining like pearls on dark blue cushions.

Eramyne swam behind me and gently grasped my waist, propelling me downward to admire her world more closely. The dancing play of shadows and light culminating at each angle was so dreamlike; it alone could captivate me for hours. I was far from done when Eramyne brought me back to the surface. I spluttered my objections.

"We do not know how long this miracle will last," my siren wisely pointed out. "I will not risk your life when you nearly lost it. What in the great Agenne Sea were you doing?"

With a start, I realized she didn't know about Melusine's return. I reluctantly informed her of her cousin's attempt on my life. By the time I was half done, my siren's eyes blackened and narrowed so fiercely that my heart skipped several beats. "Hold on," was all she said. I obeyed.

Eramyne swam me back to my island, which she searched from the first rock to the final grain of sand for any indication that Melusine lurked nearby. Satisfied that she did not, Eramyne informed me that I was to stay there while Cimon swam the perimeter and Burke was called to be my bodyguard. Meanwhile, my siren would not rest until Melusine was delivered to the court sirens for judgment and pending banishment.

I meekly agreed to it all, even to a bodyguard. Outwardly she remained calm, yet the intense rage the Tritoness emitted burned with the strength of a thousand summer suns. To my infatuated eyes, she glittered like a bejeweled golden idol, and I loved her in her wrath. She kissed my forehead. "I will return to you soon, my sweet Laura."

"I'll be waiting for you."

I watched her graceful dive back into her kingdom before returning to my hut. Alone with my thoughts, I paced the tiny living room and listened to the island wind wail against the walls. *I hate to admit this, but something Melusine said is getting to me.*

Shadow responded immediately, glad I was finally listening to it and conversing with it as it had always longed for. *Ha! She's just an aspiring murderer. You are the real thing. Why concern yourself with what a weak pretender says about you?*

I frowned. *Pay attention, Shadow. I'm thinking about how she called me a self-absorbed distraction. Doesn't she have a point? Eramyne holds several titles. Multiple responsibilities. What if Melusine wasn't lying and half the siren court at Echo Trench is irritated with me? What if they try to kill me whether I'm a human or a siren?*

Again, why should you care? I sensed Shadow eliciting a broad yawn. *You have the Tritoness on your side. And a male siren, too. You have nothing to fear. Let the court be annoyed with you. You have better things to do than worry about them.*

Then I'd best become a siren right away. Eramyne and Aden can guard me more conveniently from their own turf than from mine. Besides, it's so dull here I could cry.

You never said a truer word. Yes, let's get out of here.

I smiled. It was refreshing to be on the same page as Shadow. I was nonsensical for fighting it for so long due to some silly, moralistic high ground. If I can love a monster, perhaps I can love Shadow, too.

A familiar knock on the door signaled Burke's arrival. "Come in," I sang without fear. Burke swept inside, every inch of him plastered with seawater—clearly, he swam all the way to the island. I giggled at the thought of him carrying his clothes, his submerged pants trailing beside his siren tail. "What nonsense did you commit to get here?" I playfully scolded.

He caught his breath before answering. "Merely a quick transformation from the bay. Eramyne summoned me. Laura, I'm so sorry I wasn't with you—"

I held up my forefinger in a forbidding gesture. "None of that! I'll kick you right back outside. It looks like rain, too, so be good."

"Yes, ma'am."

I grinned. Burke's eyes narrowed. "I didn't expect you to be in such high spirits. Does a near brush with death make you giddy, you crazed woman?"

"If *you* were a dull, prosaic human and you suddenly had a siren lover who could help you breathe underwater, you'd be 'giddy' too."

"I suppose." Burke's accustomed gravity made me wonder if he'd ever experienced giddiness in his life. "The best thing about it is it proves you don't need to change yourself. You can go on being human." Still breathing hard, he sat on the large pillow by the stove that served as my miniature couch. "By Sofia, I'm out of shape."

Giggling, I slipped into the bathroom and snatched a towel. I brought it back to him. He accepted with a thankful nod. "And live on this island forever, all by myself?" I complained. "That's no fun. I still want to be a siren, and your shallow concerns won't prevent me."

"Stubborn as always, I see."

"Did you expect otherwise?"

"No. Not really."

"Then it's settled."

Burke groaned. He threw the used towel aside with weary resignation. "What does Eramyne say about it? Has she agreed to your mad intentions?"

"Not yet, but she will. First things first; Melusine must be imprisoned."

My kindred spirit gave me a long, intent look. "I never know whether you're going to be empathetic or downright bloodthirsty. You seem to be aiming for the latter lately."

Shadow and I shared internal smiles. "It's an improvement. I'm about to become a raging man-eater that never sleeps, so I should adjust my thinking to suit my future. I intend to immerse myself in their culture, learn their language, and eventually be adopted into their tribe."

He rubbed the back of his neck, yet unconvinced. "Humph. Ambitious of you."

"Thank you! Oh, and you're coming, too."

I beamed at my friend's stunned face. "What, coming to Echo Trench?" he stammered. "I can't. Male sirens aren't permitted to—"

"Eramyne told me about that. I'm going to eradicate this ridiculous tradition. Eramyne will agree; I know she will."

"Just because she agrees doesn't mean the law will be changed. The court has to approve it. Unanimously."

"They will. I'll convince them. It will be easy with the Tritoness at my side."

Burke smiled grimly. "All due respect, Laura, you do not know the court sirens yet. They're tight-lipped and close-knit; they abhor outsiders by instinct. I'm not sure they'll warm up to you at all, let alone listen to your argument against one of the most longstanding traditions in Nereid history."

"It's not *tradition*, Burke. It's *discrimination*. And it's hateful."

"I appreciate your affection for me and your care for my wellbeing, but to propose such a thing as a former human changed by witchcraft . . . Many Nereids view changing humans into sirens as against Goddess Sofia's design."

"I'll cross that bridge when I come to it."

He sighed, continuing to rub the back of his neck in a self-soothing gesture. "Well, I won't argue with you anymore. I dislike it far too much." Burke stood up and crossed the room to take my hand. "Just promise me one thing."

"Yes?"

To my surprise, he rested his forehead against mine, driving his sober gaze down deep. "Do not, under *any* circumstances, let Witch Lorelei take your voice."

"Witch Lorelei?" My eyes widened as I unconsciously reached up to touch my throat. "What would she want with my voice?"

He pulled back, yet retained my hand. "A siren's voice is their power, their identity. We are nothing without it." Sorrow crept into Burke's expression. "Long ago, a Nereid princess fell in love with a human prince. She traded her voice to a witch in exchange for the form of a woman for three days and three nights. She was the first siren to be transformed."

Instantly enamored, I begged for him to continue the story.

He shifted to take both of my hands in his. "It's a cautionary tale for our young, but it's important for you to hear, too. To remain a woman forever, the Nereid princess had to win the prince's love. But he met a human princess of the neighboring land and fell in love with her instead. On the royal wedding night, the despondent Nereid princess died alone with nothing, not even her voice. Her body dissolved into sea foam."

I felt my beaming face diffuse into sobriety. Burke nodded. "So you understand. Nothing is worth the loss of a siren's voice, including the chance of everlasting love. Don't forget it, my beloved friend."

CHAPTER 25

As Burke and I chatted by the glowing stove, the wind continued to rise. Storm clouds gathered. "Reminds me of the sea the night I met Eramyne," I sighed blissfully, watching lightning paint the darkness with blinding white strokes.

Burke joined me at the window. "The sea churns like this when she is angry. The hunt for Melusine must not be going well."

"Or they are fighting. Melusine doesn't strike me as the type to come quietly."

"You're right."

We observed the storm in tense silence. He offered me my dining chair, but I declined it. "I'm worried about Eramyne. I'm sure she can handle her cousin, but what will the court decide to do with her?"

"I couldn't say. I'm sure this is obvious, but I am not privileged with observing court rulings. Though I *can* say that there are precious few protections in place for humans, even ones we respect."

"That's what I'm afraid of. What if Melusine goes free?"

"Then I'll be your bodyguard in earnest." His rare, warm smile laid my objections to rest. "A vast improvement over sitting in a dusty old office day in and day out. Additionally, serving as your bodyguard at Eramyne's command will secure me a position within her tribe. It's a lowly start, but it's a start nonetheless."

"Then I'll be delighted to accept."

Burke fell asleep awaiting our Sovereign's return.

The stove burned low, casting a strange orange flicker over the room. My hut creaked and groaned beneath the weight of the storm. A clap of thunder rattled the walls, causing me to jump in my chair. *I wish she'd come. I can't sleep without her.* The blessing and the curse of love: the utter inability to sleep without the warmth and comfort of each other's arms. I sighed, wrapping my arms around myself and rocking back and forth. Lone misery darkened the corners, lurking in the shadows. Waited for me to summon Shadow, if only to have something to talk to.

What would it be like to live without her? We'd only known each other half a year and already I existed within her existence, longed to revel in every part of her. To adopt her world and live in it as one of her own kind. If she were ever killed . . .

Don't.

Had I not borne witness to Eramyne's supernatural strength? Had I not felt the serpentine weight and crushing muscular grace of her tail? Did she not bear venomous claws and spikes and harbor tiny, secretive fangs with the power to paralyze in her inner cheeks? This and more did my siren boast: wicked serrated teeth, large reflective pupils for seeing in the murky dark, precise hearing to locate and communicate with her tribe. Her hypnotic siren's song.

My love was right to worry about my comparative helplessness. Next to the Tritoness, I was a newly-hatched butterfly with fledgling wings and no idea how to use them.

Don't sell yourself short. You've killed a man.

Yes, Shadow, a drunk and distracted man already on his knees.

You killed your first target. How many fledgling murderers can say the same?

I wouldn't know.

Give yourself a little credit, Laura.

I'll try.

I watched Burke as he slept on the oversized pillows on the floor. He looked so content that it made me smile. I'd never loved any man as I loved him (with a strong platonic affection), and thinking of my future as a siren with Aden as my bodyguard filled me with pride. I envisioned that future so clearly. Nothing would keep me from it.

A blast of wind blew the door open wide. I flew to shut it, thinking nothing but the storm had struck it ajar. Yet there stood my siren, dripping and bleeding, her beautiful dark lips curled in a snarl, her trembling tail barely holding her upright.

"My darling!" I rushed to her and covered her tired face with kisses. "What happened?"

"You are safe." Eramyne writhed her way inside and collapsed on the floor, staring mindlessly at Burke. Her tail contracted as if still clutching its victim. "Melusine is dead."

"Dead?" I fell to my knees beside her and stroked her hair. "Wasn't she meant to attend a trial?"

"Banishment is not sufficient for a treacherous snake like her."

"But the court . . ." Disturbed, I recalled Melusine's irritable words: *I've had enough of you, and so has half the court.* "What consequences must we expect from this?"

"None at all. I am Tritoness."

The restless rage in her eyes heightened my anxiety. *Can siren queens be dethroned?* For the first time, I thoroughly examined my role in Eramyne's life and how complicated I had made her rule. Before me, human-siren relations were black and white. Enemies. Potential meals. Mating tools. Soulless flesh-eaters meant to be used and abused at will. A handful of mismatched couples managed to find something resembling happiness together, but their love story died when they did.

Now, Eramyne and I opened the floodgates to love. We cherished one another and protected each other. Killed for each other. We hadn't merely upset the natural balance. We'd wholly upended it and flipped it upside down.

For the moment, I pushed my nauseating concerns aside. They would keep. "Let's get you cleaned up and in bed," I affirmed.

Relief warmed me as Eramyne's wry smile reappeared. "You forget. Sirens do not sleep. We merely rest, and we are most active at night."

"Then rest for a while and curl up with me," I commanded. "Look at you. You're still out of breath."

"Very well." Eramyne started to transform, wincing from the effort. I placed a hand on her sharp shoulder. "Remain as you are, my beloved, so long as you're not uncomfortable this way."

"I only require a moist towel to be at ease."

"That is easily procured." I secured what she desired and helped her crawl into bed. Her massive tail wrapped around the bedpost, and I smiled, thinking of seahorses anchoring themselves to seaweed in the same manner. "What are *you* grinning about, silly woman?" My weary siren murmured from her pillow.

"I'll tell you tomorrow. You're not inclined to laugh at the moment."

"How well you know me."

I laid down beside her and stroked her bare back until she fell into lethargy. Her eyes remained open in narrow slits, her breathing steady and even. I kissed her cheekbone. "Thank you, my love," I whispered. "For this and everything else you've done for me. How can I repay you?"

"No need, my lovely one," she murmured.

A rhetorical question. I knew precisely how.

I stirred awake at sunrise. Melancholy pink streaks marbled the horizon, and the soft breath of the island breeze kissed my cheek. I turned over and saw Eramyne alert, her huntress gaze searching mine. "Did you sleep well, sweet Laura?"

"Better than ever."

We shared a long, gentle kiss. My siren's poison-clawed fingers cautiously linked with mine. "I have many matters to attend to back in the Trench. I regret leaving you, beloved, but at least you will be safe. Keep Aden with you."

"I will. I doubt I could make him leave, anyway."

"If you are good, I shall bring you a new gown."

"I'm no child to be bribed," I laughed, extracting my hands to braid a lock of her hair. "Besides, I have a request of my own. Something I want far more than dresses."

"Hmm. What is that?"

"The siren witch. Aden told me her name is Witch Lorelei, correct?"

Eramyne's gaze narrowed as she searched my face.

I groaned. "I told you; I've made up my mind. I want to speak with her."

Eramyne sighed, lifting my palm to her lips to brush a kiss against it. "You are determined, then?"

"Irrefutably so. There is nothing I want more in this world."

My siren gave one of her rarest, most mischievous looks. She bit my hand. "Besides me?"

I snatched it back with a yelp. She hadn't drawn blood, but it hurt all the same. "You're wicked!"

"That is what you like, Laura Frances Rivell."

Shadow chuckled before we made passionate love.

A humid evening ferried my love and I to the siren witch's cave.

Say what you will about destiny and fate: I know those twins are real. For the Witch dwelt near Half Moon Bay "to keep an eye on the sirens' purse and enchant the water for premium conditions," or so the Witch said.

I smiled and nodded, exchanging pleasantries. The Witch Lorelei's scales were dark blue and silver. Her hair was magnificent, straight as a sheath and utterly black. Instead of red, her claws and spikes were bright purple—the tint of dried siren blood, I noted. I pondered whether that was a coincidence or quite intentional.

"What an oddly-matched couple come to visit me," the Witch intoned. Her enchanting voice echoed to the farthest reach of the cavern. She looked from Eramyne to me and back again, curiosity bubbling in full force. "A monster from the depths and a very angel from the heavens, although," she grasped my chin between her claws and studied my face before continuing, "her wings have been clipped. A Shadow lurks in her sapphire eyes. You have killed one of your own kind. Charming! I approve of you already. Our Sovereign must be pleased with you." She released my chin with a breathtaking smile, kissing me upon the forehead as if in blessing. I trembled, embarrassed by the flush in my cheeks. I felt I'd have fallen in love with her on the spot, had my heart not already belonged to Eramyne.

"She wishes to become one of us," Eramyne stated. Never one to mince words, my siren. "What do you require for this spell, and what is the cost?"

The Witch inclined her head toward the Tritoness in humble recognition. "I require a small vial of each of your blood. I will combine your blood and fashion it into a blood gem ring, which shall burrow deeply into Laura's finger until it fuses to the bone. It is quite painful, but to be removed her finger must be cut off. This all but ensures the spell's permanence." Her smile dazzled me, radiant perfection. "As long as the ring remains, your siren form also remains."

I smiled, delighted by the simplicity of the enchantment. "Wonderful. Shall I fill a vial for you here?"

"We have not yet heard the price," Eramyne cautioned.

The Witch and I exchanged amused grins; we both knew this did not matter to me. I would pay anything. "Your other siren friend: the male siren. Aden, I believe?"

A chill coursed through my veins. "Yes, that is his name."

"I'll need him to come and stay with me," the Witch explained. Midnight blue sparkled deep within her predatory eyes. "Long have I hoped to study a living male siren, in the hopes of creating more."

"Why?" I couldn't stop myself from asking, remembering Zorstrom.

"So the sirens can breed *naturally,* of course!" The Witch laughed at my naive question. "If female sirens mated with male sirens instead of vulgar human men, then—besides being infinitely safer—there would be a massive increase to our population. We'd rival the humans themselves. What a wonderful world it would be!"

"Oh. I see." I smoothed my skirt, debating how to phrase my next question. "And you wouldn't *hurt* Burke—Aden—I trust?"

"Cross my black heart and hope to cry, dearie."

But sirens cannot cry, Shadow chuckled. I ignored the nonsensical pun. "What if he doesn't agree to stay with you?"

"Then I'm afraid you will not get your ring. Aden is all I want. Charming as you are, you possess nothing of any use to me, my pretty little human."

"You don't want," again I cursed the fact that I couldn't stop myself, "You wouldn't want my voice instead?" The thought of coercing my dearest friend into the clutches of a Witch set my warning bells screaming. I adored Burke. How could I give him up and risk his life to a Witch? And even if he agreed, I wasn't sure if she'd ever let me see him again. I couldn't bear it.

"Your human voice isn't worth the flotsam I'd float it on," the Witch wryly responded. "Your *siren* voice, however, is a powerful and rare ingredient for a multitude of spells. It might well aid me in my work . . ." She deliberated her options, tapping one poison talon against a serrated tooth. Her tail shimmered as she waved it to and fro, quite at ease. "If you sign over your siren voice to me, I shall forgo keeping your friend," the Witch promised, actually making a cross motion over the region of her heart. *She spends significantly more time around humans, to know of that motion and its use.* "Otherwise, I must default to Aden."

Eramyne fiercely shook her head at me. "It must be Aden, my darling. I am sorry for him, but you cannot begin to fathom the life of a siren without a voice. It is your identity itself. You must not give it away under any circumstances!"

Burke told me the same thing. I remembered his cautionary tale of the Nereid princess and wavered. Surely if he were here, he'd gladly hand himself over to the Witch rather than watch me sign my voice away.

But if I gave my voice to Witch Lorelei, Burke was free.

CHAPTER 26

The rolling waves supported me as I lingered in their midst. Again and again, I plunged below, staring at my love's amazing world, imagining it was already mine as well. I tapped Cimon's dorsal fin when he passed me, charmed by his graceful, if lazy, circling. *Do I eat her or protect her?* his wicked eyes meditated. I chuckled over his confusion. Nothing had frightened me since my first kill.

Well, nothing except the fear of losing Eramyne or Burke.

That and jellyfish when they floated too close for comfort.

I felt the brush of a siren tail against my calf. I smiled, turning to face Aden as he surfaced. His siren transformation was very much like his human face, but purple-and-silver toned and more angular. In all honesty, his short, thick hair and beard didn't quite suit him as "Aden," but there was no point informing him of that since he chose to live as a human. Later on, perhaps.

"What have you decided to do?" he asked. My kindred spirit's eyes crinkled with silent agitation.

"Give her my voice, of course. How can I trust a witch not to hurt you?"

"As I told you, Laura Frances Rivell, and I'll tell you again: I'm a fully-grown siren capable of protecting myself. You don't need to worry about me."

"And as I told *you*, Bartholomew Aden Burke, there's no use telling me not to worry about you. I'm going to worry. I cannot possibly swim about singing and dancing with Eramyne knowing you're enduring Sofia-knows-what at the hands of a siren witch."

"She sounds reasonable enough," Aden grumbled, absently plucking a strand of seaweed out of my hair and tossing it aside. "She had the decency not to go after your voice right away. *I* think her first proposal is logical. That being said," he swept me onto his back and swam in gentle circles, "The safest—and in my humble opinion the best—choice is to remain human. Why do you want to be a siren?"

"So I can be with Eramyne," I stated, mildly annoyed and letting him hear it in my tone. "You know that without me having to tell you."

Aden slowed his circling. We both smiled at Cimon as his jaws flexed in a yawn. Bored of us, he swam away. "Take Eramyne out of the equation, if you can. Do you still want to live your life as a flesh-craving seaborn monster, drawn to shipwrecks and drowning men like a frenzied shark? Do not lie."

I softened my voice. "I never lie to you."

"I know, and I'd catch you in it if you tried to."

I grinned, swinging my submerged feet back and forth. "Touché. But let me ask you something. Don't you believe in fate? Destiny? Months ago, you told me you did."

"I'm open to the belief but not completely sold on it."

"I believe our friendship was fate. You, my dearest friend, are meant to be my voice." Aden stopped swimming and treaded in place. I hugged his muscular neck, resting my head against his. "Whether fate is real or make-believe, there are two things I am certain of. I cannot stand the thought of losing Eramyne, and I cannot stand the thought of losing you. There is one option—and *only* one—that ensures I can have you both with me, and that's paying for the siren spell with my voice. But you and I? We're kindred souls. We practically read each other's thoughts. There must be a reason, and what other reason makes more sense than this outcome?"

When Aden finally replied, his voice was thick with anguish. "I can't let you, Laura. I just can't." His sorrow pained me, summoning my own tears. I couldn't help but cry on his behalf.

The navy mirror of the ocean reflected our beautiful, mismatched faces. Clouds framed the image. Despite our shared sadness, I lifted my head with a smile. "You'll see, Aden. It will be wonderful. All three of us free and taming the nine seas together. We're meant to do great things, and the only problem holding us back is my humanity. Once I'm released from it, I'll be so happy that you'll be relieved I cannot sing, for I will sing all night long!" I wiped my tears away with giddy laughter, but Aden shook his head.

"You just don't understand, and I can't explain it to you in a way that you *would*. You might as well be a dead siren as a siren without her voice."

The Witch gave me two days to consider the payment. Once the allotted time expired, Eramyne escorted me back to the hidden cavern, each of us carrying a small vial of blood. "I hope you locked Aden up somewhere far away," I sighed. My crimson vial looked so pretty next to Eramyne's purple one. I imagined our combined blood as a smooth, shining burgundy. "I have a strong feeling he planned to follow us and compel the Witch to take him."

"I had the same impression." Eramyne grasped my hand and lifted it for a kiss. "I sent him on an errand; he protested but he dared not disobey."

"That was smart."

My siren shot me a dry look. "Did you think my plan would *not* be smart?"

I couldn't help giggling, and Eramyne smiled, tucking her arm about my waist. "I am having a gift made for you, my love. A flute you can hang around your neck. A note, series of notes, or song can mean different things. So even when Aden and I are not with you, you will not be left without a voice."

My heart melted at her thoughtfulness and foresight. "Oh, darling, that's perfect."

She kissed the top of my head. "Before we arrive at the cavern, there is something else you should do. You ought to tell me what you want your siren name to be."

My siren name. Remarkably, I hadn't thought about it. I'd been swept up in the chaos of adjusting to island living, chasing Melusine, comforting Aden and worshiping Eramyne. "I like Delphine," I hesitantly offered.

"Delphine. Of grace and particular intelligence. It suits you. Delphine, beloved of the Tritoness, blood gem of the Agenne Sea."

"That sounds deliciously wicked."

"I thought you would like it."

As we entered the cavern, hand in hand, the unmistakable clamor of a fight menaced our ears. We simultaneously broke into a run. Eramyne beat me to the back of the cave where the Witch writhed and hissed, looking more like a glorious giant snake than a siren. Holding her by her hair was none other than my gentle kindred spirit, and his blood-stained mouth gave me such a shock that I stumbled and fell, bruising my ankle.

Aden held a knife to the Witch's sparkling throat. "Make the blood gem," he ordered. "No tricks. I agree to be your compensation once Laura has safely transformed."

"No!" I screamed. The gaping cavern swallowed my cry. "She will take my voice. I already agreed to it!"

Aden frowned. The Witch tried to wrench herself free, but her captor tightened his grip, causing her to snarl. "Did you sign the contract?" he asked me.

"No," I admitted in a small voice. The ferocity in his mien was horrific.

"Then she will *not* take your voice. I will be the payment."

"Can't I say something?" Witch Lorelei spat. "'Tis the woman who must sign the contract! You cannot touch it or change its conditions on her behalf, you shorn-headed moron."

I stood despite the pain lancing through my ankle, then smiled warmly at Aden. "You heard the witch, my friend. Please let her go. This is my spell and my choice. You do not have the right to take it from me. Eramyne understands this," I said, nodding to my siren, who waited patiently for a chance to snatch the blade from Aden, "and though she harbors the same misgivings as you, she is not depriving me of my right to choose."

"You are *destroying* your own future, Laura. You don't understand what you're doing! If you watched a young boy wander toward the train tracks, would you not warn him of the oncoming train? And if he ignored you, wouldn't you snatch him from harm's way?"

"I am not a child," I repeated, growing angrier each time I was forced to assert this obvious fact. "And there is no train bearing down on me. I am freeing myself from a life of isolation. I can never return to human society and expect to be welcome there. Instead, I choose Nereid culture. In time, I shall be part of the Nereid tribe—part of a family."

"The Nereid are no family. They are all *monsters*."

Something broke inside Aden. He dropped the Witch, extending his arms outward, flexing his upper body toward the cavern ceiling. Magenta blood stained his teeth as his mouth gaped open wide. I turned my head away, truly frightened of him. This was not my Burke, my Aden. "Look at me. Nereid are the demons of the sea, soulless, accursed. Do not become one of us, Laura! I beg you!"

Steeling my nerves, I looked back at him. "It is not up to you."

Fury and despair thrashed in his face. Eramyne leapt to his side and tore the knife from his grip. He didn't resist. Instead, he crumpled into a tearless dirge of despair, equivalent to the most angelic music. It took my breath away, and I realized at once that it was an enchantment. A final weapon in his arsenal to keep me from selling my voice.

To my astonishment, the midnight-blue shimmer in the Witch's eyes caught and flashed at the melody. She joined him in song, placing one hand comfortingly on his shaking arm. They appeared to calm and steady each other as they sang. Eramyne joined as well, though she only hummed along, her own eyes bright with reverence.

As I listened, my soul was borne away on a golden sea-chariot of emotion over silver waves. Nothing ever sounded half so sweet, so terrible, or so heavenly in my life, neither before nor since. Once the song concluded, I gained but a sliver of understanding: *A siren without a voice might as well be dead.*

But Aden didn't know I had a final weapon in *my* arsenal, too.

Shadow.

There is one option left that you haven't considered, Shadow whispered to me.

I'm ready to hear it.

Shadow's eager grin no longer disturbed me. *Sign the contract. Get the ring. Then kill the Witch before she takes your voice.*

<h1 style="text-align:center">CHAPTER 27</h1>

*K*ill the Witch.

Killing a drunk, distracted man emboldened me, but I'd have to be an utter fool to think I could go from *that* to killing a full-fledged, witchcraft-endowed siren strong enough to crack my neck in two. As my mind whirled with chaotic suggestions, anxiety, and the pulse of adrenaline already preparing me to attack, my feet froze in place.

"Give me the contract," I said. My voice sounded very far away from my body.

The Witch glanced at Aden, but he'd subdued himself with his own voice—no small wonder—and he watched me with deep affection, rooted respect. *You know I'll stay by your side no matter what,* his eyes spoke.

I never doubted you, Aden.

The Witch lowered herself into an azure pool deep enough to swim in. She lifted a watertight cylinder from some secret nook and unfastened the lid, withdrawing a rolled parchment. "Your voice?" she queried, in the interest of incontestable clarity. She darted disgruntled glances at Aden, making sure he remained subdued.

My head seemed unnaturally heavy as I nodded. "My voice."

She filled in the blank describing the price. Passing the contract and pen to me, she continued to glimpse at Aden to ensure he did not interfere. *Bless you for distracting her so well,* Shadow purred. It was quite fond of Aden, indeed.

I signed my name.

The Witch held out her hands, requesting the vials. Eramyne and I handed them over. Instructing all three of us to stay put, Witch Lorelei swam through a subterranean corridor where we heard a door lock behind her.

We waited.

Kill the Witch. Kill the Witch!

I rolled my eyes. *If you're going to make such violent suggestions, you might help me figure out how to execute them. How does one kill a siren witch?*

Take your friend's approach. Slit her throat. That would kill anybody, don't you think?

Won't she have spells in place protecting herself? If she doesn't, then she's the most foolish witch alive.

She might have them against sirens, but I doubt she'd bother with charms against human attacks. That's like a human charming herself against roaches. Gross and bothersome but hardly deadly.

Flattering comparison; thanks for that.

My pleasure.

The Witch returned with a stamped ring (metallic origin unknown) harboring a shining burgundy gemstone. *Ah, the blood gem of the Agenne Sea.* I extended my hand. The Witch shook her raven head, handing the ring to Eramyne. "The Tritoness must place it."

My siren gazed deeply into my eyes as she slipped the ring onto my finger. "I love you, Laura. Delphine."

"And I love you, Eramyne. My Sovereign."

My finger burned. Suddenly, I could no longer speak and could barely breathe. My legs were crushed together with the violence of a hurricane, and I crumpled to the ground in a soundless scream.

Eramyne held me through the screams. I writhed as if struck by lightning, helpless as I watched my beautiful fingers extend into long, predatory knobs tipped with venom. Crimson spikes burst from my iron-gray tail to my silver fins. My hair remained strawberry blonde but took on a thicker, more wild texture, like Eramyne's.

An eternity unfolded in that hellish pain.

Look on the bright side, Shadow sang, wholly unconcerned. *You won't be afraid of jellyfish stings after this. You can catch one and keep it as a pet! Name it Bubbles.* If there was a way to eliminate Shadow there and then, I'd have done it.

Once it was over, I grew conscious of the fact that Eramyne held my body while Aden held my hand. Were he in human form, my grip would have crushed his fingers to the bones. As Aden, he looked mildly pleased. "You're very strong. That's good."

I blinked. The tiny scales on my eyelids made a quiet rasping sound, like sand shifting over itself in the wind. The dim cavern was no longer dim at all, but rich and beautiful in multiple shades of *darkness* that my human eyes never perceived. Later, I found I could not hear as well above water as I could before, but submerged, my inner ears caught every throbbing note of the sea.

I lowered a shaking hand to lift the skirt of my dress, careful not to catch the fabric in my claws. My tail disappointed me at first. It was neither purple, blue, nor an ombre celebration of teal and silver, but a dark silver. Upon closer inspection, there were brighter silver scales at intervals, and each one sparkled in the meager light. *I guess I do like it, after all.*

"You're *so* beautiful," Eramyne gushed, and I could not deny the broad smile tugging my lips. *She seldom uses contractions.* My siren cupped my cheek in her hand. "I did not imagine you could be *this* beautiful, and you have kept your lovely hair! Delphine. My beautiful Delphine. My gem."

"Don't smother her half to death!" Aden objected. Eramyne gave him a look that should have killed. Aden held up his hands repentantly. "My apologies. I'm sure she'll be fine."

Eramyne cooed and kissed and massaged my aching muscles as Aden silently registered my new appearance. The Witch interrupted our special moment. "I'll need you to vocalize for a minute, Laur—er, Delphine. For your payment."

It's now or never, Shadow warned. *Kill the Witch. Or give up your voice.*

Looking at Aden, I reached for his hand again and gripped it, ever so slightly. I tilted my head toward the Witch and held my breath, waiting for him to understand.

He blinked a slow, knowing blink.

I started to sing.

A feathery, bubbling tone floated to the ceiling like sea foam. The other sirens' voices carried rich depth meant to be heard from vast distances. My human-to-siren voice was far lighter and sweeter. Less practical but not at all unpleasant. Eramyne, Aden, then Witch Lorelei herself united their voices with mine, unable to resist the opportunity. Singing came as naturally as breathing.

With a great effort of will, Aden ceased and casually maneuvered himself behind the Witch. He picked up the discarded knife and angled it for piercing.

The Witch laughed.

She turned, raven locks flowing like a cape. She grabbed the handle of the knife and struggled—tried to pry it from Aden and turn it against him.

The enchanting song's effect wore off. I dragged myself toward Aden with a desperate, terrified cry, but I was not accustomed to my weight or my tail and was powerless to protect my friend. Eramyne rushed to save him.

Witch Lorelei spoke a rapid incantation. Living seaweed bound Eramyne in place. Rage surged within my chest, but I could do nothing in haste; I fumbled with the seaweed like a drunken fool. *Burke!* After everything I had sacrificed to keep him from witching slavery, I'd sent him to his death.

Still laughing, the Witch wrestled the knife from Aden and stabbed him in the chest.

Not even my transformation wrought such a scream from my throat. Yet, midway through the shriek, my voice cut off. Dead. Uprooted like a dried-up flower. Five seconds later, its echo faded into nothing.

I paid the price.

"You three aren't the first to try to worm out of paying," said the Witch, cold as a glacier. She tossed the knife aside. It landed on the rocks with a sharp *clang,* scattering its precious spilled blood. "Your voice was mine from your first note. What utter imbecile do you take me for, *Delphine?*"

Ignoring her barbs, I gave up on the charmed seaweed. Aden was gasping and suppressing the bleeding as best he could. Dragging my cumbersome bulk to his side, I silently sobbed, but no tears would come. *Sirens cannot cry.*

My voice was gone. My friend was dying. And I couldn't even cry for him.

To crown it all, I'd made a mortal enemy out of a siren witch.

Ten minutes into my new life, I'd all but destroyed it.

The Witch dragged us from her cavern on the heel of thinly-veiled threats. I suspected the sole reason she didn't kill us was due to Eramyne's presence; the Witch had no desire to cause another war by killing the Tritoness or her lover.

Aden, of course, she now cared nothing about.

We must get him to a healer, I cried out internally, struggling to support Aden's drooping head. Eramyne gently pushed my hand aside to carry him alone. "My tribe has some of the best healers in the nine seas, my love. He will be saved."

I'll do anything. Just save him. Don't let him die!

Eramyne prepared to dive. "The scent of blood will attract wild pups," Eramyne warned me. "Please keep on lookout for them as we swim to the Trench. Leave your friend to me, darling."

All right. All right. I trust you. As one, we sank into the sea.

Home. A delicious cooling sensation stroked every millimeter of my body. My skin worked like an extra pair of lungs, absorbing the water until saturated. *But what a horrid time to learn how to swim.* Frustrated, I struggled to keep up with Eramyne and to mimic her graceful motions through the deep. My love noticed. She sang a short series of escalating notes. Minutes later, Cimon approached from the west and swam beneath me. Eramyne motioned for me to hold onto his dorsal fin as he followed her.

My loving Tritoness. Always so thoughtful. If she was a monster, then I was proud to be one, too.

Eramyne coaxed a fresh current behind us, propelling us much faster through the ocean. A forest of kelp shielded us as we delved deeper still. I kept my focus locked on Aden, numb to the fact that the emerald-green frond gleamed in my new vision like verdant stars. "The dark places of the sea" were not dark for the sirens. We saw variety in the depths, the rainbow's composition within the black.

Eramyne stopped by a lush kelp tree and plucked many strands. She wound them tightly around Aden's chest. Still exhausted from the effects of the spell, I clung helplessly to Cimon and prayed to the Goddess

Sofia for Aden's life. I'd have gladly offered her my voice in exchange were it not already stripped from me.

Aden's pale complexion warmed as we neared the Trench. Relieved by the rich minerals in the seawater, his body was already working overtime to restore him to health. I allowed myself to hope, but then I looked at Eramyne's face and saw how anxious she was. She glanced over her shoulder at the trail of magenta blood his seeping wound left in our wake. *He's losing too much blood.* She swam faster, not waiting to see if Cimon kept up. *A very bad sign.*

Angling down the rocky abyssal plain, Eramyne and Cimon entered Echo Trench. Small mud volcanoes and cold seeps altered the surrounding temperature; I was pleasantly surprised by its warmth. More marine life than I'd expected floated, prowled, and scuttled at the mouths of the sirens' caves gaping in the walls.

I heard the other sirens before I saw them. Their language reminded me of whale-song—a complex arrangement of vocalization that carried for miles. It was mesmerizing. Soothing. Had we arrived in happier circumstances, I'd have anchored myself to the nearest spiked basalt to listen and look for hours. As it was, we hurried past multiple caverns toward a tower-like protrusion of solid basalt. Black and gray and stern, the stone had been whittled out to form windows and arched open doorways.

One cave we passed housed a pale-yellow siren with snowdrop-white skin and flaxen hair. She paused in the middle of her meal, her impish red eyes ripe with intense curiosity. *She's . . . albino?* She held a man's arm between her claws. Black blood wisped from the severed limb. The keen smell of human blood haunted me as we passed her. I *ached* for my first meal.

Eramyne swam into the tower. A pod of sirens had seen her approaching and immediately came to her assistance. She passed Aden over to them, communicating in brief murmurs and quick hand signals. Four sirens bore my friend away to another room. Letting go of Cimon, I instinctively tried to follow them, but Eramyne grabbed my shoulders and shook her head. I frowned. Human language was impossible to utilize underwater, but my siren mouthed the words: *Males are not allowed here. Let me manage.*

My head dipped in a reluctant nod.

She pointed to a wide corridor that curled upward, indicating I was to swim there. Nodding again, I followed the corridor to what appeared to be a siren's resting room. There were no beds, as they did not sleep as humans did, but several comfortable anchoring points and objects were tucked into dim corners. Kelp appeared to be widely favored, used liberally in decorations and painted onto the basalt walls with unusual red-gold paint. Stories inscribed upon stone tablets served as their books, though of course I could not read them. Yet.

I nestled against a kelp-wound anchor and prepared for the most agonizing wait of my life. *No one is promised a happy ending,* Shadow chuckled. *Not even pretty little mermaids.*

Sometimes I hated Shadow even more than I hated myself.

CHAPTER 28

Half an hour later, Eramyne swam into my room. The instant I saw her face, I knew she'd come to prepare me to say goodbye.

No.

My pursed lips trembled. I shook as I clutched the basalt anchor. Eramyne pulled me into her arms and squeezed me tight. I laid my head on her shoulder, wishing desperately for tears to come. How was this reality? How was I not trapped in a nightmare? The impending death of my kindred spirit. The intimate friend of my soul. Could I survive without him?

How had I even lived before the stern, quiet, considerate Bartholomew Burke came into my life? I recalled the old Laura Rivell as a half-dead thing, bored of life and of living, passive and wry and lonely but content to be so. *That* was the tragedy. *Content to be so.* My friendship with Burke had given me new life in so many ways. *But I cannot cry.*

My dear siren gently detached from me and took my hand. *We're going to sing for him,* she pantomimed. *Please come, too.*

I nodded.

We swam back down the corridor, Eramyne leading me to Aden's room. Two sirens attended to his comfort, raising his head to place a kelp pillow underneath. Their eyes widened as they searched me up and down, having never before seen a siren with such *human* coloring of complexion and hair. I spared them brief smiles of gratitude for making my friend comfortable, then drifted to his side to take his hand.

Aden's handsome eyes were glassy, but he smiled his tiny, rare smile for me as his fingers tightened in response to mine. "I . . . am . . . your voice," he managed to say, garbled and low.

And you'll always be with me, my grieving eyes answered.

Always. You'll get sick of feeling me tag along everywhere you go.

I'll never be sick of you, my kindred spirit.

Weakly, he held out his arms for a hug. He passed away as I embraced him, and I was more than half inclined to never let him go.

My black soul broke in two that day.

CHAPTER 29

ONE YEAR LATER

I pulled the pearl-strung chain over my head. The abalone flute settled beneath my collarbone with its familiar tap. I didn't think I'd need it, but safe was always better than sorry. I seized my hunting spear and checked its sharpened blade before testing its weight. *Tonight, I hunt alone.*

For months, I'd hunted with the Echo tribe, siren-made compass in hand, hopelessly dependent on it to avoid getting lost. Anyone who hadn't lived in the sea couldn't comprehend how *titanic* it was, even the smaller Agenne Sea. The first time I'd misplaced myself, Eramyne found me caught in a kelp bed making whimpering sounds with the abalone flute like the child I repeatedly denied I was. She wanted so very much to laugh at me, but she kindly spared my fragile feelings.

That delicate newborn siren no longer existed. Eramyne herself commented on my strength. "When first we met, you were saving a man. Then I watched you kill a man without a thought. Now, you hunger for them as I do," she chuckled, tucking her arm around my waist. I merely grinned and kissed her, our tails spiraling together.

For I was Shadow. Shadow was me. We no longer fought each other, warring beneath my flesh like a gods-given curse. We were one. And that made for one hellscape of a siren. Aden would be so proud of me.

I smiled as I swam for the hidden cavern near Half Moon Bay, my true birthplace for multiple reasons. But a ghost lingered there. It needed to be put to rest. Aden's spirit tagged along, as he often did, making sardonic comments or critiquing my poise with the spear. *You know I'm just as good as you were!* I mentally remarked.

How do you know that, incorrigible sea minx? You never saw me with a spear, and I was much stronger than you regardless.

I wouldn't be so sure of that.

Perhaps you're right.

Still grinning, I checked on Shadow next to be sure it wasn't asleep. It bounded up to report for duty, brimming with energetic glee. Shadow was much happier these days, less inclined to be rude or cutting with its speeches. I supposed that was thanks to the fact that I'd embraced my Shadow at last and even liked having it with me. *You know something, Delphie? Silent sirens make the best assassins.*

I smirked. *Yes, I do.*

The creak and snap of a sinking ship seized my attention. I veered off course, sniffing eagerly and listening for its precise location. *Military practice again? It's no use tracking that down if there's nothing to eat once I get there.* My neuromasts worked their magic: I detected the frantic far-off splashing of an unwilling swimmer. *Ah.*

Don't get distracted! Aden and Shadow yelled in unison. *You can eat later,* Aden cautioned. *The moon wanes; tonight is the night and now is the time. Remember the spearhead.*

I glanced at the shimmering blade. The enchantress I'd visited was young and comparatively inexperienced, but she assured me the spearhead would negate all protective spells and penetrate with lethal force. For the next twelve hours and no more. *You're right. I can't take any detours and risk wasting my time.* I turned away—with great effort—and redirected my course.

No one kills my loved ones and escapes the consequences. Not even a witch.

Demented as it was, I lured Witch Lorelei out with the promise of an apology and a request for another spell. Her demeanor bristled with suspicion, and I realized with mounting unease that a spear was probably the wrong choice. How could I seize it, lift it, and thrust it in time? I glanced at the rock currently hiding it, questioning my choices. "Where's the Tritoness?" the Witch asked, lightly tapping her purple claws against her arm. "Surely you did not come alone."

I used the siren flute to communicate. "I did. Our Sovereign wouldn't approve of me apologizing to you."

"Oh. I suppose that makes sense. Well, what do you want? If you're looking for a spell to bring your friend back from the dead, it doesn't exist. I'm not a goddess."

"No, nothing like that. I'd like a spell that makes my flute unbreakable."

The Witch looked disappointed. Bored, even. "That, I can do. What do you have to barter with?"

"My hunting spear. It's high quality, I can promise you—made at the Tower."

"Let me see it."

I swam to the rock. A bit of snowy hair floated up from behind it, making me start. "What's wrong?" called the Witch, immediately back on edge.

I lifted my flute again. "Nothing. I thought I put it right here."

I peered behind the boulder. It was the snowdrop siren with the pale-yellow scales. Her coloring proclaimed her as a deep-dweller. *What is she doing in shallow waters? Isn't that dangerous for her?* Apparently, her body could handle the pressure change. *She must have acclimated herself very carefully.*

She curled up behind the rock, smiling wickedly at me and raising one bone-white forefinger to her lips, urging me to remain quiet as Witch Lorelei swam closer.

A flash of predatory insight coiled my fins. *She's going to kill the Witch for me.*

Fast as a blink, the pale siren straightened her form, picked up the spear, and launched it with impressive strength. The Witch didn't have time to cry out before her body snapped backward, beautiful even in death. Clouds of purple blood stained the sea. It smelled sweet. Tempted closer by the alluring aroma, I amused myself by swirling around in it, bathing in it. *All hail the witch killer, the christening of the blood gem of the Agenne Sea!* Shadow cheered.

Once my personal ritual was complete, I turned to thank the pale siren. Her crimson eyes shone with appalling elation. Besides my Eramyne's unique eyes, they were the most beautiful eyes I'd ever seen. "I had a score or two to settle myself," she lisped, her white lips as soft and thin as funeral rose petals. The Nereid language sounded so flawless spoken with her diaphanous voice. "I heard the court sirens saying she murdered your friend. My sincere condolences. I'm Shilo, by the way. That's my land-nomen." Her smile faltered. "At least it *would* be, if I could go on land." She sighed. Deep-dwellers could seldom handle shallow water without imperiling themselves; they would never see land.

I smiled, responding cheerily through the flute. "Well met, Shilo. And do not envy the sirens who visit the human world. Humans are quite dull."

"I'm sure you're right. Well met, Delphine."

I liked the way Shilo darted to and fro as she spoke, like a restless bluefin. She twirled a frond of kelp around her fingers in intricate triangles and loops, a hatchling game meant to mollify fidgeting hands. Still, she was shaking somewhat and wincing from the sunlight. I took her hand, indicating that we must return her to deeper waters. *I think we're going to be friends.*

Yes, Aden's spirit calmly informed me. *You are.*

How do you know that, *Mr. Know-It-All?*

Shilo and I swam back to Echo Trench together.

Because Shilo, daughter of Nadine, is my half-sister.

PART TWO

~Erampne~

CHAPTER 30

"This was no small crime against the Nereid, my Sovereign."

The scent of anger seasoned Echo Trench. I grasped the ceremonial trident. *Let them all remember who it is that steers the currents and directs the tides.* "She was hardly a member of our tribe. Who saw her outside of her cavern attending to any matter beyond her own experiments? She cared nothing for any of us."

"Do not belittle her work." Ignacia, the ice-blue siren who'd dared to speak before, resumed her rebuking strain. "Witch Lorelei hoped to unravel the secrets of the conception of male sirens, freeing all Nereid from the evil necessity of breeding with men. Did you not recall this when your precious blood gem struck the Witch dead?"

My grip on the trident tightened. The ceremonial trident was far too ornate and heavy to be wielded as a weapon, but it might put the court in mind of its sister trident—the war trident of Tritoness Serena, my famed predecessor who defeated Zorstrom. I tilted my head to stretch my stiff neck. *Serena dealt with plenty of court opposition, too. I am in good company.* "It was not Delphine who struck the Witch, but Shilo of the deep-dwellers. She had her own quarrel with Lorelei."

"So she recruited Delphine to her murderous cause." Ignacia's white-blue eyes ought to have the power to freeze sirens in place with their concentrated stare. Luckily, this magic was not in her possession today. "Melusine warned you against—"

I held up my hand. "May our sister rest in the Goddess' light. Do not speak of the warnings of the dead, Ignacia; you know it is bad luck."

"Then listen to *my* warning, my Sovereign. You've created a monster in our midst. A half-breed siren with the brain of a human and a heart that lusts for siren blood."

My fangs bared at this accusation. "You do not know her as I do. How tender she is, how sympathetic to our cause. Her sisterhood with Aden alone proves beyond any doubt—"

Ignacia hissed. "She used him to get what she wanted!"

My adviser, Undine, swam to my side and placed a hand on my tense arm. "I never thought I'd utter this phrase during Eramyne's reign," Undine began with a cautiously lighthearted tone that worked miracles, "but please calm down, *both* of you. Delphine planned this attack alone and Shilo happened to be in the right place at the right time. Even if it could be proven that they conspired together, what then? The consequences remain: The Witch is dead, and all her research was enchanted to dissolve at the moment of her death. Lorelei's pride has ruined her work, not Delphine.

"However," she continued, darting a wary glance my way, "Ignacia is right to be cautious. The Blood Gem of the Agenne Sea is neither human nor fully siren. She is something the sea has never suffered before." She paused, her discomfort clear. "Shilo herself boasted that Delphine swam giddily in the Witch's blood. Can you pledge that Delphine is quite stable, my Sovereign? Can you guarantee a close eye on her until she is more settled and . . . civilized?"

Civilized? Never in my long years as Tritoness had I glared at my loyal adviser. At last, I had occasion to, and I did not waste it. Undine backed down and bowed her head, her submissive posturing a mute apology. "There is nothing—*nothing*—uncivilized about my Delphine,"

I intoned. "She was testing her power. Longing for justice for the death of Aden. Do newborn sirens not frenzy at the scent of blood? Or has my entire court forgotten what it is to be young and strong with the whole ocean within reach?"

Undine answered softly. "Even feral newborns do not succumb to frenzy for the blood of their own kind, my Sovereign."

Rage boiled in my chest. "It was not frenzy!" Yet, as my gaze skipped unflinchingly from one court siren to the next, I read varying degrees of concern in their eyes. They truly believed Delphine was unhinged. "She is no threat to our tribe," I swore.

The court sirens followed Undine's lead, backing down a few feet and lowering their heads. Ignacia complied as well, albeit hesitantly. I turned my back to signify court-wide dismissal.

Ignacia's final words did not escape me. "If any siren among us lost her wits, it would be the siren without a voice."

The siren without a voice.

I swam for the Titan Chain, a series of seamounts offering a warm habitat many fathoms deep. For deep-dwellers, the Titan Chain was something of a playground. Many of them might be found here at any hour of the night, catching one another 'round the columns, hunting, and laughing with skin white, eyes red, and scales wrought in soft watercolor tints.

I tasted the water for either Shilo or Delphine's proximity. I listened for my love's flute or Shilo's laughter. *For my darling cannot laugh.* Regret loomed at the thought. How I missed her voice, her mirth, even her tears, for then I might comfort her and dry them drop by drop. By Sofia! I missed her human form, too—her beautiful, beautiful legs, the angelic smoothness of her skin.

All the same, I loved Delphine as I loved Laura. Delphine is fierce, fearless, and a lover a siren might boast of—*must* boast of. My gem raised not one pup—as many sirens did for occasional company—but seven of them at once, unable to choose only one and leave the rest to their fates. They circled her for the sheer joy of it before lazily meandering away. Yet, they were curiously quick to return to her side, far more so than with the natural-born sirens. It baffled me, but as the siren in love with her, I would have done the same were I her pup.

My blood gem, Delphine. She faced a Witch, gave up her voice, and turned her back on her own species for *me.* Every time I slipped into a waking doze, anchored to my column with Delphine in my arms, I marveled at her adoration and pondered how to demonstrate my own in return. I offered shipwreck jewels for her to wear. She declined them, preferring her enchanted abalone flute around her neck and nothing else. I offered to hunt for rare oysters full of rosy pearls to fasten to her tail—a mark of her high favor and protection with the Tritoness. Still, she refused. "You are enough," she communicated with her silent smiles and gentle kisses. "You are all I desire."

So, I had flowing garments made for her to simply swim about and feel pretty in whenever her charming heart desired. A human's variation of a princess of the sea, according to their picture books. She did wear them sometimes on our "dates," as she called them. "Sirens do not 'date,'" I explained with a tolerant smile. "We catch someone's eye, they catch ours, and if the desire is mutual, we will satisfy each other's cravings whether we are alone or not. It is quite natural for us."

She'd wrinkled her darling nose and lifted the flute to her dark lips. "How unromantic. Henceforth it is my solemn duty to teach you how to be properly romantic, my beloved Eramyne."

My heart swelled as I remembered her passionate kiss, followed quickly by . . . Suffice it to say, she'd been delighted to discover how sensitive our tail fins were. It was not always a good thing, to be sure, but for siren lovers it was euphoric.

I mused upon all these things as I followed Delphine's mesmerizing scent through the sea. I wreathed around one small gushing seamount. Then another. Finally, I saw her.

The Nereid shed once a year until they were fully grown. No one knew whether Delphine would shed or not, but she had; she'd scratched and peeled off her dark gray uniform to reveal glittering silver beneath. My gem was a veritable treasure flashing through the sea: purified silver, burnished rose-gold veils of hair, and ruby-red spikes sparkling in tandem with the blood gem fused upon her finger. Dark lips and eyes alike expanded with joy at the sight of me. Not a second of hesitation remained in her poise as she swam to me, quite at home in the Agenne Sea.

Sofia knew it would suit her. She called Laura's true spirit home.

Delphine twirled into my arms and nuzzled the crook of my neck. "Have you been a good princess today, darling? Or a naughty one?" I asked, pretending to be stern.

Her roguish grin made my heart sing. "Horrendously, selfishly naughty," it said. I knew her well enough to practically hear her voice in my head. With me, she could forgo the flute.

"I need to check on Half Moon Bay and the hidden purses there." I dropped a kiss on her shining forehead. "I will see you tomorrow."

She affected a pout, but I knew she regarded my duties as Sovereign and guardian with respect. Wrapping her arms around my neck, she pulled me into a fierce kiss ending in a playful bite. I smiled as our tails wound into a glittering spiral. "I know what you're doing."

Still grinning, she let go and looped backward, frisky as a dolphin. I pushed the court's warnings out of my mind as I watched her unbridled glee. *She will adapt. She will prove them wrong.*

The Shadow she spoke of. Had it driven her to seek the Witch's death? Yes, Lorelei stabbed Aden, but it was in self-defense; Aden had tried to stab her first. Although I loved him for wanting to preserve my beloved's voice, siren witches were almost as rare as male sirens. Depriving Echo Trench of the sole witch in our midst was a grievous loss. For not all sirens boasted magical blessing. It was said that the first sirens born of Sofia fairly burst with magic. Generation after generation, it weakened, until only a handful of us could do more than manifest a wave or temporarily bend an existing current. I, myself, was bred to be the next Tritoness, magically gifted and granted a longer lifespan.

Since my birth, I'd found that such gifts came with a price. Loneliness.

Sirens were a jealous species. Born to compete for the handsomest males, yet deprived of them, we sashayed upon the shore in the form of human women to lure men. We sang to them upon gleaming rocks in the midst of storms, luring drowning sailors into our arms as they mistook us for angelic saviors. We enchanted them to continue our race. Most of us believed it was nature's plan and that there was no reason to change it. Why fight nature? A fraction of us—Witch Lorelei included, may she rest in the Goddess' light—yearned to revive the population of male sirens so that we needn't continue to "breed with our own food," as she'd delicately put it.

Privately, I agreed with her. Particularly after falling in love with Laura, I struggled to consume men unless they were already drowned or killed by sharks. Publicly, I remained neutral, open to both beliefs and restricting neither group from maintaining their right to choose. It was difficult to combine strength with compassion, to mitigate fierce beings such as sirens, but it was not impossible.

The only siren that concerned me now was my sweet gem. The Siren Without a Voice. For I knew her spirit was burdened by a dark influence she called Shadow, and I knew her well enough to perceive that behind that gleaming, serrated smile lurked a growing melancholy. The only other Nereid who had given up her voice ended up as foam upon the sea, with neither her family nor her loved one to mourn her passing. She'd died alone.

This would *not* come to pass for Delphine. This I swore before the Goddess.

CHAPTER 31

I swam slowly to the deceased Witch's cavern, trident in hand, adjusting to the pressure change in the shallow water. Strange, glowing sea moss crawled over the cavern walls and dripped from the ceiling. Their pinpoints of reflected light mirrored the stars. I wondered how the Witch conjured them, and how the enchantment survived past her death.

Perhaps other things survived, too.

My head broke the surface, and I turned to inspect the cave. A musical hum of wind echoed from the crags, deepening in tone as it reached farther back into the stones. I remembered the hidden underwater tunnel she'd locked behind her to create Delphine's gem without witnesses. A squirming unease seized the pit of my stomach. Why had I simply tread water there and allowed her to do so? I should have insisted on following the Witch. Had I kept my love at ease regarding Lorelei's work, perhaps Delphine wouldn't have risked having Aden attempt murder. Her dearest friend would still be with us. Or if I'd found some other bargain to strike . . .

I knew what Delphine would tell me. "There's no use regretting the past. We can use what we've learned to plan the future, but that is all. Everything else is melancholy pining which accomplishes nothing."

I sighed and plunged back into the cavern pool in search of the tunnel entrance. Surprisingly, I located it with ease, but that was the end of my luck. It was sealed shut. Digging my talons into the tiny crease, I pulled with all my might. Nothing. I placed the prongs of my war trident against the doorway and spoke a handful of incantations. Still nothing. I contemplated destroying the entryway altogether, but this would produce shockwaves similar to an explosion. The residents of Cape Althea couldn't fail to notice.

Swimming back and forth, I considered my options, but it was no use. Unless I found another siren witch, which was not likely, Lorelei's sacred knowledge was locked away forever.

I said nothing of my expedition to Delphine. After all, I had nothing to say; I'd gained nothing. The merry months passed as wisping clouds above the sea. Delphine and I introduced seasonal dances and court feasts at Echo Trench—feasts of oyster cups and jellyfish caprese, and best of all, the hearts and livers of men. "All respect, my lovely Sovereign, but why has no one thought of this before me?" she indicated with her flute.

She wished for a ballroom to be added to Echo Tower as well, but at this renovation I balked. "It is too much like—"

Her flute managed to convey her annoyance with a breathy puff. "Too much like what? Like the *humans*?"

Despite having turned her back on them once and for all, Delphine bristled whenever objections or insults were made against humankind in her hearing. I soothed her. "We do not live opulent lives, my gem. I am your treasure, and you are mine, and that is all we wish."

A crease formed on her forehead. My darling was restless and dissatisfied. Perhaps another organized hunt was in order? Usually sirens hunted alone, but group hunts were rising in popularity since Delphine joined the tribe. She knitted Echo Trench together in a way that no tribe had ever experienced and no siren had been blessed to call her own. She decorated caverns without demanding favors in return. She healed the injured with wraps from the kelp forest. She was no bloodthirsty, power-hungry, human-spirited monster as the court feared.

So *why* did I tense up when that subtle crease, that purse of lips, and that flash of her eyes altered her beautiful face?

I waved to Delphine as she swam off with the hunting pod, Cimon following along in his lazy sidewinding fashion like a snake that had eaten too much. "Shilo," I called in the Nereid tongue, beckoning to the pale siren holding hands with Delphine. "Let me speak with you a moment."

Shilo released my gem's hand and swam to me, a frond of kelp fluttering in her hair. Her sharp, crimson eyes narrowed on my face, seeming to notice how solemn it was. "Anything wrong, my Sovereign?"

I stared at her a minute, drumming my talon-tips against my arms. Shilo's fingers laced together as her white shoulders stiffened. "Not yet." The deep-dweller had a fresh childlike face, so pearly that it was almost translucent in some lights. Her white hair resembled the gleam of polished bone. "I must ask you a special favor."

"Anything, my Sovereign." She bowed her head.

"Keep a careful eye on Delphine. Her moods, her reactions. If anything is out of place or concerning, tell me right away."

"So, the court sirens were right?" she blurted, then winced, looking as if she'd like to bite off her tongue. Instead, she reached up and yanked the strand of kelp free from her locks, instantly engaging in the lacing game hatchlings called "pyrifera knots."

I smiled. "Right about what? Speak up."

Shilo's fingers spun the kelp into loops with skillful haste. "Some of them are saying she is going mad. That any siren without a voice will gradually lose her sanity. It is not that I believe it," she added, regaining the coral flush of color in her cheeks. "If anything, she is happier than I've ever seen her."

That is the concern. How could I explain it to Shilo, whose charming, childlike mind would not understand? There was a kind of *manic happiness* Delphine's shadow might induce. How could I mask the fact that the woman I loved might be eaten away inside until I no longer knew her? "As I said, there is nothing wrong *yet*, but I would make a poor Tritoness if I did not take this concern seriously. I am . . . how would Laura put it . . . covering my bases."

"Of course, my Sovereign. I shall report to you immediately if anything happens."

"Thank you. You are free to go."

Shilo darted away, her hands partially imprisoned by her own game. I dropped my shoulders and uncrossed my arms. "She will be safe with Shilo and Cimon both," I reassured myself.

How little I knew the Witch.

"My Sovereign! My Sovereign! Oh, come quickly!"

I dropped my kelp basket. *By Sofia, I was right.* Hardly ten minutes ago, a strange pricking stung the back of my neck—the same sensation I endured years ago when I was circled by an enormous great white shark.

It was the first and only time a fellow predator of the deep was foolish enough to consider biting a siren. No matter the pregnant shark's bulk, she'd have lost. Sirens were far more agile. "Delphine?" Her name escaped my throat in a deep rumble.

Shilo swam to my side, closely followed by several other members of the hunt. They murmured among themselves, eyes wide with alarm. "She's turning human again!" Shilo gasped.

Shock numbed my emotions. I floated in place, staring at the deep-dweller, chilled to the bone. *This never occurred to me. Not in a thousand dozing day-terrors did this ever occur to me. Why? For the Goddess' sake, Eramyne, why didn't you plan for this?*

"The spell is wearing off." My fear rendered me cold and matter of fact. Hidden from the court, my heart flailed like a drowning seabird. "The Witch must have weaved a counterspell into the gem in case we moved against her." Nearly a year had passed since the blood gem was formed. Why now—

Ah. Not *nearly* a year. Precisely a year as of tonight. That damnable Witch took us in with a false sense of security, buying us just enough time to build a happy life together, deep down in Echo Trench.

So she could take it all away with one glorious drowning.

"Must all witches be spiteful, even after death? Take me to Delphine!"

"She's back at the island," Shilo panted. She darted aimlessly in her nervousness, a vigorous creature in the best of circumstances. Vibrant with energy when afraid. "She's terrified. She started changing in the thick of the hunt. We barely got her to the surface in time as she called out for you."

I took her hand to cease her pacing. "Take me to her."

She acquiesced with a single sharp nod. "Follow me."

I debated bringing Serena's trident with me. However, I was no witch. Control over waves, waterspouts, currents and tides was my sole line of magic. But at least that aided us for travel. I stretched out my hands to manipulate the current, pushing us to the island. "Wait," I called aside to Shilo. "Did you say she was calling for me?"

"Yes. She can speak again."

Thank Sofia. One minuscule sliver of light in the darkness. As we neared the island, I prepared to surface in human form. "Stay here; don't swim any closer. You'll risk your life," I warned the deep-dweller. Reluctantly, she obeyed.

I soared over the island on the mighty wave's crest. Descending, my tail split in two and my scales vanished, replaced by a human's complexion. I landed on my feet and ran to my beloved, stumbling as I found my footing. This body felt strange and heavy after a year in siren form.

Laura waited on the shore curled up, arms around her knees, and sobbing, her strawberry-blonde tresses curling in the humid sun. Part of me rejoiced in seeing her stunning womanly form again, just as I beheld her the night we'd met at sea. Dropping to my knees, I held her tightly. "Shh, my sweet girl. Do not worry. I will find out what's happened, and I will fix it."

"Oh, Eramyne…" she managed between sobs. I held her even closer, ashamed of the bounding joy tickling my senses. "How wonderful to hear your voice again," I admitted, forcing my mind to practicalities. "Do you still have your ring?"

"Yes." Sniffling, she lifted her smooth hand to display it. The blood gem had faded from burgundy to pale red, all the magic of the amethyst siren blood leeched from it. I smoothed my hand over hers with a frown. "This is strange magic to me, dearest. I have no choice; I must search the Agenne Sea for another witch. I may need to search the surrounding seas as well if I do not find another here. I shall speak with the other tribes."

"No, don't! Please don't leave me." She clung to me, burying her sweet-smelling head against my chest. I stroked her hair. "I couldn't bear isolation without you.

I can't be alone with Sha—with my thoughts. Please don't leave me."

I made my answer as low and gentle as possible. "I have no other choice."

"Of course you do! Send someone else. Send the entire court if you must. Just *don't go.*"

"You know I cannot do that. It would put Echo Trench at risk, and if any rival tribes realized the Tower was unguarded—"

"Burke," she suddenly whimpered. I ceased stroking her hair, puzzled. "I want Burke."

"He's . . ." I frowned. "Do you not remember? He is gone."

"Not completely," Laura whispered. "Not altogether."

I grasped her soft shoulders and pulled her from my chest. I wanted to look her in the eyes. She gazed back at me steadily, though she trembled head to foot. "The court sirens will alternate guarding the island perimeter," I promised her. "I'll search as swiftly as I can. Your pups can hunt for you." She said nothing, but her head shook from side to side. *No.* "What are you afraid of, darling?" I pleaded. "This is your own island. Your second home."

"*You* are my home, Eramyne. I'm lost without you beside me."

"That is not true."

"I am lost without you!" She repeated as her tears resumed.

My heart ached as I hugged her again. As my fingertips traced her tender human skin, a second option leaped up to declare itself. Riskier for both of us, but the solution could possibly be found much faster. "We can search for a human witch."

A long silence.

Her lips brushed against my chest as she spoke, teasing me. "You're joking."

"Not at all, my gem."

"You would go to *them*?"

"They are more plentiful among humankind, are they not?"

"Y-e-e-s." She drew out the word with reluctance.

"And we can travel together, can we not?"

"Y-e-e-s." Slowly again.

"Then this is the best option we have. We must restore the blood gem, seal it for good, and restore you to the Agenne Sea at my side where you belong."

She drew back to kiss my cheek. "As long as we're together, I can face anything."

I nodded and smiled, returning her embrace, but I couldn't help comparing the daring, independent Delphine with the soft, pleading Laura and battling a myriad of emotions. Irritability reigned above them all as I shifted my waterless weight. "I feel I must weigh a thousand pounds. If we are intimate in these forms, my love, I might crush you beneath me."

Laura laughed, just as I'd hoped she would.

CHAPTER 32

We knew we had to avoid Cape Althea at all costs. The ballroom disaster was famous there, Laura's parents were there, and her reputation as a monster's willing friend could not have been forgotten. "We need a day or two to rally and form a travel plan," I said, wading in the water to catch some fish. As I observed a sea turtle hatchling struggling to reach deeper waters—alone— I glanced at Laura over my shoulder. "Would you like to see your parents? Even from afar, perhaps?"

Toying with her flute, Laura considered it, but mechanically shook her head. "You have your voice again," I reminded her. Laura just nodded. She sat with her arms around her knees, her weary expression taut with misery. "You are the most beautiful island princess I ever beheld," I offered.

She summoned a halfhearted smile.

"Your lips deserve to be kissed night and day."

She tried to laugh but didn't quite manage it. Abandoning my attempts, I approached her, hungry for something other than victuals upon my tongue. "You are breathtaking when you wear nothing but pink-hued sand."

"Stop it!" she protested, but she laughed in earnest that time. I caught her up and rolled her on top of me so that she straddled my waist. "Oh, my darling gem," I murmured, guiding her soft hands over my body. "I missed your laughter so much."

She blushed. I cherished every curve, every breath, the pounding of her heart as I touched her chest. "Do you think I could get my voice back for good?" she asked.

I sat up slightly to kiss her. A gentle moan escaped her as my hands coaxed it out of her body, touching her as only I knew how to. She caught her breath as I kissed her neck. "That I cannot say," I whispered, "but I've missed the sounds of your euphoric pleasure most of all. Brace thyself, my beloved."

"There is a witch in Summerside who takes . . . clients."

From the way her nose wrinkled up, this good, religious woman harbored certain notions of such *clients*. Laura quickly made an odd sign with her hands; I immediately copied it as well as I could. "Then we must witness to her right away," Laura crooned. She straightened her creamy skirt for the thousandth time since she'd stepped into it (with my aid); she'd quite forgotten how to wear clothes. "As humble daughters of the High God Maltaros, we seek out his beloved children who have gone astray and bring them back into the fold. Blessed be, mother."

"Blessed be, child!" The woman wobbled away with her bag of groceries and her goodwill, both intact. "I am glad she didn't think we meant to rob her," I remarked. "We *do* look rather strange."

"Speak for yourself." Prim and proper in the embroidered gown she'd stolen from the wash line, Laura checked her high collar and skirt yet again. Her bare feet mocked her with every elegant step she took. "We need stockings and shoes."

"I don't suppose people wash their shoes, too, and hang them up to dry?"

"I don't suppose so," my lover laughed. I smiled, instinctively reaching for her waist, but she gently pushed my arm away and shook her coiffed head. "We can walk arm in arm as chums do, but nothing more. Perhaps . . . perhaps a discreet kiss on the cheek now and then."

"Nothing more?"

"Nothing more, my love. Our relationship is not considered proper here."

"That is a very odd thing."

"I know. The roots of religious faith run strong and deep; they are not easily uprooted, and they spread far and wide."

"They are like invasive species in that way, then."

She raised her gilt brows. "That they are, my clever siren."

I was glad to see her good spirits returning. Continuous walking, however, was a strain upon us both. She fanned herself with a sigh. "I'm feeling those thousand pounds you mentioned, dearest. We won't reach Summerside today."

"Shall we . . . exercise more?"

Laura's mirth rang heartily through the marketplace. Some humans smiled when they heard it, as if it touched their hearts as well as it did mine. I quashed the ridiculous sting of jealousy as I observed them. "Certainly. We must bolster one another's flagging strength."

"And retrain our human muscles."

"Nothing else for it."

We stopped in Yolanda on the outskirts of the royal city. Laura booked a hotel room for us with some money she'd hidden on her island. We relaxed in each other's arms, content to listen to each other breathe. "What if this witch turns out to be a fraud?" Laura asked, playing with my hair. Braiding it, unbraiding it, braiding it again. "What will we do then?"

I shrugged. "Go to the next town and inquire again. Keep going until we find the real thing.

"Perhaps we could try advertising for one instead. Have her come to us."

I chuckled, smoothing my hands up and down her waist. "How can we phrase such a message? 'Dear kind local witches, please come to us in strict secrecy to this address, but you won't know what for until you arrive'?"

"Yes, that will attract too much attention." She sighed and turned around so I could trace invisible pictures on her back. A bonding ritual she demanded at least every other night. "What if there's nothing we can do?" she murmured next. "What if I'm human again forever?"

I traced the image of a palm tree. "Then I will be a human, too."

Immediately, Laura turned around and caught my hand. She linked our fingers together. "That's the sweetest, most giving, romantic thing you have ever said to me." She kissed the tip of my nose. "But I can't let you give up your seat in Echo Trench. The court sirens despise me already; I can't be the reason you step down from the throne. I'll be murdered in my sleep."

I stiffened. "I'll strike their heads from their shoulders before they've laid a finger upon you."

She stroked my hair back from my face. "I know you would, but I couldn't live with myself knowing I'd forced you to give your *birthright* to another. No. If I am stuck being a human, then we'll find another nice island for me to call home."

I did not like that solution, either. "So you can wither away in loneliness and isolation, like a prisoner?"

Laura released my hair with a frown. "Surely if we pass the word through the siren tribes that we are in dire need of a witch's services, one would be willing to come."

"I don't know if another exists in the entirety of the Agenne Sea," I protested. "That is why we chose to seek a human witch. Don't you recall?"

"You're right, I'm sorry. I am *so* nervous."

"I know. Tell me all about it. Tell me everything you're feeling right now," I murmured, cherishing her sapphire-blue eyes despite the insufficient hotel lighting.

She bit her lip as she weighed her response. "If we're caught—"

"We won't be. You have explained that it is dangerous to be lovers here."

"It is. If we're caught, we will be punished."

"And what is the punishment? Paying a fine? Public confession? A flogging?"

"Worse." Laura squirmed at the mere thought of it.

I cupped her cheek. "Tell me."

"We will both be circumcised. In public. In the name of the High God, all shall know our shame."

"Circumcised. What does this word mean?"

As Laura explained, horror and rage caused my blood to quicken until my dear love calmed me down by placing her hand on my chest. Her human warmth seeped into my cold-blooded body. "This demented human invention of punishment. How is it permitted in your *civilized* culture?" The court sirens were right to fear humans—to fear the fact that Laura was given Nereid looks, strength, longevity, and language (albeit via a flute). A new sympathy for their doubts embedded into my soul. Not from Laura—Sofia above, no—but from almost any other woman from such a country.

Laura rose with a sigh. She slipped out of her gown and laid back down, skin to skin—another method to calm me. Her heavenly warmth soothed my muscles despite my desire to resist. To remain incensed. "I'm not sure I can answer that question," she sadly replied. "There are many similar questions I've considered all my life. I've yet to resolve them.

"How do we claim that women have souls just as men do, yet treat women like property? How do we value sons more than daughters yet expect our daughters to be smarter, wiser, kinder, better for society in almost every way? And how can I live with myself after being raised to care for my parents until my marriage, only to abandon them for my siren lover?" She covered her face and burst into tears.

She does *miss them.* Considering the humans' tendency to form lifelong family units, her silence on the subject had surprised me. Perhaps Shadow had kept her quiet, too busy reveling in the bloody siren hunts to muse on the life she'd left behind. The family she'd deserted. For me. I let her cry and silently rubbed her back.

"You've been so good to me. So protective and loving." Laura sniffed and dried her eyes. "It seemed so wrong to complain when you've bent over backwards to give me every blessing in the Agenne Sea."

I studied the seashell print on the hotel walls before answering. "Well, I gave you everything you would accept, anyway."

She choked out a laugh, as I knew she would. "What good would a golden fork have done me?"

I cringed at my own lovesick loss of sense. *That* offering had been nonsensical, and she'd never allowed me to forget it. "I thought it was very pretty! It was quite small and made of *gold*. I did not think humans ate their meals with anything tiny and gold; it looked nothing like the utensils we ate with at that cursed ballroom dinner. I thought to myself, 'Perhaps it is a comb.'"

Naughty Laura laughed all the more. I grinned at the delightful sound, snuggling her close. "Thank you for cheering me up. I suppose . . ." She tapped her forefinger against her chin. "I suppose I didn't want to think of them for all this time because I couldn't cry. You don't know what a burden that is. *I* couldn't have guessed what a burden it would be. In some ways, it's worse than not being able to talk. There are hand signals. There's body language, expressions, mouthing words. I can dance when I am happy. I can learn to play instruments. I can hold entire conversations with Aden's spirit in my head. But there's no sufficient substitute for crying."

"I shall command the court sirens to invent the saddest-sounding instrument in either the land or sea. Just for you."

She eyed me with playful suspicion. "I can't tell if that's a joke or not."

"You won't know until it's placed between your hands."

"Will it be framed in golden forks?"

"You *do* go on about that. I shall fetch you more to adorn your hair, like combs."

Laura huffed. "Then the court shall claim I've gone mad for sure!"

"They won't know any better. Tell them it's the latest human fashion."

Thus closed our first masquerade night as two normal, friendly women. The hotel room was humid and plain with ugly blue-striped wallpaper upon a yellow base, lined with blue and white seashells. The bed was stiff, very uncomfortable for our sore muscles reacquainting with human use. And the walls were so thin that we could hear the enthusiastic couple in the room adjoining ours, creaking and moaning until Laura and I dared each other to spark an even louder, more passionate bout of lovemaking.

Midway through our banter, Laura's eyelids fluttered, and she yawned. "You need to sleep." I tucked the blanket around her. "I shall doze as usual and keep watch over you."

"I love you, Eramyne."

"I love you, my gem."

I stroked her back until she fell asleep. Left alone to ponder the hours away, I grew increasingly concerned by our plight—how to discover a legitimate witch who would not demand significant payment (for Laura had little to spare) and how to travel through several towns without being caught as lovers.

I tossed and turned until finally giving up and going to the window, watching the sun rise over the faded turrets of a seaside castle. If Laura was imprisoned and sentenced to public circumcision for her "crime," I'd render the ballroom disaster a mere fairy dream in comparison to the blood I'd spill.

CHAPTER 33

As Laura and I approached the den of the Summerside witch, we simultaneously paused, stared, and turned around, retracing our steps without a word. Bedazzled symbols were etched into the doorframe to manufacture awe. Painted goat skulls gaped from the windows. However, the Ouija board "took the cake," as Laura phrased it; we required lunar witchcraft, not demons. "We're wasting our time chasing pseudo-magicians," she said. I nodded in mute agreement. A brooding dejection had swallowed the words churning in my head since dawn. *I'm endangering you. Every loving look, every touch that lingers, every night of passion we cannot resist. We can't go on like this.*

Laura stopped. "Are you unwell?" She instinctively touched her hand to my forehead. I smiled as my cool skin reminded her that my human form was a facade.

"I did not rest well."

"You're worried about something."

Annoyance at her perception tightened my tone. "I am nocturnal. Rushing about during the hot daylight hours is uncomfortable."

She raised her red-gold brows and pursed her lips. *I've been a siren too, you know,* her demeanor reminded me. "Later," I sighed, resisting the temptation to take her hand. "I will tell you later."

"Why not now?"

"We are not in private now."

Waves of heat shimmered above sunbaked stone. Still barefoot, we avoided the sidewalk, choosing to walk in the dirt to spare our feet. The large-hoofed beasts known as "horses" pulled vehicles full of humans. Miniature human offspring were led about by the hand. Staring in fascination, I briefly wondered what they would taste like, then shook the notion from my head. How would I feel if a human caught and consumed a newborn siren? I'd tear him limb from limb.

Laura's voice fractured my thoughts. "You've learned that I have no patience when I know something is wrong. Please tell me. Don't make me wait."

"By your insistence, then." I took her hand to draw her toward a stable, away from the center of town. The coarse scent of horse alleviated my growing hunger for the flesh of men. I crossed my arms. "I was so eager to help you right away that I did not take this journey's problems fully into account."

Laura wiped the sweat from her forehead. "I don't have much money. I know that makes any journey thrice as difficult. Perhaps we should have brought a chest of shipwreck spoils."

"No; we'd be accused as pirates."

Laura huffed. My gem's temper shriveled in the heat. She crossed her arms to mirror me. "We'd sell one piece at a time. We'd make it last. I'm aware that I'm not as cautious as you are, but I'm no idiot."

"That's not the only problem, my gem." I held out my hand for the handkerchief she'd brought from Isle Rivell. Laura extracted it with a sigh. As I took it, my fingers tenderly rubbed the faded initials. *B. A. B.* Her expression softened as I dabbed her forehead dry. "I love you too much to play the part of a disinterested friend for long. I am a danger to you. It might be best if . . . We need to at least consider splitting up."

"Splitting up?" Her eyes widened. I cast a wary glance around us before pressing a kiss to her forehead. "I do not mean our relationship," I clarified. "I mean we should search for a capable witch separately so we do not endanger one another. It is not a matter of *if* we shall be caught but *when* we shall be caught." I returned Burke's handkerchief.

Stubborn as ever, she pursed her lips again as she folded it with care and tucked it into her pocket. "I asked you to stay with me. You promised you would."

"Please consider this logically," I begged and grasped her hand. "Who knows how long it will take for us to find help? How far will we have to go? Do you think the inevitable just won't happen?"

Laura shifted her weight to her left leg, stretching her right leg and arching her foot against the straw-flecked ground. One of her thinking habits that she called her "dancer's pose." It was very cute. "But then we'd have to pick a meeting time and place, and take the risk that one or neither of us would make it there. I can't fight if I'm attacked like this, Eramyne. I'm a weak human again."

I winced. She knew my weak spots and how to target them. She knew that pleading defenselessness would curdle the blood in my veins like spoiled milk. "There is another way," I offered. The horse-drawn carriages had given me the idea. "Get a boat and fill it with supplies. We'll steal it if we must. Attach the boat to Cimon and have him follow me while I visit the neighboring tribes in search of our witch. That way you will be with me."

"Siren witches are rare. You told me that. Our search will take much longer."

"Not necessarily. Our voices carry underwater. I can pass the inquiry on ahead of our travels. We'll be guided in the right direction before we arrive at the first destination."

Laura tilted her head. "We've already chosen to seek a human witch. Why are you trying to back down so soon?"

It cost me a great effort to keep from wrinkling my face in disgust. "If the other 'witches' among your kind are like the Summerside witch—"

"There it is." Laura turned her back to me and started to walk away. "You've been dying to insult *my kind* since the moment you set foot on land. Why am I not surprised, my Sovereign?"

It hurt. I would not admit it, but hearing my sacred title upon her sour tongue hurt me very much. Unthinking, I rushed after her to grasp her wrist and pull her against me. My free hand seized the back of her beautiful neck. My lips sought hers.

A man's stern cough separated us.

I jolted to my senses. Laura and I pushed each other away. The human male was balding and scantily bearded but wore a kindly (if concerned) expression. "May I ask who you young ladies are and where you're from? That's illegal here."

"I didn't know," Laura gasped, red as a ripe apple. "We didn't know! We beg your mercy, sir. Please—" She dropped into that form called a curtsy. "Please, I beg you not to tell anyone. My friend was dazed and confused by the heat of the day." *Not entirely a fib. My clever girl,* I chuckled inwardly.

He smiled at Laura. She beamed prettily in return, a gilded carnation sanctified with holy water. Even I, who knew her Shadow, felt taken in by her aura of innocence. Her charming duplicity only captivated me all the more, and I longed to kiss her again. I yearned to kiss her until the burning sun sank back into the sea where it belonged.

His gaze turned to me. He fired a long, stern look into my wide pupils. I blinked and bowed my head, involuntarily following the sirens' gesture of apologetic submission. *Maybe we should run.* "Is your friend feeling ill?" he questioned Laura. The man stole a step or two closer. I moved back, feigning ladylike shyness. "She is so pale. Do you need a doctor, miss?"

Laura adopted a higher, sweeter octave to match her performance. "Oh, thank you so much, sir, but my friend is naturally pale. I assure you all she needs is quiet, a cool room, and rest."

"Then kindly come with me." His sternness implied more of a command than an invitation. "My wife is home, and she will be happy to receive you."

Poor Laura made one last attempt. "We work for the local dressmaker, sir. That is where we are going. We only stopped for a minute."

"A stable is hardly adequate shade for ladies." He half-turned, gesturing firmly for us to follow. "Please come with me."

My gem and I traded hopeless glances.

Our hosts studied and whispered from across the room. Armed with cut-glass cups of water and a miniature cake a piece (which I admired for its beauty though I did not care for the flavor), Laura and I traded our own share of whispered commentary. "Do you think he knows you're a siren?" Laura fretted. She twisted her napkin until it resembled a white waterspout.

I watched our solicitous couple for a minute before risking a response. "There is no reason for him to assume I am. I did not bare my teeth at him, though I'd very much like to," I added. Laura unrolled her napkin and lifted it to hide her grin. "Please don't. We're in enough trouble as it is. Do you think he'll turn us in?"

"I imagine he'd have done so immediately instead of inviting us into his own cave. Home," I corrected, smoothing my skirt as I'd seen Laura do so many times. "He must have taken pity on two mad women wandering about without shoes."

I didn't like the way he looked at me. Especially in human form, I was crafted to fascinate men into babbling subjugation. To bring them to their knees so they might be devoured. He looked fascinated, indeed, but not in the usual way. Like he'd caught a rare exotic fish in his net and was calculating its price. "We need to get out of here the second they turn their backs," I muttered. Unfortunately, I was too far from the shore to command the waves to circulate their moisture into the air and form storm clouds. "*Please*, darling, let me eat them."

"No, dear. Their neighbors will raise an alarm. Investigators who have seen siren attacks will know precisely what to advertise for."

"There can't be many of them in existence—"

"*Shh*, my love. I want to hear what they're saying."

I strained to interpret their words as well. They were discussing the option of having some human called Mason come "take a look." I didn't have the first clue what that meant. It couldn't mean anything in our favor. "We need to leave," I whispered in a fierce hiss. "We have no choice but to run."

"But what if—"

"Now!"

I snatched her hand and held it tight. We darted for the front door. Behind us, our host bellowed and lurched in our direction as his wife stayed rooted to the spot, gaping. Our middling speed was infuriating. Neither Laura nor I had sprinted in over a year, and our legs were already sore from walking for hours and resting in a hard bed.

We ran along the outskirts of town. That pesky man charged after us, insisting he meant us no harm and that ladies should not run in that undignified way. Laura laughed hard at his objections, though I couldn't understand what she found so amusing about them. "He'll never catch up, crazed old goat," she jeered.

Ah, there's the Delphine I know. I glanced behind us. She was wrong. He *was* catching up, and he was aiming for me. From the greedy flash in his eye, I guessed he intended to sell me to this Mason fellow. Every siren was warned to be cautious of this prospect: being forcefully taken and sold to the highest male bidder and abused until they bled to death. Or worse—conceiving a siren purse, yet chained up far away from salt water in which to lay them. The imagery of a siren keening over her shriveled purse tripled my rage.

I stopped, turned, and bared my teeth.

The arrogant imbecile backed away but did not turn and run, as I'd expected. "You're one of those sea monsters," he accused. Oh, brilliant man! A most insightful personage. "You're holding an innocent woman captive. What game are you playing, you vile sea snake?"

"A game, you say? Yes. Let us play a game."

I rushed at him, talons flexed and eager to plunge into his delicious flesh. He screamed as I joyfully ripped out his throat. My huntress heart sang with every bite and tear. *It has been far too long.* The frenzy called my name as I reveled in the warmth of his blood. Laura called my name, too, over and over again. But I couldn't understand what she was saying. The height of bliss deafened me.

CHAPTER 34

Someone tried grabbing my arm, but I shook the hand away. A simple thing to do when one's skin is slick with blood. Then two hands clutched my arm and pulled me from my feast. My head snapped around as I hissed.

My gem. I clapped my jaws shut and rose to my feet, wiping my mouth with the back of my hand. "I'm sorry . . ."

"Not now." Laura yanked me into a run. As our bare feet pelted over the pounded dirt, grass, and small stones, I finally registered that people were screaming. "I'm afraid we'll have to adopt the longer plan," she gasped between panting for air. Our skirts flailed over our legs, threatening to trip us. Cursed things. "We have no choice now. We must return to the sea."

"You're right." *What a wistful fool I am.* I could never live among the humans. They tasted too wonderful, smelled too delectable, and practically *asked* to be eaten with their greed and stupidity. I hadn't even lasted a week. Poor Laura deserved a much more thorough apology, but now was not the time for such things. "Head for that forest in the distance. We'll hide ourselves there," I directed. Laura agreed with a short nod.

More accustomed to running than I was, she gained a little ground and looked over her shoulder. Despite the chaos of our flight, my sweet Laura shone in the sun like a goddess—delicate skin flushed, sienna lips parted, creamy layers floating around her divine figure like clouds. *I shall love you until the Agenne Sea dries up and the bedrock cracks from the heat of the sun.*

Pain burst from the back of my skull.

Men's voices reached my buzzing ears. I fought to listen through the pain, hoping to understand where I was and what I was doing here, but I knew from the empty ache in my heart that Laura was not with me.

"...the black market."

"You swear you have...before?"

"I assure you..."

"...fetch a higher price."

My face was pressed hard against a dirt floor, and it took some effort to push myself into a sitting position. The room whirled around me. I drew in deep breaths, forcing back the urge to lose my recent feast. My skin, hair, and dress remained soaked with blood. Its warming scent comforted me. *You'll kill these men just as easily as you killed the first.* I glared between the iron bars of my cage to pinpoint my fresh prey.

The black-haired man standing with exaggerated poise must have been Mason. Two other brown-haired men were with him, all of them middling in age and self-assured in demeanor. Mason's dark blue eyes suddenly fled their human targets and lanced my pupils. I hissed, leaning closer instead of shrinking away. *I've never been intimidated by a human in all my long life, and I'm not about to allow it now.*

He smiled. I sneered, baring my serrated teeth. His attention returned to his associates before he concluded the conversation and walked up to my cage. He knelt beside it. "You killed my lover, you know."

He smelled of rich tobacco and leather. Prosperity and hunting. I refused to answer him since I knew he wanted me to ask who he'd meant. *Not that silly balding creature I ate hours ago?* Mason could do far better. By human standards, he was handsome. The gloss of his long blue-black hair alone denoted better health and grooming than any other man I'd seen before. The shine of his bold white teeth enhanced my first impression. He rolled a piece of cardamom cachous, nearly dissolved, beneath his tongue.

"Melusine. You remember her, don't you? One of your court sirens. Although she may have lied about that," he amended cheerily. "She fibbed like the devil."

You are the one who is lying, foul human. Melusine and I had fought to the death after she'd attempted to usurp my place as Tritoness. She wouldn't have succeeded; her relation to me was far too slim a claim, but her rashness outstripped her logic. She claimed that my human lover had turned my head, that my protection of Laura was borderline treason against my own kind. I took great pleasure in clawing her pretty face into ribbons. I'd considered cutting out her tongue and feeding it to her pup, rendering her a voiceless siren just as my love had become. But it wouldn't do to let a traitor live.

That being the case, how did Mason know I'd killed her? Did he row after her that night and somehow witness the battle? Witness, yet *do* nothing. The despicable coward.

Mason continued to grin at me through the bars. *Those teeth are so white and straight, it makes him look strange.* He tapped his forefinger against the cage, drumming out a short beat. "Lady Melusine was my priceless pearl. An admirable informant with a glorious future ahead of her. Now, are you going to do the smart thing and claim that future for yourself? Or shall I enslave you and beat you every night until you submit? That, my overgrown sea serpent, is the question."

I turned my back to him, resting against the bars. He chuckled. "Enjoy your imprisonment, then. A shame your tour of the castle must be delayed."

He stood up and left the room, whistling for guards to come secure the door behind him. *My tour of the castle?* With a start, I quickly calculated the size of the drafty, stone-walled room, the cage I sat in tucked within a cell, that cell lodged within a dungeon. I caught a glimpse of immense winding stairs with mahogany rails. Guards in silver armor. Royal gold-and-blue pennants hanging from the walls, split in half by the magenta image of a beach rose.

I am a prisoner in Castle Rosa Rugosa. The decaying yet imposing beachside fortress of the Eriksons, the last royal bloodline. And "Mason" of the siren black market was none other than Prince Mason Aubrey von Erikson.

His hateful voice drifted down the winding staircase. "Make the smart choice quickly, my venomous wraith. I can't keep you in pristine condition for *selling* for very long."

Prince or not, he could peel every scale off my body one by one before he enticed me to act against my tribe. He might chop off my fingers and feed them to my pup before I so much as spoke Laura's name. The prospect of beatings and torture did not ruffle me. The only issue I pondered was how to make my escape.

As one might imagine, there were precious few good things to say about imprisonment. However, one benefit to my imprisonment in the Castle Rosa Rugosa was the schedule crafted for my convenience. They fed me one fish every four days, enough to keep me from starving but left in a weakened state. They sprayed me with salt water once a day (I did not need it that often, but I saw no reason to correct them; it was the sole semblance of a bath I obtained.) Once I recovered enough to sing my enchantment, I attempted it. There was no apparent result. It relaxed the humans who heard it and a guard or two sent a glance of appreciation in my direction, but that was all. I did not understand how they were protected.

An hour prior to my allotted meal, the prince stomped down the gleaming staircase, his pampered gloved hands buttoned with blue tassels gliding down the rail, a confident leer upon his freshly-shaved face. Commanding the guards to open the cell, he stepped inside and pulled off his gloves. "Good day to you, my loathsome sea serpent. Charming weather!" He chuckled because I couldn't possibly know what the weather was like. After pinioning me in place with his cerulean stare, he knelt by the cage and commenced with his inquisition.

"Are you the Tritoness, queen of all sirens?"

To which I would not reply.

"Do you wield magical power over the waves, the currents, and the tides?"

At which I smirked.

"Who was the woman you were with? Your afternoon snack?" This query forced a hiss from my throat. The prince laughed as his shiny black hair fell across his marble forehead, his eyes twinkling like Half Moon Bay in the early morning. It was insufferable that he saw fit to waste his handsomeness in sadistic cruelty. Surely statues were carved in his likeness, portraits painted of him astride mighty horses, and invitations to royal feasts distributed with prints of his own flourishing signature. He might be wonderful instead of cruel.

"Now, I must warn you that the chains and the floggings shall shortly commence if you don't start telling me what I wish to know." He slapped his gloves against the bars. "Unfortunately, some of my contacts at the market already know about you and are dying to aid me in selling for a percentage of the profits. Do yourself a favor and consider this contrast: Melusine was highly respected in my court. I ordered my staff to bow when she passed them just as they do for me. She wore beautiful gowns designed by my own outfitters, stitched up with camellia silk, seed pearls, and gold thread. She dined at my right hand every evening she could spare. All the freshest human remains from the local morgues were slipped into her six-course supper. Now, doesn't that sound a *smidgen* better than your current predicament?"

The depth of Melusine's treachery filled my mouth with bitterness. I spat it out on the floor. "And what evils did she commit to win such favor from you?" I clutched the bars so tightly my knuckles paled. How I longed to transform and draw a bloody masterpiece upon his smug face. "One of my tribe was slaughtered and served at the Whittaker's ball. I knew Melusine was behind it. You told her to do it, *didn't you?*"

His satisfied grin made me seethe. At last, he'd unlocked my voice. "Don't make the mistake of giving me too much credit. She was a skillful strategist, which is why you must understand." He reached in with his forefinger as if to tap me on the nose. I snapped at him. He withdrew with a smirk. "You must understand that I am fully and *personally* committed to breaking you. You stole Melusine from me, and you are the compensation I demand. You will bless my fleet with good fortune; you will pause the tides at my command; you will send tsunamis to swallow my enemies." He straightened and pulled on his gloves. "As well as several additional favors, some of them performed in my bedchamber. I have no doubt a powerful siren such as yourself can please me as well as Mel did."

Shame, distaste, and boiling rage exploded in a concoction that tasted too much like fear. I writhed against the bars as my hands clenched for him. *I will kill him. I WILL KILL HIM.*

He left the cell, cool as an autumn breeze. "Oh, and don't get any ideas about escaping. Your cage has been warded with magic. We've got our own little siren enchantress locked safely away, and she'll see to it that you don't get high-spirited on us. See you in four days."

My eyes widened as his boots clomped back up the stairs. I fell quite still, thinking. There was but one other siren enchantress in the Agenne Sea, one who was yet young and only capable of basic spell work such as warding and protection, piercing warding spells, or enchanting objects to make them unbreakable. She enchanted my Delphine's flute and provided her with the spear that killed Witch Lorelei. Her land-nomen was Tamar.

It grieved me that she had been taken, too, and Sofia only knew for how long. *I suppose I have Melusine to thank for that, too.* As the cousin of the Tritoness, it would be easy for Melusine to lure her fellow Nereid targets. But one thing filled my anxious heart with hope: Tamar might not be capable of changing Laura back into Delphine *yet,* but in time, perhaps she could. And now I knew where she was.

However, I had no plan to extricate myself from this net, let alone another siren. Besides, that idiot prince hadn't mentioned where she was in the castle. In fact, he'd never said she was in the castle; he'd merely said, "locked away."

Was she in the dungeon with me? All I heard was the gentle dripping of water leaking through the ceiling. The guards were nearby, quiet and bored. An idea sprang into my head. I hummed a quiet tune as if amusing myself, gradually increasing the volume until I called out in Nereid, "Are any members of my tribe here with me? Call out. Call out, my dear daughters."

After a minute of silence, I heard an answer, likewise carefully masked in song. "My Sovereign! I thought I recognized your voice, though you sounded quite human. I feared it was a trick."

Tamar. Calmly, I called out the Nereid equivalent of her name.

"It is I, my Sovereign. How did you come to be here? How did they capture you?"

"By violent means, as one might expect of them. Are you caged as well?"

"Yes. I can break the locks with my magic and free myself, but they have broken both my legs. I cannot walk."

"They have broken . . ." I hadn't believed I could be angrier than I'd been moments ago, but the humans kept proving me wrong. "Have courage, my daughter. I will think of a plan."

CHAPTER 35

I told the prince nothing, no matter the punishment. He'd initially commanded a guard to flog me. Impatient, he fetched an engraved whip himself. Even as the lashing pain burned through my flesh, I told him nothing. He threatened chains next, breaking my fingers, crushing my toes. He grew irate as I accepted every punishment and endured them without a whimper. I was Tritoness; I would endure a lake of fire for my tribe if I had to. A Tritoness did not break, nor did she bow to humans. If I was to die, I would do so with my honor intact and Laura's sweet name in my heart.

As Mason swore beneath his breath, cracking his bloody whip and striding from the cellar, the guard inclined his head toward the prince. Dazed and shaking, I barely caught the guard's low words. "You must take care, Your Highness. If you kill her, you'll have nothing left but that enchantress."

"I know that," Prince Charming snapped.

The guard hesitated. Unease crinkled the corners of his eyes. "Shall I tend to her bleeding, Your Highness? If only to prevent the creature from dying. I'm sure you don't want the inconvenience, my prince."

"Very well. Make haste. Don't dawdle about it."

"Your Highness." The guard bowed, but the prince just snorted and swept from the room, the bright blue tail of his hair ribbon fluttering away. I thought unaccountably of a helpless, pampered bluebird—all chirp and no peck—and laughed until I felt delirious.

The guard hobbled off to fetch clean water, soap, and bandages. When he returned with said ministrations, I realized he'd hobbled because he had one leg. The other was made of wood. Still lying on the floor, I smiled up into his grizzled, bearish face. "And what shall I call you, pray tell? Peggy?"

"If that makes you laugh, I don't mind." He opened the cage door with a special key and a low, muttered phrase in a human language I didn't recognize. He had to stoop to avoid knocking his head on the cage ceiling, as did I.

Surprised, I shifted in the dirt to gaze my fill of him. He wasn't much to look at, to be sure. A burly heavyset guard, brown of hair, brown of eyes, bronzed from too much time in the sun, a coarse-cut beard and halfhearted mustache. A grunting sort of voice that complemented his physiognomy. A sad, lifeless expression in his eyes that struck me as permanent. "I'm going to wash your wounds and stop the bleeding. I'm sorry if I hurt you; I give you my word it isn't intentional."

Grunting my amazed appreciation, I turned my face to the wall opposite. "I find a human's word isn't worth much."

"Can't say I blame you."

He tended to me with care. I marked how he averted his eyes from private areas and lifted my battered sleeve to cover my bare shoulder. Accustomed to the leering from male humans, this was refreshing. "Are you immune to siren seduction?" In my right mind, I wouldn't have asked because I wouldn't have cared, but today's punishment set a fever in my blood. I dreamily pondered what it would feel like to die. Would I still become sea foam away from the sea? That made my heart ache, though I couldn't say why. Why should it matter? I'd be dead.

"I can't say whether I am immune or not, my lady." He dabbed the damp towel against my sore back, removing as much dirt as possible without pressing too harshly. "But by Maltaros, I've never heard a laugh like yours in all my born days. You're like an angel."

"That would be a *no*, then. You're not immune." I laughed again, thinking the comparison of my monstrous, man-eating self to an angel a very funny joke. "Don't call me 'my lady;' it's ridiculous. I am no lady. Call me 'Eramyne.'"

"Like the goddess Eramyne?"

"I suppose." Until then, I hadn't known Laura had pulled the name from the human's vast pantheon. It was flattering to be gifted with a goddess' name, even if I didn't think highly of the humans themselves. I could be generous.

A tremulous blend of fear and excitement joined the guard's adoration. "*Are* you the goddess Eramyne? Is that how you're able to control the sea?"

Silent giggles bubbled in my throat. What a tasty treat this human was. An unexpected delight. "Yes. I am a siren goddess. Now, can you get me out of here, Peggy?"

To my astonishment, he actually put down the towel and glanced around the cage. Leaning over me, he whispered in a tone of solemn sincerity, "I can't get you out now, Goddess Eramyne, but if you are patient, I will find a way to help you."

"And Tamar," I hastily added.

"Tamar?"

"The siren enchantress."

"Oh! I'm sorry, I didn't know her name." His forehead wrinkled as he thought. "That will be far more difficult as she cannot walk."

"She'll have to be carried or wheeled to the shore. Once she is returned to the water, she can gather the strength to transform. She will be whole again."

"I don't know," he muttered. Doubts overshadowed his dull face. "Please don't be angry, gracious goddess. I don't think freeing Tamar as well will be possible. We must be silent and quick."

"We free my daughter too, or we do not leave at all."

"Yes, Goddess Eramyne."

I heard a couple more guards coming close to my cell. "We'll discuss the specifics later." He nodded. As he finished cleaning and wrapping my wounds, I marveled at my good luck. Sofia be praised! Yet, it was clear his mind was formed for obedience, not leadership. I had to collar him and pull his leash tightly to my side, lest he slip away and betray everything for two mugs of beer.

I'd all but called poor Peggy a dullard. Yet was I not one myself? Melusine had loved beer and wine and finely-cooked seafood, prepared as the humans liked it. Why had I never stopped to ask Melusine when she'd had the opportunity to sample fine dining? Why had I ascribed her sudden bickering and snooty manners and ambition to "natural envy"? She must have been the prince's lover for a year or more, a traitor romping beneath my very fins. Dancing at my Tower. Eating with my court. Encouraging my tribe to fear Delphine. To disapprove of me.

I was the dullard, it seemed.

A week passed without a visit from Mason. "Peggy" cleaned my wounds and changed my bandages as I slowly healed. The daily spray of salt water helped. "I can't keep calling you Peggy," I objected when he answered readily to the nickname. "That was rude of me."

"Truly, I don't mind it."

"Well, I do. What do you call yourself?"

"Luke."

I paused. "I'm glad we ran into one another, Luke. Despite the circumstances."

His head dipped in a sad nod.

Suddenly, the *clomp-clomp* of a heavy sole accompanied by the jingle of buckles snapped us both to attention. I backed away from the bars while Luke locked the cell door and stood before it, lance in hand. "Your Royal Highness."

"Move aside." The prince flapped his hand at the guard. Luke obeyed. I winced as the cell gate creaked open and clanged shut behind my tormentor. "At last," he snorted. "A flinch of fear betrays you. Your humble enchantress whines and begs, but you don't stir an inch. It's really quite dull."

I ached for Tamar. I'd make Mason endure thrice what he inflicted upon her. "I tire of this." He knelt into his favorite position for questioning me, tugging at his blue tasseled gloves. I yearned to yank those ridiculous tassels off and throw them across the room. "Everyone has a weakness. What if I kill your precious little enchantress? What say you to that?"

"You won't do it." I allowed myself a brief yet satisfying smirk. "You need a backup plan in case I die or escape."

He straightened his snow-white collar embroidered with beach roses. "She can barely retain a simple ward while defending my men against your song. Your enchantress hardly merits the title."

At least Mason was chatty enough to answer my unasked questions. I wondered if I should risk goading him into answering more. "Do you torture your own kind as well? Or only 'overgrown sea serpents' like myself?" I intended to find out whether he'd either captured Laura, too, or intended to capture her.

Prince Mason yawned. He stroked his sleek ebony ponytail, patting every hair into place. Vanity seeped from his violet-scented pores edged with cardamom. I resisted the urge to betray my disgust. "I practiced on human prisoners first. It was educational, but I grew bored of it, just as I'm getting bored of you." He stood and cracked his knuckles. "I tracked down the widow of the old man you ate. She had an interesting tale to tell about you and that red-headed captive of yours. She wasn't a roadside appetizer at all, was she?"

My heart slowed. My gaze dragged down his face, his throat, and sloped over his Adam's apple. I fantasized about digging my poisoned nails into his neck. Then I would trail my hands down, rending him with agonizing slowness until I stopped above his heart. I'd rip it out of his chest and eat it while his guards watched.

"My, my. A murderous glare fit for a demon. I think we've struck a nerve!" he crowed to Luke. The guard stared at me with wide eyes, sweat dotting his sunburned forehead. "That pretty lover of yours shall receive a very special invitation."

I smiled as I clenched and unclenched my hands. Laura Frances Rivell was no idiot. There could only be one reason in the world she'd catch the eye of a spoiled prince who'd never known she existed before. "She will not come."

"Then we'll catch her using you as bait. I'm disappointed in your lack of faith in me, *Tritoness.*"

In answer, I showed him my arms, wrists, and back. My resilient flesh was now scarred with the strokes of his whip, thin purple lines resembling the kiss of a man o' war's tentacles. "You have done your worst, foul prince, and I have recovered from it. I have nothing to fear from you." *And Laura need not fear you, either.* I'd watched her play among wreckage and floating bodies, singing and twirling as she chose which offerings looked best to eat. She might be human again, but I could see her that very moment in my mind's eye, sizing up the prince for future feasting. With Shadow and Aden's spirit to help her, Mason might have more reason to fear her than to fear *me.* Laura could be quite unhinged. I'd defended her sanity before my court, but deep down, I knew it was rightfully disputed.

I knew what *I* was capable of. However, I was still learning what the Blood Gem of the Agenne Sea could do, and now the prince wished to play his game with her. Part of me still clung to the dirge of fear, but another part of me rejoiced. *Yes, let us play the prince's game, my darling.* My lover and I would destroy our fair enemy together. Then we would seek every tablet, ritual scroll, and talisman available to train Tamar until she was capable enough to make my sweet Laura the dark, decadent Delphine once more. And this time it would last forever.

"What are you smiling about, Your Loathsomeness?"

I smirked at the prince's snappish tone. "Nothing at all, dear prince."

CHAPTER 36

Beyond Luke's company, my days in isolation extended. Nervousness began gnawing at my bones; I was unsure where Laura might have fled after my capture, and I started worrying about worst-case scenarios. Would they succeed in finding her? If the prince declared a kingdom-wide search, it was only a matter of time. The suspense ate away at me more than the isolation did, as a home in the vast ocean allowed for plenty of solitude. That in and of itself was no trial.

But how would Laura fare? I doubted. I trembled. I rebuked myself for welcoming the challenge. If he plucked but a single golden-red hair from her head I'd sing myself hoarse, hoping against reason that songs could kill.

Some sirens in Echo Trench believed such a song existed. Arrangements titled *The Mortal Dirge, The Final Sound, Serena's Necropocrypha,* and other similarly-named melodies were well known among the tribes. A smaller group proclaimed that a secret song could change a human into a siren. I'd dismissed them all as fantasy. As I considered these theories now, however, I wondered if I ought to have studied them more seriously. What if I'd been wrong to dismiss them?

Tamar could aid me in decoding possibility versus sheer fancy. Cautious to mask our conversation as before, I discussed it with her in the Nereid tongue. "I think Shilo was a disciple of the Necropocrypha," Tamar professed. For some sirens worshiped perfected music and song as humans worshiped their flawed gods. "However, if any of these arrangements worked, then there wouldn't be multiple sects. Even if they're onto something, the answer has not been grasped."

"And the secret song that can change a human into a siren?"

She hesitated. "That one, I know. I can teach it to you. It's called the *Pontos Apognoisis.*"

"The ocean's despair?"

"Yes; it is said that the transformation is so painful, some humans may die from the shock. It is dangerous, and the siren must have tasted the human target's blood before she sings for the spell to take effect."

"How have I not heard of this before?" I demanded, panting with eagerness.

Tamar's voice lowered, though the guards couldn't understand us. To them, we were merely singing again to pass the time. "It is dark magic, which is sacred and requires decades of study to compile. It is a crucial secret among enchantresses who wish to become witches, my Sovereign. I am breaking my initiate vows this moment by sharing it with you." After an uncomfortable pause she added, "The Tritoness is barred from all knowledge of it, as she may abuse its power. Please . . . Please do not tell anyone you learned of it from me. I shall never become a witch, and that is all I want in my life."

"Surely, Tamar. I will protect you."

"Thank you, my Sovereign." She sighed with relief, and I chuckled. "What do you find amusing?"

Now I was the one sighing. "I have learned so much about humans and sirens alike thanks to this imprisonment. If only I'd been knocked out and chained up sooner. What a pity!"

Tamar and I laughed. Her flimsy ward wavered as our mirth echoed like the striking of angelic bells. The guards flinched and stared at us, gaping. "It almost worked that time," I realized. "We need to sing together."

"Yes. It's a shame the mortal dirge has not been discovered."

"A shame indeed." At least enchanting the guards would buy us the time we needed. I would carry Tamar myself, not trusting Luke to avoid dropping her. "Can you heal your legs, Tamar?"

"I've been trying to. It's slow work, I fear."

"Keep trying. There is hope for escape yet."

Tamar and I were midway through a song when the clomp of Mason's boots cut us short. "Don't stop!" I hissed in Nereid. "Perhaps we shall ensnare the prince, too."

"We shall not," the frightened enchantress insisted. "He wears a warding shell."

The same healing and protective concoction I'd given to Laura. "You told him about that, too?" I snapped before stopping myself. How many secrets had Tamar given away? Was she truly that afraid of pain? While being tortured, I concentrated on the image of Laura basking in a serene golden glow of perfect comfort and safety. That fastened my mind onto the future, onto the one thing that mattered in this cursed world.

"I am sorry," Tamar faltered. Mason's boots paused outside my cell; I said no more. The humans might be ignorant of our language, but it was better that Tamar and I were not appearing to communicate.

Luke unlocked the door, and the prince sauntered inside. "Well. I've heard a great deal of singing from you two of late. I trust your throat is not too sore for talking?" His sarcasm flicked like his fancy whip.

"Not at all, Your Highness."

"Very good. Bring her down!" Mason shouted over his shoulder.

Bring her down. Three simple words that nearly cleaved my heart in two. I pressed the palm of my hand to my chest for reassurance that it was still beating. *One. Two. Three. Four.*

A pair of slender feminine feet tiptoed down the stairs. They were beautiful feet, deep in the arch, one golden-brown mole by the slope of her left anklebone. The second her layered cream skirts stitched with worn daisies came into view, my heart rate doubled.

"Eramyne!" Her gasping voice thrilled and grieved me. My love flew to the cell door and seized it with both hands, crying. "Oh, my beloved! What have they done to you?"

I swallowed back my shock, deciding to digest it another time. *Why didn't you run far, far away from here? Did you come willingly? Why would you do such a foolish thing?* There wasn't a scratch on her. I glared at the prince anyway. He turned up his empty hands and shrugged, innocent as the beach rose on his banners. "She didn't believe me when I told her you were alive. We had to bring her to prove it before she'd say anything." He grinned a dazzling grin, his perfect teeth like regiments of polished pearls.

I cursed the cage that kept me from touching her. "What do you expect to learn from her?" I couldn't help asking. "She is just a human girl. She is no siren, no enchantress, and certainly no seasoned witch. Let her go."

"Ah, but she is your lover." He glanced from Laura's tearful face to my stern demeanor. "You underestimate the love in your eyes at this moment. 'Tis a powerful confession. Lovers make excellent leverage. Put her in the western dungeon," he ordered the nearest guard. "Treat her civilly until I've decided what to do with her. I'm only a monster when there's reason to be," he sweetly maintained.

To me, Laura shone as brilliantly as the goddess I was said to be. I adored memorizing every illustrious inch of her and studying the workings of her fascinating mind. Terror seized me as I ruminated on what the foul prince might do to her—assuming he found her as attractive as I did—but when she passed him to ascend the stairs, he looked at her with cool indifference.

Perhaps the humans who take siren lovers do not desire another human again. And perhaps that is the true curse behind the abomination of our coupling. Should anything happen to me, Laura could never love a human again, just as the prince could not.

It was the middle of the night. Wide awake, I sat cross-legged with my hands resting on my knees, palms up. I breathed in the dungeon air, then breathed out, focusing on that one simple act in a calm celebration of life. I would practice with Tamar again. One melody at a time, we would wear away the ward protecting the guards from our lure. I would find Laura, and we would escape together, the three of us.

My ears caught the patter of bare feet. My eyes snapped toward the door just as Luke grunted, then collapsed. The image of Laura was reflected in my night-loving vision. She snatched the key from Luke with her free hand, her opposite hand brandishing a bloodied knife, and muttered frustrated profanity when the door did not budge.

I watched her in amused silence. She continued to rock the key back and forth in the lock. Her brows furrowed deeper and deeper. "You need to speak the secret enchantment," I finally said, "and why did you kill him? He was an ally. You might have held chloroform to his mouth until he slept." Ah, my sweet Laura. She stabbed first and asked questions later.

In a way, I admired her impulsiveness, her freedom, while still giving every indication of a sheltered débutante. She only diverted to her true self with me. "What secret enchantment?" Laura growled. "Don't tell me the prince was foolhardy enough to ward the place with Tamar's own magic?"

"That he did."

"Audacious bastard!" Laura spat.

I chuckled at her venom. "He has some sort of hold over Tamar. She's frightened of him." I called out to her in Nereid, but she didn't answer. I frowned.

Laura lapped the blood dripping down her knife. The face she made was worth a chest of gold. "By Sofia, habits die hard or not at all. I love you, Eramyne, but stop wasting time and speak the enchantment to me."

"I do not know it. Each time, the guard spoke it softly in a human language I did not recognize."

Laura hissed. The flash of her eyes in the dark reminded me of Delphine. For a moment, I wondered if she'd somehow burst into her siren form and break down the cell door with sheer willpower. "If Tamar generated the ward, then she would know the enchantment, correct?"

"Yes, but as I said, she is afraid of the prince's wrath. She will not tell me what it is."

Steely rage crawled over her face. Lifting her knife, Laura marched toward Tamar's cell. "Don't!" I hissed, clawing at the door of my cage and hating it more than ever. "Laura, let her be. We'll find some other way."

"There is no other way. Not right here and right now with the guards dead."

She'd killed all *six* of them? Luke stood directly before my cell at all times. The other five stood in the stairway or walked back and forth from cell to cell. How could she have stabbed them all without a single sound?

Wait, I had to go further back. She'd escaped from whatever hold the prince had trapped her in. *How in Sofia's name did she do that?* The convenience of it all tasted sweet but washed down sour. *I've been betrayed once. Why not twice?* "Laura—"

Clomp. Clomp. Clomp. Jingle. Buckled boots descended the stairs. A soft whistle curled down the handrail and caressed our ears, a playful assault upon the silent night. "Good evening, ladies!" Prince Mason paused and tilted his head. "Although, I fear there are no ladies present. Just two murderers and fornicators ready for the hangman's noose."

He wore a fluffy white nightshirt tucked into his pants. Yet, his cerulean eyes sparkled alert and awake with not a hint of fatigue. He'd merely pretended to go to bed. He must have crept after Laura the instant he heard her escape.

Unless . . .

Had he influenced Laura through his diabolical threats? I didn't want to believe it. She was far stronger than Tamar, which was a strange thing to say. With her Shadow and her spirit both, my love was no common woman. If Mason threatened her while Shadow was conscious, they would have laughed him clear back to Cape Althea. But if her Shadow slept, that was another thing. The beauty and the chaos of Laura Rivell: One never knew which version of her one would get. She might be sweet and demure. She might stab you in the neck.

She might stab you in the back.

No! I banished the thought the instant it was conceived. Laura could be a fierce little savage, but she was no traitor. She'd never betray me. I looked at her. She looked at me. I subtly touched the hollow in my throat where she'd worn her warding shell so long ago. The hint of a grin trembled in the corner of her sly mouth. *Be quick, my gem,* I silently instructed. *If it all comes to death, know that I love you with all my black heart.*

And I love you with all of mine, my siren.

Raising her glinting blade to the moonlight, Laura charged at the prince.

CHAPTER 37

"Guards!"

Distracted by the knife, the prince redirected the blow and knocked the blade from Laura's hand with ease. While he did so, her free hand reached for the circle of twine around his neck. She wrenched it free. The tiny shell quivered in her hand like a living thing. Hope swelled within me like the tide. "Destroy it!" I cried.

She smashed the warding shell upon the rocks.

A sound like a small peal of thunder quaked the ground. At last, Tamar's confused wail rose from the opposite end of the dungeon. Did Mason drug her?

Or perhaps her healing spells had made her too weak. *Either way, it seems I am performing alone tonight.*

I sang my tribe's sacred birthright.

The guards running to the prince's defense diverted, coming straight for me. They slammed against the cell door, rattling it loose at its very hinges. I scrambled back until I hit the cage wall. The crazed men piled one on top of the other, clawing each other's eyes out to reach me first. They reminded me of our voracious pups in the midst of a feeding frenzy when even we sirens dared not venture too close.

When we lured men, they were scattered, solitary, and vulnerable. Many of them were flailing in the deep at death's door. To have a cascading wave of sprinting, frantic humans reaching through the bars for me filled me with a dread I'd never known. The way their eyes rolled, their teeth bared, and their tongues deliberately licked the bars—

"Eramyne!"

For the first time in my long years, I'd been frozen in shock. Laura's voice thawed me. The foul prince had her in a headlock, grabbing a fistful of her lovely hair. "I'll snap her neck if you don't stop!" he yelled. His eyes narrowed as he pulled her hair again, making her gasp with pain. "I saw her kill my men. It's no less than she deserves. Stop it now!"

I blinked. *How is he not affected?* It shouldn't have been possible.

There was but one explanation.

"What is your name?" I asked him.

Mason frowned. His grip on Laura faltered. "You know my name."

"I know your land-nomen." I switched to Nereid. "Tell me, what is your true name?"

His stainless teeth flashed as he snarled. Those far too perfect teeth that set me on edge. *They are illusions.* "I rejected you repulsive creatures long ago. I am not a monster; I am a man. You could have made the same choice, but you didn't. I condemn you all!"

So, he didn't fear Tamar's ineptitude because he didn't need the warding. It was all a show for the benefit of his humans. The human servants that never could have dreamed they served one of the monsters they feared.

My focus flickered back to the brawling maniacs at my cell door. A few more tugs and the door would collapse from its hinges. They'd free me from my cage, then afterwards, they would . . .

Dare I risk it?

Mason followed my gaze and tightened his hold on Laura, pulling her head back further. "Stop calling them. Tell them to jump off the nearest cliff to win your love."

I looked at Laura. Her soft eyes brimmed with pain and concern. "Release them, my love," she murmured. "There are too many of them. I can't stand by and see you hurt."

"And I cannot bear to see *him* hurt *you.*"

I ordered them away, but not off the edge of a cliff as the kind prince had suggested. I noted a lone maid amongst them and prayed for Sofia's protection over her. Mason let go of Laura's hair, pinning her wrists behind her back. "Thank you ever so much. Now we can discuss your future serving the last prince of the Erikson bloodline."

"Tell me, how was a male siren brought up as a human prince?"

Rather to my surprise, his face fell. I did not think he was capable of emotions like regret, if that's what he was feeling. "I won't waste my time feeding my life story to a monster. Now, stay put like a good siren, and I'll return our cherished bird to her cage." He shoved Laura ahead of him. As she stumbled, she cast an impish look over her shoulder. "I love you!"

Despite everything, I smiled. "I love you more."

"Prove it."

"Have patience, and I shall."

"Shut up, both of you! I can still have you hanged."

Outwardly, I was calm. Inwardly I feared I'd die a prisoner.

Mason refused to allow Laura even brief visits. "I'll bring her if you agree to demonstrate your power." I would not. I grew thin pining for her, picking at scraps of fish my new (unsympathetic) guard threw at me. I missed Luke. A simple, religious soul he might have been, but his faith had taught him to be kind. That was the type of religion I could respect; although it was difficult for me to comprehend why the most intelligent species on the land dedicated every breath to their deities. I acknowledged the existence of my creator, Sofia, and that sufficed. I saw no logical reason to do more.

I pined for Half Moon Bay. The dark, serene waters bubbling as they frothed upon the shore. The black rocks jutting like jagged teeth from the sand. How I used to watch Laura wander along the waves as she waited for me. She'd grasp her folded arms, bite her lip, and stare wistfully out to sea.

I craved my sweet Laura. I yearned for our lazy mornings on Isle Rivell.

I wished I knew how to cry.

The cell door crashed free from its hinges.

I snapped alert, having lulled into lethargy from sheer ennui and to escape my appetite for the new guard. They all wore warding shells now. There was no point in wondering why the prince hadn't forced Tamar to enchant more shells from the start; his guards were replaceable and he did not care. Most likely, he *wanted* to witness the effects of the siren song in person. Audacious bastard, indeed.

A siren in human form broke my cage and gathered me into her arms. She touched the small, hidden gills on either side of my jawline. "Dry as bleached bone in the sun," she murmured.

I knew her eyes and hair. "Ignacia," I whispered. Five more of my court sirens rallied at the dungeon entrance, watchful.

"Yes. You are very weak, my Sovereign. Can you put your arms around my neck?"

I obeyed, albeit in a clumsy fashion. She shifted my weight and glared at the fallen guard as she stepped over him. His head was hanging onto his neck by a shred. "Before you ask, Shilo sent me. I confess I was stunned to discover that the prince himself had his hooks in you. I suppose we have Laura to thank for that."

"No," I growled, shaking my head insistently. "She did not betray me."

"Then you were a fool to go after her."

"I was caught first. *She* tried to save *me.*"

"You are delirious, my Sovereign. Humans kill sirens. They do not try to save them." Ignacia wobbled a bit, unsteady on her human legs. "Walking is horrendous. What a miserable way to live!"

I stilled my tongue. *Let her think what she wants to think.* "We need to save Laura."

"I will return for her once you are safely at sea."

I shook my head again. I knew by Ignacia's lackadaisical tone that she would *not* return for her. "We must. The prince will be enraged. He will torture her—"

"I give you my word, my Sovereign. I will come back for her."

Too weak to persist, I had to be content with that. Ignacia clambered up and down the sand dunes, crushing beach flora and sea oats mercilessly underfoot. I rather enjoyed the destruction of the castle's sparse garden. Outside of the castle and fully conscious, I could see that there wasn't much grand about Rosa Rugosa anymore. Crumbling yellow stone grieved in unswept sand. Stone sea dragons leered above the gutters, many of them displaying chipped noses and cracked tails. Baskets full of the local beach rose cultivar had overgrown to such a weight that they'd snapped free of their delicate hanging hooks and dropped to the flagstone. No one had bothered to trim them or hang them back up.

The crowning glory of all this morbid disarray was the bone-white, stone-dry, massive fountain complete with a statue of the prince himself, arms akimbo as he scowled out to sea. Lightning cracked above his pale head. Thunder grumbled its response.

The instant the Agenne Sea splashed a merry greeting over my parched skin, I laughed. The waves answered my glee and rolled to me. I gathered them up as if they were my children. My transformation was the most painful it had ever been, but I reveled in delicious relief as bubbles tickled my skin, soothing the thin purple welts Mason had gifted me. *I shall wear them with pride.*

"Bring Laura back to me immediately," I warned my sirens. "Be quick." They bowed their heads and rushed back up the garden slopes.

If only I had more time. I'd conjure a hurricane to end all hurricanes since the dawn of humankind. However, I must provide Laura with her chance to escape.

I evaluated a pleasing alternative to a hurricane. It would appease my craving for violence, yet I could control it more carefully, ensuring Laura's safety. Steeling myself, I began to sing the sea into withdrawal. The Agenne Sea gathered up her shoreline skirts and pulled them back, and back, and back further still, girding her loins for the fray.

CHAPTER 38

Water churned at my waist to hold me apart from the current. A rumbling roar expanded on either side of me. I whispered to the sea to spare what marine life it could, and she listened, creating a new current to wash fish, crabs, and stingrays out of harm's way. Drawing back past the sandbar, I rose high within the mighty wave. Rosa Rugosa quickly became a yellow, tumbledown shack from my view. "Not enough," I shouted to the ocean, outstretching my arms. "Higher!" The nearing crack of thunder overhead doubled my giddiness. The strength of the Agenne Sea fueled me until I forgot I'd ever been a prisoner.

He might survive. The instant the water slapped him down he'd transform, writhing with indescribable pain as he became what he despised. I prayed to witness it myself, but Laura was my priority, not satisfying my vengeance further.

To my great relief, seven tiny dots darted from the quivering courtyard. A glint of reddish-gold hair shone in the filtered sunlight. *My love.* I hadn't smiled until then. I beamed down at my sweet Laura from high above. *I dedicate this tsunami to you.*

I pulled my arms back, then thrust them forward. The wave tumbled on ahead. As I watched, I sang the *Pontos Apognoisis.* How fortunate that I'd bitten Laura's neck our first night on the island. The conditions of the spell were satisfied; I had tasted her blood.

When my song was complete, I murmured a few words and directed my standing wave to the right. My ears rang from the infernal roaring, and as the tsunami swallowed Rosa Rugosa, the sound intensified into a titanic symphony. Pride swelled in my chest. *The most beautiful song I've had the pleasure to direct.*

I waited one minute. With another motion, I pulled my loyal sirens to my side, counting them with frantic haste. *Five . . . Six . . .*

There she was.

A strawberry-blond siren with dark lips, silver scales, and blood-red spikes surged to my side to take my hand. "Eramyne! My love. I *knew* that had to be you."

I permitted myself a small smirk. "Who else do you know that can conjure a tsunami to save you, my beautiful gem?"

Our tails spiraled together as we kissed, my hands cradling Delphine's lovely face as she braced my lower back. Our passion finally subsided enough for us to watch the receding waters leak from the castle, arms about each other's waists. Obliterated flora, baskets, and the stone figurehead of the prince bobbed at the surface, quick to sink. "It looks pretty this way." Laura grinned. "If only we'd drowned the castle sooner."

"Alas, I must be in the sea to command it, my love."

An eighth head surfaced to our left. Tamar stretched her siren muscles and flapped her tail, relief bright in her wide eyes. She trembled from the painful effort of transforming, but her joy was unmistakable. "You nearly dashed my brains out against the cell wall, my Sovereign."

I laughed. "But I did not!" We traded amused glances, and my heart warmed as I reflected on our budding friendship. *It is good to have friends.*

Laura—Delphine—tucked her head beneath my chin, snuggling close. Our tails embraced again. "I'm hungry for that pesky prince. Let's eat him."

The sweet mirth of my sirens was music to my sore ears. They yet rang from the fierceness of my power. "I fear cannibalism is frowned upon in our tribe, beloved."

We waded through the flooded castle in search of Prince Mason. Unfortunately, we never found him. I instructed all of Echo Trench to be on guard for him, but after months with no signs of the wretch, we concluded that he must have transformed back into a human and gone into hiding somewhere on land. Rosa Rugosa remains deserted to this day. It became a surprisingly stunning place—a lonely yet decadent shelter for birds, turtles, crabs, and the odd siren or two who decided it made a good haunt for dinner dates (this was Delphine's idea, of course).

Delphine and I basked in the shallows of Isle Rivell. I tilted her chin up for another kiss. "Do you think we could have converted Mason?" I asked her. "He'd have been brought down to Echo Trench as our prisoner, but perhaps in time . . . Perhaps he'd realize we are only monstrous when we need to be." *Just as he claimed he was.* Much as I despised admitting it, even to myself, he was not so different from us. He *was* Nereid, whether he accepted it or not.

She sighed, linking our long, scaled fingers together. "He really thought he was a human. He denied the truth so many times, he wouldn't know it if it came bearing down upon his head like a tsunami."

Our laughter frightened a nearby fish. I coaxed it back to me and stroked along its back, admiring its rainbow shimmer. "It's possible that he *did* realize the truth. Perhaps that is why he ran."

"It's possible," Delphine said with a grin, sweeping her fingers along the rippling water. "Some of us learn to accept our shadows and grow alongside them, teaching them as they teach us. But some of us deny them until the day we die, returning to the dirt or sea foam from whence we came. Perhaps we rise again in another life. Perhaps we don't. Who can know?"

"Indeed. Who can know."

Soon, the rosy sun set over Isle Rivell, warming two siren lovers in its pink rays. It set over Cape Althea, where the office of Burke and Sampson collected dust and lonesome books. It set over the shoreline of Rosa Rugosa, where the statue of the missing prince sank into crystal-blue oblivion. And the sun set over Half Moon Bay, where a mother cried for her daughter, who was seduced by a siren.

Acknowledgements

Profuse thanks to every reader who gave my first Gothic romantasy a chance. As a proud indie author, every story is a labor of love and our readers mean the world to us. Simply dedicating your time and attention to our books is a wonderful gift. Believe it or not, when I began Half Moon Bay, I wasn't convinced I'd enjoy writing a siren romance. Thanks to the bittersweet chocolate of the Gothic genre—and generous inspiration from Eggers' *Nosferatu*—I fell in love. Gothic fantasy has officially captured my soul. I'm already planning my next novel, a Southern Gothic fantasy/paranormal mystery with a strong sapphic subplot, so keep your eyes peeled for more from Manteufel Books!

I humbly salute the OG mermaid master, H. C. Andersen. I was blown away by the actual story (versus Disney's cheery adaptation), and I can't recommend it highly enough. I infused Half Moon Bay with its darker theme of sacrifice in the form of Aden, who was modeled after a dear friend of mine. Aden serves as a potent reminder to never take our kindred spirits for granted.

Lifelong blessings to my beta reader, V. B. Scott. He's also a talented writer, and I highly recommend his stunning historical fiction debut, *Revenge of the Bakeneko.*

I kiss the feet of my editor and best friend Elise Nelson, who writes romantasy beautifully herself. I adored her Hades and Persephone retelling, *The Light in Hades.*

I gratefully bow before Ana Hansen of Sparks Editorial, who was kind enough to submit an editorial review. I look forward to improving my craft!

And I extend special appreciation to my team of freelance artists. If you didn't snap up this book for the art alone, then that's great! But for those of you who *did* snap it up for the art alone . . . so would I.

Minor Author's Note: Some readers might have been confused by my modern use of the word "dating" for Delphine and Eramyne. This was intentional, as the Victorian equivalent, "courtship," implies intent to marry. Marriage does not exist in my siren realm, hence my decision to utilize the modern concept of going on dates.

About the Author

Gothic horror fan Richelle Manteufel grew up relishing the psychological deep-dives of Poe, Stoker, and the Brontë sisters. She discovered her passion for writing fiction at nine years old.
Now a married mother of two in Spanish Fort Alabama, she can be found shopping for gothic fashion or writing in her Victorian-style office,
earbuds blasting heavy metal.

~

Find her latest publications and social media handles on **manteufelbooks.com**.

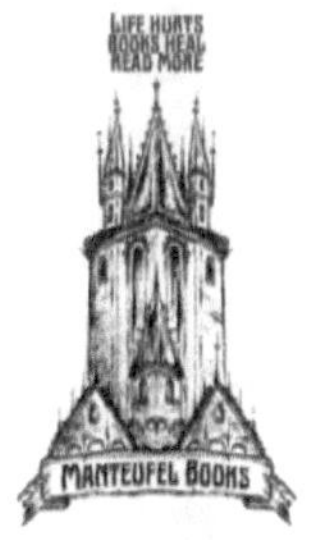

www.ingramcontent.com/pod-product-compliance
Lightning Source LLC
Chambersburg PA
CBHW030014010826

48973CB00009B/2797